Whiskey, Murder, and God

by
Peter Redpath

DORRANCE PUBLISHING CO., INC.
PITTSBURGH, PENNSYLVANIA 15222

This story is a work of fiction developed only in the mind of the author. All the characters are fictional. However, many of the places where the story unfolds in Kentucky and Tennessee are real.

All Rights Reserved
Copyright © 2001 by Peter Redpath
No part of this book may be reproduced or transmitted
in any form or by any means, electronic or mechanical,
including photocopying, recording, or by any information
storage and retrieval system without permission in
writing from the publisher.

ISBN # 0-8059-5167-9
Printed in the United States of America

First Printing

For information or to order additional books, please write:
Dorrance Publishing Co., Inc.
643 Smithfield Street
Pittsburgh, Pennsylvania 15222
U.S.A.
1-800-788-7654
Or visit our web site and on-line catalog at www.dorrancepublishing.com

Acknowledgments

This book would not exist today without the helpful support and information provided by the people mentioned here. To each of them I am eternally grateful.

George Bareis	Margaret Krey
Alan Beal	Fred Lambrecht
Kathy Beal	Herbert Mayfield
Mary Beth Beal	Maggie Miller
Jack Bellomo	Mary Miller
Gloria Benson	Tom Mooney
Ruth R. Broyles	Doug Mossberg
Steve Dolan	Virginia Murphy
Jack Donahue	Ann Redpath
Kathy Flynn	Kate Redpath
Beth Farrell	Tim Redpath
Jim Gulden	The Trappists of Kentucky
Keith Hanzel	Visitor Center–Bardstown
Leonard Keyes	Dennis Waite
Adam Krey	Fran Winkel

To any I forgot to mention, I apologize and thank you for your contribution. And a special thanks to my wife, Barbara, who endured this project with much moral support and no small amount of honest feedback.

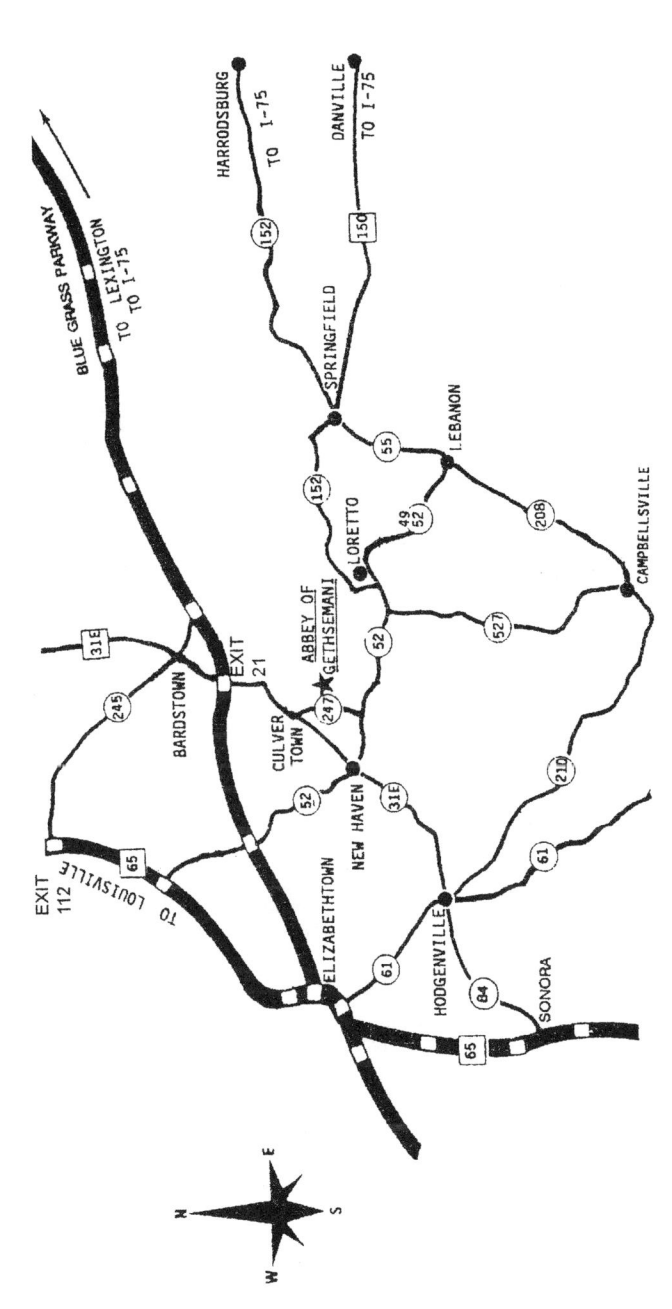

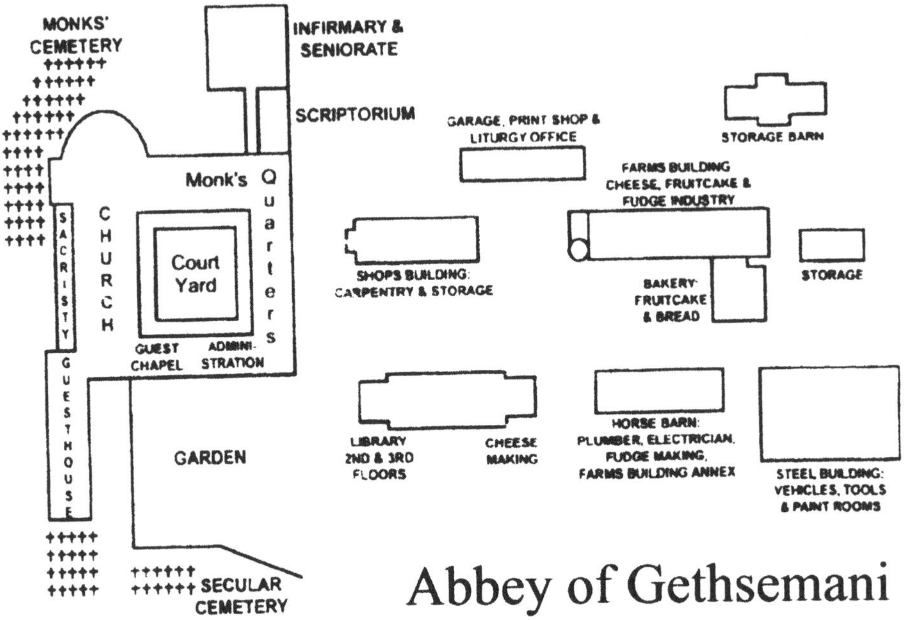

Abbey of Gethsemani
Trappist, Kentucky

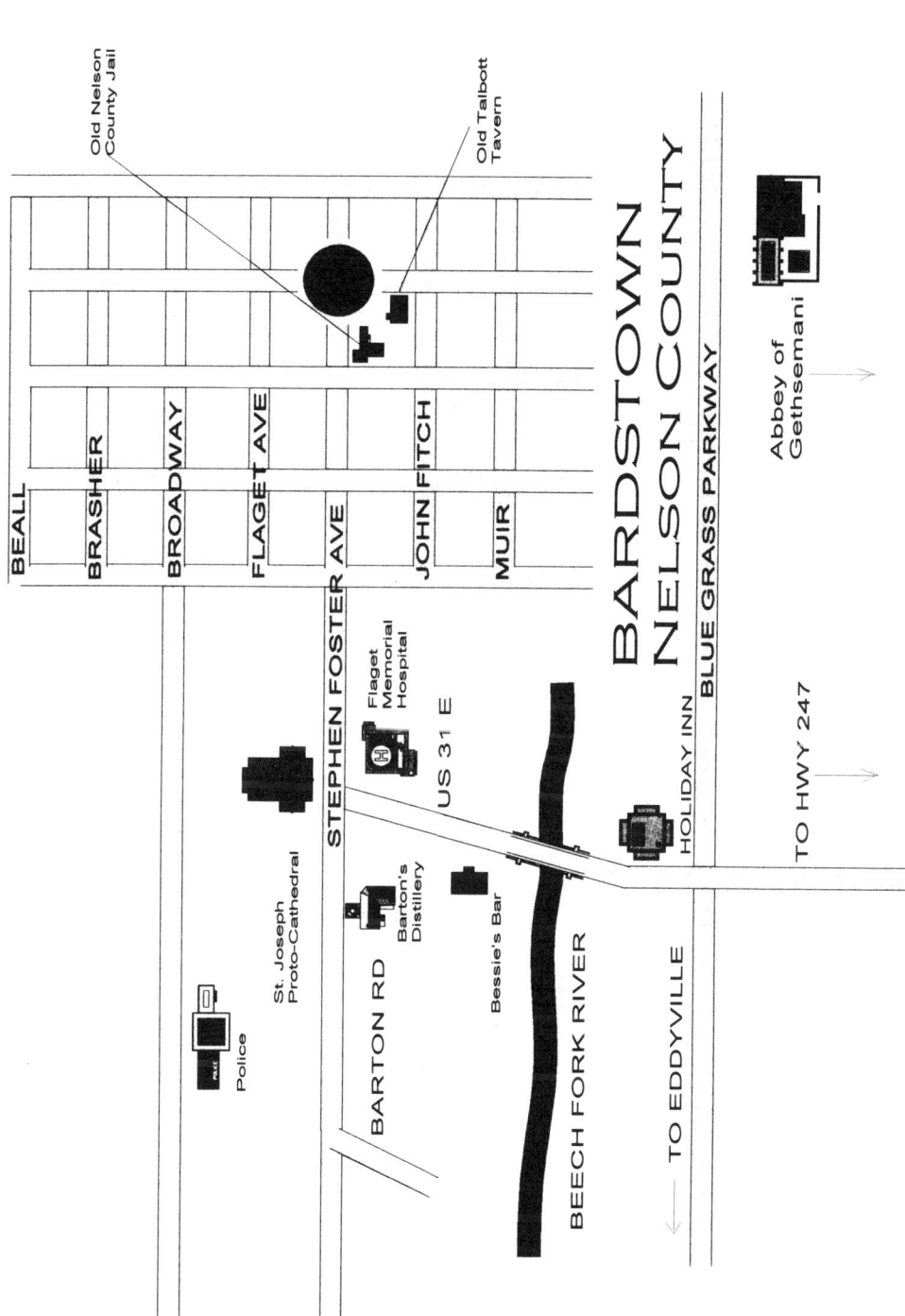

Prologue

Judge Kenneth Leonard slammed his fist on the polished mahogany conference table in his chambers. In twenty years serving Washington County, Tennessee, first as Assistant D.A., then as D.A., and finally as district judge, he'd never seemed more angry. The object of his anger was Defense Attorney James Powell, a boyish-looking, middle-aged man whose skin matched his light blond hair. Powell had been a law school classmate of the judge years before in Chattanooga. The judge then believed Powell had cheated on a final exam but couldn't prove it. Yet he never forgot the incident. Clearly they were not friends. But this was more serious. Since this meeting was in chambers, he didn't hold back.

"I just know you planned this whole thing, Powell. Do you realize we have impaneled the jury and we've sworn the first witness? Do you know what this means, Powell?"

"Yes, Judge," answered the lawyer for the defense. "It means jeopardy is attached."

"That's right. It means that Curt's witness, this Betty Kuel, if she asserts the 'privilege of marriage,'" Powell nodded that she would, "won't have to testify. She's the whole link to the gun and probably would prove Parton's guilty. Worse, since jeopardy is attached, it means if this case falls apart, we can never try Danny Parton on this charge again, even if they get divorced. It's double jeopardy, and you know the law as good as I do—he can't be tried again for the same crime. I think the bar association needs to hear about your actions in this case, Powell."

"Ken, let me go over this with you again."

"You can call me 'Judge,' Powell," said the angry justice.

"Okay, Judge. I hear ya."

The judge turned to the D.A. and said, "Curt, recap the case for us."

Curtis Kraus, the Washington County D.A., a tall, thin man with glasses and a pencil mustache, proceeded to recount the known and alleged facts in the case. He described how a local man by the name of Daniel Parton, long considered to be a bootlegger living in the hill country outside of Jonesborough, Tennessee, had been arrested as the prime suspect in the murder of a Johnson City tavern owner. The two men had been feuding for years. The tavern owner, Stanley Zobel, had often complained to Parton and others that Parton's sophisticated illegal liquor sales operation threatened his livelihood and those of the other legitimate purveyors of spirits in the area. On Christmas Day 1977, in front of many bar patrons, Zobel, a fearless Paul Bunyan of a man, told Parton that he intended to go to the authorities with proof that the bootlegger was not only selling illegal whiskey, but offering bar owners thinly veiled threats of bodily harm to get their business.

On the day after New Years in 1978, along a wooded path near his home on the outskirts of Johnson City, Stanley Zobel was found shot through the head. The bullet removed from his skull was determined to be one used in a 1914 German Luger, a pistol used in World War I. Such a gun had been owned and often demonstrated at fairs and gun club events by one Horace Kuel, a rural resident of Jonesborough and a veteran of the Great War.

Danny Parton, neighbor of the Kuel family, had often admired the pistol and enjoyed the occasional chance to fire it when its owner was showing it off. After Horace Kuel died, Parton had often tried to persuade his spinster daughter to sell him the gun. Betty Kuel resisted but shortly after Christmas of 1977, he had asked her to loan it to him for a week or two. He claimed he wanted to show it off at a gun show in Atlanta. Feeling that would do no harm, she agreed and did not think of it again until the police made a call on her on January eleventh.

The police officer in charge had explained that they were checking any German Lugers known to be in the area. He explained that a Luger had been used in the widely reported murder of Stanley Zobel. She acknowledged that she still owned her father's weapon and that it was in her possession. In her absence, Parton had left the gun in a package on her porch a few days before. Feeling some vague sense of loyalty to Danny Parton, she was silent about loaning him the Luger. When pressed by the police, however, she became afraid of being accused of not cooperating and so admitted the loan. She strongly protested the veiled hint by the officer that Parton was guilty in the murder of Zobel and perhaps Betty may have even been an accomplice. The officer backed down and confiscated the gun. The police thanked her and departed.

The gun showed signs of extensive clean up. After careful forensic tests, however, the police were able to confirm that the bullet in Stanley Zobel's head did match the barrel markings from the Luger owned by Betty Kuel. Danny Parton was arrested, booked, and released on bail.

Judge Leonard did not have an abundance of patience. An average-sized man whose head made him look top heavy, the judge's broad forehead started to betray growing red spots. He sputtered and interrupted the D.A. "I know all this," the judge shouted. "Powell, what about your involvement?"

James Powell took a drink of water and took up the narrative. "Let's see, Judge. Somehow, when Parton was out on bail, he and Betty Kuel hooked up and went to Nashville and got married. I didn't know anything about it."

"I don't believe you, Mr. Powell." The judge was getting flushed. "You probably took them to Nashville."

"No sir, I didn't. I had no knowledge of their marriage until two weeks ago," said the attorney for the defense.

"Well, why in hell didn't you tell the court what you knew then, instead of this morning after we heard the first witness in this joke of a trial?"

"Ken, I mean Judge, I don't have that responsibility. In fact I have an obligation *not* to tell you. The D.A. has all kinds of means of finding that out."

"You are an officer of the court," bellowed Judge Leonard. "You have a legal and moral obligation to disclose."

Earl chimed in. "Damn right, Jim, you shoulda disclosed."

"I take issue with that. I don't have an obligation to disclose a fact like that which is public information. In fact, I have a strong obligation to allow my client every legal means to defend himself. And the law is clear about a spouse not testifying against a defendant spouse, right Judge?" James Powell was sarcastic.

"Powell, I'll have you on an ethics charge on this. I'll get you disbarred if I can. You are a bad lawyer." The judge had momentarily lost it.

The D.A. interceded calmly, "Judge, maybe all is not lost. If you were able to declare this a mistrial, couldn't jeopardy become a non-issue if you rule that essentially no trial could go forward due to the suppression of extremely critical information?"

"No way," yelled Powell. "This information was available to you. I had no obligation to tell you. I am absolutely convinced I had an obligation *not* to tell you if your ignorance of public information could help my client. In fact the same is true if this *wasn't* public information. There's no mistrial here. Put on your case, Curt."

Judge Leonard had recovered a little. "You mean to tell me that when you realized that Curt didn't know about this marriage between the defendant and the key witness, you purposely allowed us to proceed through jury selection and hear our first witness before you revealed this . . . this convenient marriage?"

"I did. I couldn't believe Curt didn't know," answered Powell. "But I knew my case improved when that first witness was heard. That's why I asked for this meeting in chambers, so as not to waste any more time than was necessary," said Powell.

The judge turned to Curt. "Didn't your guys do a routine check on Parton that woulda brought this so-called marriage to light?"

"Yes, Judge, but we did it early, right after Parton made bail. That convenient marriage undoubtedly took place after that, isn't that right, Jim?" said the D.A. in a not-so-friendly aside to the defense attorney. He added, "I agree with you, Judge. I think you oughta look into an ethics charge on this one."

"Go to hell, Curt," retorted Powell. "You had the obligation to surface that information. I had no obligation to disclose it. For the last time, I had nothing to do with this marriage. I didn't know about it myself 'til months after it happened."

"Well, I've heard enough of this mess for now," said the judge. "We'll recess this thing for two days to think about what we can do. This is Monday; we'll see all of you and the defendant and his so-called wife in chambers at 10:30 on Wednesday. Powell, you are still on my shit list. I'll be lookin' for a way to get you on this one. This session is over." The judge made a quick appearance in the courtroom to recess the proceedings and returned to his chambers, reached for his sports coat, and headed out his office door.

Shaking his head and muttering to himself, Judge Leonard grimly descended the courthouse steps. Built in 1913, the Washington County Courthouse was the sixth county courthouse in Jonesborough since 1799. Locals brag that Andrew Jackson was admitted to the bar in the first courthouse. The current building is two stories higher than in Jackson's day and topped by a four-sided clock tower set in a large, traditional colonial-type cupola. Each entrance is sheltered by a roof-high portico held by four stately pillars. The courthouse sits on its own square on Main Street within one of the historical sections of Jonesborough.

The judge stepped out into a warm summer day. Tennessee's oldest town, Jonesborough is located in the lower Appalachians in Washington County in the northeastern part of Tennessee. The town is typical of small towns in the region. The railroad is a major factor in the economics of the community. The older buildings throughout the town are set among even older trees. Local residents tell all who listen that The Lost State of Franklin was organized here in 1785. Jonesborough was that state's first capitol and the site of its constitutional convention and early legislative sessions. In the late twentieth century, Johnson City, seven miles to the east, is the larger, more industrial town of Washington County, but the three thousand residents of Jonesborough are known to be loyal and proud citizens of their county seat. These are people who, in 1979, valued the difference between right and wrong just as did their ancestors. It was their heritage and they took pride in it.

Judge Kenneth Leonard was among those proud. And he didn't like complications like the one he just left. He liked to preside over cases that had clear facts that could be subjected to his skilled management of due process. He was stumped about the turn of events in this case. This morning, he had anticipated a smooth trial. His pre-trial grasp of the facts had led him to consider the good possibility that this could be a capital case. While he resisted the temptation to wish it might be so, he had become aware of some growing newsworthy aspects of this case that might bring him some not entirely unwelcome publicity. Now the chance of negative publicity loomed large. He pondered what to do.

The judge spent most of the next day researching cases that might salvage this one. He was unsuccessful finding a single case that would allow him to declare a mistrial. He saw no way to avoid double jeopardy which would void a second trial. He was frustrated.

He turned his thoughts to James Powell. The judge was convinced the lawyer was behind Parton's marriage. He made a call to a colleague, Judge Simon Walters, and asked him his opinion about ordering an investigation that might prove the lawyer guilty of some type of conspiracy. Judge Walters sympathized but could not encourage his friend. He said, "Ken, even if an investigation might prove he knew about the marriage before it happened, I don't think it is a disclosure matter. You'd have to prove that it was Powell's idea to get him on a conspiracy charge. Do you think that's possible?"

"No, Simon. Powell's too smart to leave any evidence that he thought up that marriage. And I'm sure neither of the married couple will tell me it was Powell's idea, even though I have serious doubts Parton could've thought about marrying that gal by himself. Plus the fact it would take too darn long to run the investigation and put this trial on hold. Damn! I guess I'm talking myself out of it, Simon. Thanks for listening. It helped me clear my head even though I don't like the answers. I'll talk to you soon." He hung up.

The mood was not cordial on Wednesday morning when the group assembled in Judge Leonard's chambers in the courthouse. Danny Parton was uncomfortable. Six-foot-two and supporting a pot belly, the fifty-one-year-old was sweating and wiping his forehead. His red lumpy nose betrayed lifetime use of the product he was suspected of producing and illegally selling. His slick black hair was combed straight back from his forehead.

Mrs. Parton was not attractive. She was almost as large as her new husband. A round face with gray hair pulled back in a bun made her look older than her forty-three years. She stared ahead, expressionless as if she willed herself not to be where she was.

The D.A. and the defense lawyer busied themselves with papers pulled from their briefcases. A court reporter was requested for this session and had set up in his usual spot in chambers, ready to take his instructions from the judge. No one spoke.

The judge and his clerk entered the room at 10:35 A.M. Both quickly sat and the judge said, "Okay let's see where we are with this mess. First, I would like to ask Mr. Parton a couple of questions. Mr. Parton, how is it you came to marry your wife here?"

"What do ya mean, Judge?"

"I mean tell me something about when you and your wife decided to get married and when and where the marriage took place."

Parton shifted in his seat. "Well Judge, I think we made up our minds to get married in March and we just went on over to Nashville and saw the justice of the peace. I have the license here if you wanna take a look at it."

"I'm sure you do, Mr. Parton. But tell me, why did you marry the former Miss Kuel here?" The judge looked at Betty as if one could not believe anyone would be interested in matrimony with a woman so homely.

"Why? Well I guess I've known Betty here for years. I always admired her father and enjoyed talkin' to him whenever I had the chance. After he died, I took up to talkin' to Betty once in a while and one thing led to another and, well, you know, Judge, we got to sparkin' some and we just decided to get married up."

"I see. And you Mrs. Parton. How do feel about your recent wedding?"

Betty Parton looked stunned. The cold reality that she might indeed have to say something this morning was hitting her hard. "Uh, uhhh, whatja say Mr. Judge?"

"Tell me about this wedding. It must have been a big day for you. A happy day and all. Right?"

"Uh, we just went over to Nashville and saw the preacher or whatever he was and got married. It was Danny's idea but I always liked Danny—never knew he liked me too, though—and when he asked me, I was real happy, Judge."

"But you were surprised?"

"I was surprised but I was sure happy, Judge. I like Danny a whole lot."

"Did Danny ask you to get married so you wouldn't have to testify against him in this murder trial?"

"No, Judge. He just told me he loved me and asked me to go to Nashville with him. I was real happy, like I told you, Judge."

Judge Leonard turned back to Danny. "And I don't suppose you married Betty here because you knew she couldn't testify against you?"

"I know it now, Judge. But I really care for Betty. I wanted to marry her. And I wanna stay married to her."

The judge was hesitant but carefully asked the next question. "Did either of you get any advice from anyone that getting married might save Betty from having to testify?"

Danny squirmed. "No, Judge. We kept our marriage pretty quiet for a while. When I told Jim here, I mean Mr. Powell, about it a few weeks ago, he did say we shouldn't lie, but that we should not go around tellin' anyone about being married either. He said that it might help if nobody knew we were married till the trial started. We agreed to be quiet but I told him it don't matter anyway since I didn't kill Stanley Zobel."

Judge Leonard was angry yet couldn't help but speculate and admire the work Jim Powell must have done in preparing the two Partons for their performances this morning. He said, "Okay, you two can be on your way for now. Your lawyer will let you know when the next steps in the trial will take place. Stay in town."

The Partons looked relieved and quickly left the room. No one else in the room had spoken since the judge and his clerk had entered the room. James Powell spoke. "With due respect, Judge Leonard, I question the appropriateness of what we just witnessed here. I don't know if you should be questioning my client and his wife about my interaction with them, even though you can see they have nothing to hide."

"Oh come off it, Powell," said the D.A.

"Yes, you better be quiet, Powell," said the judge. "What I've done is off the record and in my opinion those people needed to be interviewed in front of witnesses to test the theory that I still hold—that you, Mr. Powell, are behind all of this. Now, we'll go on the record and talk about what to do next." The judge nodded to the court reporter. They were on the record.

"Curt, can you put on any kind of case without the new Mrs. Parton?"

The D.A. answered, "Man, I sure want to, Judge. But everything we have is hearsay. Like the guy we had up there as our first witness. He said what others can also say, that Parton hated Zobel because he was gonna expose the bootlegger. But Mr. Powell here would have no trouble convincing the jury that there is reasonable doubt without an eyewitness or the link to the gun that has to come from Betty. Even the cop's testimony that Betty admitted Parton borrowed the gun would be challenged and probably you'd have to toss it out. I hate to say it, Judge, but I don't think we can put on a strong case without Betty Parton."

"And no way the Partons are gonna budge on Powell not advising them to get married?"

"Just a minute, Judge," Powell chimed in. "I resent that. You have me guilty of something I did not do. Seems like I'm guilty until proven innocent in this deal. What kind of fair treatment is that? Come to think of it, Judge, there may be nothing illegal about it if I *did* suggest they get married. But I didn't!"

"Judge Leonard, I've heard enough from Jim Powell. It's people like him who give lawyers a bad name. I'd like to ask Your Honor to sanction Mr. Powell for his actions in this case," pleaded the D.A.

"Forget it, both of you! Even if I'd like to have one, it doesn't look like there's a viable case against you right now, Powell," the judge responded. Then he ordered the court reporter, "Strike those last couple of comments between Mr. Powell and Mr. Earl and me."

The D.A. spoke up, "I might as well make a motion to dismiss, Judge. We'd be wasting everybody's time to try this case."

Judge Leonard grew quiet and reflected for a moment. This was to be a good case for him. One with some exposure. He was now feeling some momentary guilt about this selfish motivation and also about being too verbose in his opinions regarding Jim Powell. In his anger he'd not lived up to his own standard of professionalism. But after this bit of self-recrimination, it was now time for him to act.

"Okay, Curt. We'll do it at nine tomorrow. Make your motion." He turned to his clerk. "Sara, please talk to the bailiff and get everyone in here tomorrow. Let's wrap this one up." The judge slouched in his chair, lowered his eyes, and muttered, "Damn."

Chapter One

Bessie's Bar was not fancy. But it was a comfortable place enjoyed by neighbors and workers from the nearby distillery. A few regulars sipped beer, enjoying their usual bar talk. Phil Norton, a stranger in town, sat alone at the end of the bar. A stout yet muscular man of medium height, age was difficult to determine. His only remarkable feature was his red nose that took a slight right turn as it protruded from his blotchy face. He felt as drunk as he knew he probably was that late March night in 1981. Desperate and angry, his mind trudged through a quagmire of self-pity.

None of 'em ever loved me. They all hated me. Phil had a vision of his mean father, his nagging mother, the woman who wouldn't marry him, the teachers who flunked him. *What did I ever do except work my ass off for my old man? Like the day I worked two extra hours in the field just so my dad would notice and maybe even say thanks. And what did he do but beat the hell out of me that night for leaving the porch light on. And the time he came into the schoolhouse and pulled me out of there in front of everybody—yelling and saying I was a lazy bastard who should be home working.* Phil sank lower into the bar and lower into his morose, hateful self. *And all those crummy jobs I had workin' for crummy bosses, always treating me like dirt. Then them Army bastards treated me like a pile of shit, too. Always pushin' me into treatment or work I hated, always bitchin' at me. And I walked all over 'Nam for them SOBs, too. Why me?* He paused. *Why not me? I really* am *the worst bastard I know. Everyone I ever knew hates me. But damn it, somebody owes me something for all the crap I've taken in my lousy life.*

Phil felt sick. His head and stomach each twirled out of sync. He forced himself not to vomit. His nausea made him even more angry, as if his soused-over pain was now delivered courtesy of all the people of his past. All those people who hated him. They needed to be punished. They deserved it. He had to punish them.

Ahh, and Mary Fallon. I wasn't good enough for her. She led me on. That bitch. She pretended to like me, too, made me think she even wanted to marry me. Then I ask her and she says she wants to go to college. Bullshit. She went to school to get rid of me. She really didn't care about me. 'Course, who would . . . a bastard like me. But I treated her real nice. And what did I get for it? A jilting, that's what I got!

Tears filled his eyes. Sadness added to anger. Phil felt so alone. And so mad. He wasn't sure how he arrived in *this* town. He'd been hitchhiking with an aimless goal of reaching California, and this must have been where his last ride dropped him off. He sat another hour, drinking, crying, and recalling his unhappy past. His attention rolled back and forth from his physical pain to remembering his "enemies," hating them and hating himself. He couldn't hold on to his feelings; they dragged him to want even more whiskey, more pain, more hate. He no longer cared to be relieved of his pain. If he could punish no one else, he'd punish himself.

Phil's weeping broke into loud muffled sobs, and he was starting to annoy other patrons in the bar. He was dead broke and asked Tom, the bartender, to pour him "one more on the house." Deciding that Phil had had too much to drink, the bartender refused and suggested that Phil leave. When Phil objected loudly and stood to push him, Tom grabbed him by the collar, walked him to the door, and shoved him into the street. Phil felt no physical pain as he weaved and bobbed and finally fell to the pavement. But still boiling with the deeper pain of anger, he regained his feet and wobbled away.

Bessie's Bar was on Highway 31E, a quarter mile south of the St. Joseph Proto-Cathedral of Bardstown. Phil staggered north along the highway, mumbling to himself and grinding his teeth as he went. "Rotten family, rotten army, rotten girlfriend." He crossed Steven Foster Avenue into the cathedral parking lot. Thirty-five degrees was a normal nighttime temperature for March fifth in Bardstown, Kentucky. And by now, it was March sixth, almost one-thirty in the morning.

He shivered. He was becoming even more angry; angry at the bartender, angry at the world, angry at himself. He wanted a drink.

Phil moved mindlessly toward the cathedral. Intuition guided his feet toward the entrance to the church. It might be open and offer some warmth. Through the open gates of the empty parking lot a 60s vintage Chevy drove slowly in Phil's direction. In his drunkenness, he didn't notice the car until it came alongside of him.

The lone driver rolled down the window. Sitting high in the car with long blond hair pulled back into a ponytail the man said, "Hey pal, do you need a ride someplace?"

Phil retorted, "No, leave me alone; get the hell out a here." He kept walking toward the warmth of the cathedral door.

"Come on, mister, you look sick. Let me take you someplace and get you some help."

Annoyed, Phil turned to look at the driver. In the "Samaritan's" face, he suddenly saw his father. The driver *was his father*. Phil was enraged. His whole body stiffened as hate overwhelmed him. He had to retaliate; he had to punish this beast who was his father. He hated this man who caused him to hate himself and everyone else.

Phil lunged at the car door and yanked it open. He reached in and grabbed the young man from the car and hit him squarely on the jaw. The man was stunned and before he could recover, Phil tossed him on the ground, jumped on his chest, grabbed him by the throat, and continued to beat him back and forth around the head.

"Here's for all the beatings, ol' man. Here's for humiliating me, you son-of-a-bitch. Here's for ruining my life—I hate you, I hate you, I *hate* you." Phil was crying and screaming at the same time. As the man offered some resistance, Phil became even more angry. He lost all control and pummeled the face in front of him. With energy borne out of rage and drunkenness, Phil mutilated the face of the would-be helper—now his father—this father who punished *him*. Blow after blow he delivered to the man's head and neck. With each blow, the drunk's old army ring would tear away more flesh as the man's face lost its identity. All resistance finally ceased and still Phil continued to punish this lifeless vessel that had *become* his father.

Phil finally sensed no reaction and stopped. He rolled on his back and lay next to his victim. His heart was pounding and he struggled for air. Yet he felt relief and satisfaction. He had finally fought back.

Gradually, his breathing slowed and he began to feel complete fatigue. His raging, violent outburst had brought him around some and he started to become more aware. He rolled up and looked at the person next to him. He touched him. The man was dead.

Suddenly Phil was completely sober. Truth dawned—the victim was *not* his father. He stared in disbelief at the battered mess that had been the man's face. He tried to swallow but couldn't. His heart pounded. He couldn't breathe. He had to act. He had to get out of there. Phil bolted to his feet and ran from the lot across Stephen Foster Avenue and retraced his way south back along U.S. 31E. He ran by Bessie's Bar again, and by Barton's Distillery's huge silver-painted buildings where thousands of barrels of whiskey were stored. His fear brought him new energy and he ran as fast as he was able crossing the Beech Fork River bridge. More alert now, he stopped at the end of the bridge. Instinct told him he needed to lose his identity. He ran back to the middle of the bridge and tossed his wallet into the river. He started back south, then paused as he felt the soreness in his hand. Grimacing, Phil pulled the army ring from his swollen finger and flung it over the railing. Again, instinct.

Then he moved on past the Bluegrass Parkway, nearly two miles now from the cathedral. Although it was dark and cold, he kept walking, passing over the parkway, running and walking again south along the highway. Panting at the pace and wearing only a light sweater, he was sweating profusely, becoming oblivious to the cold and to the pain in his swollen hand.

Phil hurried along U.S. 31E. His panic and the cold air caused his mind to race along with his heart. *My God, what have I done? I've killed someone. . . . I don't even know who. . . .Oh man, I'm doomed . . . they'll find me . . . hang me. . . .Oh, oh, oooh,* he wailed. *What happened to me? How could I do that? I was drunk. It's not my fault. The bartender shoulda let me stay in the bar. Oh no, they're gonna kill me. I can't let 'em find me. I gotta hide, gotta hide, hide. I'm doomed.*

He continued this litany until he stopped at a utility pole and steadied himself. The night was dark except for the light from the pole that seemed to expose him to the whole world. He took in a series of quick breaths, trying to stifle the sobs that followed. The wail came on uncontrollably and he wept bitterly. All alone, he wanted to die.

He had managed to get four miles south of the parkway on 31E. He had passed a few rural homes and businesses spread sparsely along the highway. Phil was aware that he was cold now. His sweat now chilled him deeply. He had no jacket and was quickly losing the energy generated by his need to escape. Fearing the light from the pole, he started to walk again. His quick pace soon dwindled to a slow stagger. Exhaustion replaced fear now. He noticed a large wooded area along the right side of the road, staggered into it and covered himself with leaves, and slept.

About four-thirty in the morning he awoke, again terrified and cold to the bone. Darkness had been his friend so far. With daylight upon him in a couple of hours, it was time to get off this main route. He struggled along the highway for a couple more miles and then turned to the left onto Highway 247, a rural road that carried less traffic.

Norton staggered and stumbled for another mile and a half. His breathing was shallow and labored. He shuddered from the cold, now about thirty degrees. He was suddenly sick and vomited nothing. His energy was spent. His head was spinning. Spotting a brush pile below, he tumbled down the side of the ditch, hoping to find shelter in branches and leaves deposited there. He was unconscious before his body lay still at the bottom.

Chapter Two

St. Joseph's Proto-Cathedral was built in 1819. It was the first Catholic cathedral built west of the Alleghenies. The building, a popular tourist stop, is preserved in its original colonial architecture including the tall single spire that reaches upward over the bell tower. The building contains many old paintings by the masters donated by popes and kings. It no longer serves as a cathedral church of a diocese, thus its name "Proto" cathedral.

Seth Trenter drove into the church parking lot about six-thirty the morning of March sixth. Seth was a cheerful, round-faced little man in his late sixties. It was his job to open the cathedral each morning for the early Mass. He noticed the lone car in the middle of the lot with its door open. As he pulled his car alongside of the empty car, he noticed the form of a man lying on his side several feet away from the open door. He quickly jumped out of his car to investigate. His first thought was that some early churchgoer had experienced a medical emergency. He rolled the man onto his back and let out a loud gasp. He looked at a place where a face had been. He saw only a tangled mass of flesh and dried blood. He saw a broken, twisted nose and a hole with several dangling teeth where the mouth had been. Tendons were exposed where skin had been ripped away. The man's eyes were gone from their sockets. Only the man's right ear seemed untouched.

Seth's hands shook as he dialed 911 from the phone in a basement office of the cathedral. In two minutes he heard the sirens entering the parking lot. Seth's eyes could not conceal his panic. He could not look at the beaten body as he told the police about his discovery.

The police investigator who was fetched at home and arrived with the squad car was a gray-haired middle-age cop with bags under his eyes. He had the face of a beagle hound. He seemed annoyed at the early hour.

His name was John Sedwick. He glanced, then did a double take at the beaten face of the victim. Even Sedwick, a callused veteran, was shocked. "Holy shit!" he grunted. His stomach turned but held. He was no longer sleepy. His juices started to run and he was alert; what he saw lying on the surface of the cold parking lot was not an everyday sight in Bardstown. If fact, John Sedwick had never seen worse.

Soon the coroner arrived. John said, "George, I need you to do every test in the book to see what we can learn about this situation. I'll get someone out here to go over the car. You take care of the body and move it only when you've done everything you possibly can here. I'll call you later for your report."

George Cantrell was a professional. A pathologist, he'd been the Nelson County coroner for twenty years. "I'll be in touch, Sedwick."

"Well, we need speed *and* accuracy," John said, and hitched a ride with one of the squad cars returning to the police department two blocks away.

The detective slumped into his chair and wondered about what he had just seen. Could he solve this one? And he admitted to himself he wanted badly to solve this one. This just might be the opportunity he was seeking. He was tired of not getting the recognition he deserved. All these years on the force and he was really only the *self-proclaimed* detective on the force. He confided to himself, "When Dick Rowlands retires as chief, I want that job."

As he pondered the situation, a call came in from George Cantrall. "Sedwick, we are just getting started but I thought you'd like to know that we have an ID."

"What?"

"Yes, his wallet was in his pocket. He had over a hundred dollars cash in it. Robbery's probably out."

"What's his name, George?"

"I'm coming to that. The only thing in the wallet besides the cash was a temporary driver's license issued last week. Lists his address on Beall Street. I think by the number it is Mrs. Maloney's rooming house. You know her, John. And let's see, the name on the license is Bobby Swanson."

"Thanks George," said John. He called Teddy Fry, the lone lab technician in the department, and asked him to go to the crime scene and check out the victim's car. Then he sped out the door to his car.

The house in the one-hundred block on Beall Avenue was a large wooden frame-home with a pitched roof. The typical long, unscreened porch covering the entire width of the house indicated it was a home built in the early 1900s. For its age the house was well maintained. The dark green paint job looked only about a year old.

Mrs. Maloney, a widow for some fifteen years, was in her sixties and had no children. While a stout woman, her round face topped with white curly hair gave her an approachable air. She wore small glasses over her small nose and big smile.

She greeted John Sedwick as if he were a long lost friend—even though he had met her only briefly one summer day twelve years ago. He had answered a noise complaint from a neighbor. It turned out that Mrs. Maloney was giving a piece of her mind to a renter who asked for one too many extensions on his overdue rent. Seemed like the complainer was really more entertained by the whole affair than upset by it.

"Hi Officer Sedwick," she yelled when she saw him as she opened the door. "You haven't had another complaint about me, have you? You know, Officer, I haven't had but one or two deadbeats in all the years I've been boarding folks. I love my boarders; they've been my family since my husband died. Sure the money helps but it *isn't* the most important thing. I uh. . . ." She paused and looked at Sedwick, questioning why he might be calling.

"No, Mrs. Maloney, no complaints and it's *Detective* now; been off the beat for about ten years." Sedwick *embellished* a bit. His official title was investigator; his job combined investigative work with routine administrative duties. He occasionally donned his uniform, too, when the situation called for it. He thought it only fair that the chief and the rest of the squad allowed him to borrow the "detective" title.

"Congratulations then, Officer, I mean Detective. Come on in and have a cup of my terrible coffee."

"Thanks ma'am. I came to ask you about a renter of yours, a Bobby Swanson," he said as he followed her to the kitchen.

"A nice kid, Bobby," she offered as she poured his coffee. "He hasn't been here long. Only about three weeks. Keeps to himself, is clean, and pays his rent on time." Then quickly she looked alarmed. "Why, is he in some kind of trouble, Officer, I mean Detective?"

"The worst kind, Mrs. Maloney. He was killed last night. We found him in the parking lot of the cathedral early this morning."

She gasped. "Oh my Lord. Oh my Lord," she cried. Then demanding. "What happened?"

"Well, we're not sure, Mrs. Maloney. He may have been brutally attacked by some wild animal but it looks more like murder to me. We'll know for sure in a few hours."

"Murder! No, not here in Bardstown. You said 'brutally' attacked, Detective?"

"I'm afraid so, ma'am. His face was unrecognizable, it was so badly beaten and bashed."

"Oh no. He was such a nice polite young man. I can't believe he would be involved in anything bad." The words came rushing from her mouth. "He was always asking if he could help me with the dishes or if he could run any errands if he was going uptown. On Saturday, he bought a used car—the day after he got his license. He was so proud of it. Looked like a wreck to me but he was sure proud. Asked me to take a ride but I turned him down. No need for an old lady to go joyriding in old jalopy with a young kid." She fell silent. A tear showed in the corner of her eye. "Ohhh, I feel so bad about all this, Detective." She looked away and talking more to herself now, she said quietly, "Bobby was here less than a month. You know, I never had a son. I wondered if I had, would he be like Bobby. Ohh, this is terrible." The tears were more evident now." Do you need me for anything else, Detective?" she asked, clearly wanting to be alone.

"Just a question or two more, Mrs. Maloney. What did he look like? We couldn't tell except for his blond hair. Can you tell me where he came from? How old do you think he was? Did he have a job?"

"He did have that long blond hair like the kids wear it these days. But he was a pleasant-looking guy. Not like a movie star, but not bad looking. I'd guess him to be in his early thirties. I'm sorry I don't have a picture of him. I don't know how to say what someone looks like."

"That's okay, chances are we'll get a picture from his permanent driver's license, or we may ask you to work with a police artist who can sketch his face. But what else do you know about him, Mrs. Maloney?"

"He said he was from West Virginia. He mentioned some little town but darn if I remember it, Detective. You know, he was kind of a hillbilly but I don't mean anything bad by that. He had a job, though. A good one, too. He was hired over at Moore's Distillery the day he arrived. He knows something about mixin' them spirits, I guess. Until he got his car, he rode the company bus that picks up the Bardstown workers every morning. Oh, that reminds me. A fella came to the door asking for Bobby yesterday. Said he owed Bobby some money and wanted to know where he worked. Told him about the distillery. Seemed pleasant enough."

"What did this man look like?"

"Older than Bobby. I'd say in his fifties. Heavy like me. Red face, I think. I just can't tell you any more, Detective," she said, wanting to go off by herself.

"That's fine, ma'am. You've helped a lot." Sedwick made a note about the caller. "By the way, could I take a look at Mr. Swanson's room?"

"I guess it's alright," she said and led him up the stairs to the young man's room.

The room was furnished modestly and had been kept very neat by the renter. The clothes were arranged perfectly in the closet, the bed was made, the few personal effects were organized fastidiously around the room. There were no letters or other apparent clues as to the background of the victim.

"Well, thanks Mrs. Maloney. I'll have our lab tech, Mr. Fry, come over and dust for fingerprints. Maybe we can find out more about Bobby

Swanson. I'll be in touch, ma'am." Sedwick said as they returned to the front porch.

"Oh, I'm so, so sorry about that fine young man," she lamented. "I don't know what this world is coming to, Detective Sedwick. Bobby didn't deserve to die and certainly not the way you said he did. He was such a quiet, such a nice man. I do hope you find out who or what did this horrible thing. Oh my, his family, wherever they are, will be so saddened, too, won't they? Oh, I feel so bad, Detective," she sobbed as he headed down the porch steps.

"Thanks, ma'am," he said over his shoulder as he left the house on Beall Street.

Chapter Three

Brother William had just passed his turn-around point along Highway 247 on that early morning March 6, 1981, and was heading back toward the monastery. Even the brisk pace of his morning constitutional didn't keep the brother from a quick shiver as he turned back into the wind. He pulled his jacket tighter. It was still dark at 6:15 in the morning. An overhead yard light from a nearby rural home cast a pale light for fifty yards along the highway.

Brother noticed a brush pile and what appeared to be a sack of trash next to it. He gave it little thought. When he was a few yards past it, he thought he heard a low groan. He dismissed it and continued walking.

As he walked on, he began to wonder what the groan might have been. Probably some animal. Yet even though barely audible, it didn't sound like an animal. More human. Couldn't be. Could it?

He began to argue with himself. He needed to get back and get the breakfast started. The house was full this morning. But what if someone was in trouble back there? After a short battle with himself, Brother William hurried back to the brush pile to investigate.

At first, the brother thought the man he found was dead. There was no movement or response as he tried to arouse him. The man's face was expressionless. The brother himself felt panic. He hoped the groan he'd heard was not the man's dying breath. He quickly felt his neck to see if there was a pulse. He couldn't find any; then, as his fingers probed the area more carefully, he did feel a slight pulse. Brother carefully felt around the man's body and limbs to check for any obvious injury. He found none and thought perhaps the man had had a heart attack or stroke. The brother noticed the blood on his shirt and hand but assured himself he was not bleeding now. He thought it strange that the man was not dressed for the cold of night. Maybe he was freezing to death?

Brother debated what to do next. If he ran back to the monastery, the man might die before he could bring help. It was a half-mile to the nearest farm house and he had the same concern about leaving the man. He took off his coat and wrapped it around the shoulders of this man he thought would die soon without help. He wondered if he should rub the man's legs and back to increase circulation. The brother prayed.

As he pondered his options, a pickup came along the road from the direction of the monastery. Brother scrambled up the ditch and waved down the driver. The pickup and the man were not familiar. The man was obviously a farmer—ruddy complexion, slim yet muscular, dressed in bib overalls.

"Hurry, I need a hand. There is a man down there in the ditch and he'll die soon if we don't get him inside."

The driver quickly responded, jumped from his truck, and ran down the side of the ditch. He and Brother William struggled, carrying the man gently by his arms and legs to the cab of the truck. They laid him on the front seat with his head toward the driver's side and legs at a 90-degree angle toward the front of the truck.

As they were placing the man in the cab of the pickup, the driver said, "Hey, Father or Brother or whatever, are you one of them Trappists? I seen that big ol' building back there a ways, and your dress and all." He paused. "My name is Lenny Cullen and I'm headin' home to Missouri. Been visitin' a cousin over yonder. Hey, I heard you guys ain't supposed to talk. What gives?"

"Well, we do keep silence most of the time and we shouldn't be chit-chatting. But in an emergency like this, we must talk. By the way, I'm Brother William, Lenny, and I sure am grateful for your help this morning," he said a bit breathlessly.

"Glad to help," said Lenny as they carefully arranged their sick man in the car. He finished awkwardly buckling two of the three seat belts around the unconscious man. "Should we run this fellow into the emergency room at some hospital?"

"No, Lenny, we have emergency equipment at the monastery and we're much closer. I'll point the way." The brother spoke with such authority that Lenny didn't question it. He boosted himself into the back of the pickup and laid close up to the cab to avoid the wind.

The buildings of the Abbey of Gethsemani, known informally as the Trappist Monastery, stand solidly on many acres of woods, hills, and farm fields the monks own on both sides of Highway 247. The monastery was founded in 1848 by Trappist monks sent from France. Since then, the monks at the abbey have received visitors seeking some quiet reflection and a chance to make a private retreat. In modern times, each three or four-day retreat is unstructured but guests are encouraged to join the monks for community prayer. A monk is also available to them for private consultation each evening. As the retreatants arrive, they report being struck by a sense of peace not found elsewhere. The surroundings, the good food, the entire program is designed to offer them a time to relax, look at their lives, and reorder their priorities.

The monks who live at the monastery live the monastic life every day. And faithful to the Trappist tradition of supporting themselves, they also perform manual labor—processing, packaging, and selling fruitcakes, cheeses, and chocolates by mail-order. The monks also tend a fair-sized beef cattle farm. These enterprises have replaced the total, more agrarian ways in which they supported themselves in the past. In addition, they cook and serve the meals. They maintain the grounds and the buildings. They sing, pray, and study—most of it all in silence.

Brother William was the monk in charge of cooking breakfast each morning for the other monks and any retreatants who may be in residence. Father Abbot had given him permission to leave the monastery grounds and take a brisk walk along the highway at five-thirty each morning. It was early enough that few, if any, would encounter the brother along the road. And this would allow him to enjoy his morning meditations while keeping the rule of silence. In allowing this minor freedom, Father Abbot probably also felt he was tending to the good health of the brother, who was short, overweight, and could use the exercise. On this particular morning the routine was altered.

Following the brother's hand and arm motions, Lenny drove his truck through an open gate in the eight-foot wall on the monastery grounds that separates the cloistered area from the open area adjacent to Highway 247. The main monastery building is accessible from both the open area and from the private cloistered area. There are eight red and brown brick outbuildings on the cloistered grounds that the monks use for various purposes, including their food enterprises. Brother William pointed the way along the road around the buildings to the kitchen entrance at the rear of the main monastery building.

The monk jumped out of the back of the truck and burst through the kitchen door and met Brother Alfonso, a mousy little man, who often helped him with breakfast chores when the house was full. "Hurry, Al, get Father Abbot. We gotta dying man in the truck."

"We? Truck? What's going on, Bill?"

"Don't ask; get Father. Lenny and I will get him ready to move him into the annex."

"Lenny?"

"Brother Alfonso, PLEASE get Father Abbot. There'll be explanations later," said an exasperated Brother William. Alfonso was on his way as William returned to the truck to help Lenny, who had just finished unhooking Phil Norton from the seat belts.

Brother William got into the driver's seat and checked the man's pulse again. "He's still hanging on, pal."

The next moment Brother Alfonso and Father Abbott, carrying a canvas stretcher, hurried out the back door and approached the truck. "What's going on, Brother?" asked the abbot.

"I found this man on my walk, Father. He was in the ditch out near the junction. This good man here, Mr. Cullen, came along in his truck and helped me get him here. I think he is dying—probably from being outside in the cold without any jacket. Or maybe he had a heart attack or stroke. I don't know."

Father Abbot acknowledged Lenny with a nod and quickly took charge of the situation. "Let's carefully move our visitor onto the stretcher—Bill, you and Mr. Cullen get ahold of him as best you can from the driver's side, and Al and I will take hold of his legs. I'll lay the stretcher right here on the ground and we'll ease him onto it."

The abbot's idea was executed quickly, and the sick man was soon lying on the stretcher and on his way into the nearby annex building where the infirmary is located. After moving the still-unconscious man onto the bed in one of the small infirmary rooms, Brother William returned to the kitchen with Lenny, who offered to wait in case he might be needed to drive the sick man to the hospital. Brother thanked him warmly and assured him that transportation was available if needed and that the monks would seek medical help for their "patient" and take good care of him. The brother gave his new friend three loaves of the monk's homemade bread for his family and bade him goodbye.

Lenny drove off feeling good that he somehow had done a decent thing in helping and he wondered if the sick man would pull through. He knew he probably wouldn't hear much about how everything turned out. "Strange people, those monks."

As soon as Brother William returned to the infirmary, Father Abbot asked the brother to undress and cover their patient. Then he went immediately to the chapel where the monks and the retreatants were engaged in morning prayer. The abbot interrupted the service and asked quietly if any of the retreatants were medical doctors. Three put up their hands and the abbot asked all three to follow him. In a hallway outside the chapel, he quickly explained the situation to the three and asked who might be the best suited among them to deal with the man's condition. It was decided that Doctor Jack Vogel, an internist, was best qualified to look in on the sick man.

The monastery infirmary contains fourteen patient rooms, a chapel, exercise area, day rooms, and ancillary services. The patient rooms are used to provide care for ill or aging monks or occasional visitors who become ill but do not need more extensive hospital care. The infirmary is more than a fully stocked first-aid station. It has all the necessary equipment to handle most emergencies until an appropriate higher level of care can be obtained, if needed. Each patient room is furnished with a hospital bed, hookups for oxygen, a small bathroom, a closet, and one side chair. The infirmary building is situated in a manner allowing each private room to have an outside window.

A striking figure at six-foot-three, Doctor Vogel entered the small infirmary room and saw the short, muscular man lying motionless on the bed. He quickly felt for the pulse and calculated 125 beats to the minute. He then took Norton's blood pressure and it read ninety-eight over sixty-five. He asked the abbot for a thermometer and some Vaseline, gently turned him on his side and took his temperature. It was ninety-five.

The man's face was white. The tips of his fingers, the edges of his ears, and the end of his nose were whiter. Other parts of his body were very red. His cheeks were sunken and his general appearance was gaunt. His lips were parched. The doctor opened the man's mouth and observed a red, dry tongue.

He said, "You've got a sick one on your hands here, Father Abbot. I think we should call an ambulance and get him to the hospital in Bardstown."

"How serious is it, Doctor?" asked the abbot.

"Well, the white areas around his face and fingers show frostbite, but I'm not sure yet how serious it is. Smell the alcohol? Don't know if he's an alcoholic, but if he is and hasn't had nourishment in a while, he could be in more serious trouble. When I see these parched lips and dry, red tongue, I see a man who is dehydrated. His blood pressure is low. His temperature is also low. His heart beat is strong but too fast. Now, we need to do a few things for him right away."

Brother William hadn't left the sick man's side and was hovering nearby. The doctor instructed him to get several blankets and cover the patient.

As the brother went for the blankets, Father Abbot said, "Doctor, if there is any way we can keep him here, we'd really like to do that. Since the time of Saint Benedict, whose rule we follow, monks like us have ministered to the poor and suffering souls who fall into our hands and need our help. You can see we have a fairly modern infirmary here and two of our brothers,

Brother Bill and one other, were medics before joining the Trappists. Our patients are usually our monks but once in a while God allows us to minister to a retreatant or another outsider."

The brother returned and started to cover the sick man with blankets. As if responding to the weight of the blankets thrown over him, Phil started to stir. He mumbled, "Gotta hide. . . ."

"What did he say?" questioned the abbot.

"Something about 'hiding'?" offered the brother. "When we found him he seemed to be hiding next to a brush pile in the ditch along the road."

"Well, we can learn more from him later," said Doctor Vogel, "right now we need to get fluids into him. Get some 7 UP—the kind with the sugar *in* it—and give him as much as you can get down his throat." The doctor demonstrated how to tilt the man's head properly to avoid drowning him while forcing him to drink even though not fully conscious. "I have a couple bags of a powdered mix of vitamins and electrolytes in my car that you can add to his little cocktail. As soon as he is awake enough, get as much broth or thin soup into him as you can.

"He doesn't appear to have any severe physical damage other than the considerable swelling and bruising on his right hand which he must have cut, too, considering all this dried blood. I don't think his frostbite is terribly serious and can be treated easily enough. I suppose as long as he's coming around, you can keep him here for a few hours and watch him. If he doesn't improve from the liquid intake, then he's got to go to the hospital. I'll go get the vitamin packet for you and then look in on him in a couple hours."

Brother William left to prepare the drink and the doctor went to his car and then met the brother in the kitchen. Father Abbot stayed in the infirmary room and decided to clean up his new visitor. Using a warm wash cloth, he gently washed his face and hands. As he cleaned the bloody hand that the doctor had mentioned, the abbot thought it strange that when all the blood was washed away, he found only minor scrapes and deep bruises.

Brother William returned with the concoction. He and the abbot were able to rouse Norton enough to prop him up and force him to take most of the drink. Before reaching the end of the glass, he laid back and was asleep. As the two monks moved the pillow under his head, Father Abbot said, "Brother, I think you need to see how the breakfast is coming, so I'll stay here for a while and you can return here after things are cleaned up in the kitchen. And thank you, Brother, for your good work this morning. Who knows why God may have brought this unfortunate man to us today."

The abbot was just over seventy; he was born Clarence Sorensen but as a monk he was known as Father Conrad. Today he was simply addressed as

Father Abbot. His white hair and gently lined face betrayed a character of discipline softened by a genuine concern for others. The abbot sat in a nearby chair and wondered about the man in the bed. Why was this fellow found outside along the road? And why no coat on such a cold night? What happened to him that he was discovered near death? The bloody hand with no cut? The abbot prayed for his sick patient and for answers to his questions. About forty minutes passed.

The priest was startled when Norton let out a loud groan. He quickly moved to the side of the bed, just as Phil turned on his side and vomited, nearly hitting the abbot with the ugly liquid. The abbot fetched an emesis basin and held it while Phil finished retching. Then the abbot grabbed another washcloth and cleaned the immediate mess while watching closely to see if his patient was going to stay conscious for a while.

Phil groaned again and opened his eyes. He looked straight at the abbot, blinked twice, and looked at him again. "Where am I?" he mumbled.

"You are in the Abbey of Gethsemani, son."

"Huh?"

"You're in the Abbey of Gethsemani," the abbot repeated.

"Ooh, I'm sick. Is this a hospital?" said Phil as he glanced around the infirmary.

"No, son, the abbey is a monastery. This is an infirmary room at the monastery. You were found in a road ditch not far from here by one of our monks."

"Monks?"

"Yes, those of us who live here in the monastery are called monks. We're dedicated to God and to quiet service to people who visit us," the priest said gently.

Phil was feeling ill. The pain throughout his body was now making itself known. His head throbbed. Alternating between shivering and sweltering, it seemed like every muscle screamed for attention. He wanted to die.

His pain called him back to reality. He remembered much of the previous night until the point he had turned off the main highway. "How did I get *here*?" he grunted.

The abbot explained how Brother William had found him and, with the help of a nearby farmer, was able to get him to the monastery. He assured him that he had been seen by a doctor and that he was concerned about frostbite and dehydration. He told his patient that the doctor would be checking him soon and, if need be, he would be taken to the hospital in Bardstown.

At this Phil sat up in bed and said, "No, I ain't goin' to Bardstown!" The quick motion made him feel faint and he quickly fell back on the pillow.

The abbot touched his arm. "It's our hope, too, that you can stay awhile with us until your health is returned. It is part of our ministry to care for people like you who come seeking our help. But, now in 1981, we are obligated to abide by the best judgment of the medical profession. There's a worry as to how much risk we can take on in performing this ancient ministry of ours." Then as an afterthought, "But why are you so concerned about going to Bardstown?"

While Phil ached in every part of his body, he was now more alert and realized he needed to protect himself. "Oh, I uh, I just hate hospitals. I got poisoned in one once," he lied. "I just think I should stay right here for a while. Then I'll be on my way. I won't be much trouble. You'll see."

The abbot doubted the story about poisoning but could understand how this disoriented man might believe anything. He said, "Well, we'll see what the doctor says. Perhaps you don't have lasting injuries, but you're still quite sick and will need some time to get back on your feet. Now, rest a while 'til the doctor comes in."

After the morning conference, Doctor Vogel returned to check on his "case." As he walked in the room he heard Father Abbot and his patient talking. "Well, this sounds encouraging. Let's have a look here," said the doctor as he started a routine check of the vital signs. "Hmm," he listened to the heartbeat through the stethoscope. The pulse was slower. The temperature was 97.5. Blood pressure was unchanged. "Watch my finger," he said as he studied Phil following the movement of his finger. Next, the doctor checked the reflexes. Seemed fine. He asked Phil to stick out his tongue. "That looks a little better." The physician carefully examined his fingers and ears and nose. "I see the color is to starting come back. A good sign. How do you feel, uh . . . what's your name anyway?"

The abbot cried, "My gosh, we didn't find any ID in his clothes and I forgot to even ask him his name!"

Phil grimaced. "Uh, it's Phil. Phil Johnson," he fibbed. "I feel okay, Doc," he fibbed again.

"Well, Phil, you may just be the luckiest man alive today. But you don't look like you feel good to me. You really look pretty sick; in fact you *are* sick, Phil. I wouldn't believe I'd say this, though, but I do think you may just be able to stay here for a week or so if these good monks want to nurse you back to feeling better. Father, this fellow is not going to feel well for quite awhile but perhaps he's coming out of any real serious danger already. I'll take another look this afternoon and we can decide then. In the meantime, keep getting liquid into him. Be sure you give him some of that warm soup, too. We need to start building his strength. Anyway, I'll check later and then if we decide to let Phil be your guest, I'll have some more orders to leave with you. Okay?"

"Thank you, Doctor," said the abbot. "We'll watch him closely and plan on talking to you this afternoon. Now, I hope you can relax and return to making your retreat. We break our silence in a serious situation like this, but I'm sorry that all of this has interrupted the peace and quiet you came here to experience."

"Don't worry, Father. See you later."

⸺⸺

The chapel, built during the Civil War, was incorporated into the monastery building and took up about a fifth of the entire building. It was set out in the traditional monastic manner. There was the high, vaulted ceiling over the whole structure. In the center part of the chapel there were three long rows of pews facing each other that ran two-thirds the length of it. Another six rows of pews facing front were behind them in the rear of the chapel. There was a long wide sanctuary leading up to the main alter behind which was a very large tapestry of Christ. Long, high rectangles of stained glass lined each side wall of the chapel.

In the pews facing each other, the monks took assigned places during the mass or any other common services. During the chanting of the Holy Office, the monks on one side alternated with those on the other side as they sang the ancient verses. When there were retreatants at the monastery, they occupied open spaces in the chapel and joined in the liturgies and prayers of the monks. When nothing was scheduled in the chapel, the men and women on retreat often used the chapel for silent reflection.

Doctor Vogel returned to the chapel and slipped into a place in one of the back pews. Try as he might, he could not get back into the spirit of the retreat. He couldn't get his mind off his new patient and how he came to be in the monastery infirmary. He had noticed that when Phil's hand was cleaned up, there was some bruising but no cut. What was this man involved in, he wondered. It was clear that Phil was rebounding from the sorry condition he was in when the doctor first saw him. The physician wanted to know more, however, before he would just leave him in the hands of the monks.

After the mid-afternoon conference, Doctor Vogel returned to the infirmary. "Well, Mr. Johnson, how are you feeling this afternoon?"

"I'm real tired, Doc. But I think I'm gonna be fine," said Phil as he struggled to put on a cheerful face. The thought crossed his mind that he'd feel better right now if he had a drink.

"Phil, tell me how you got those bruises on the butt of your right hand here?"

Phil gulped. "Dunno, Doc. I think I hadda fight with a dog or something before I passed out in the ditch."

The doctor raised his eyebrows at Phil's answer and asked, "And how did you get in that ditch with no coat or anything, Phil?"

"Uh, I uh, uhh really don't remember, Doc. I was drunk last night. I don't drink all the time, but when I do I usually get smashed. I think I had too many and the bartender tossed me out without my jacket. I was probably stewed enough I didn't care. I just wanted to get out of Bardstown and started walking. Probably had enough booze in me to keep me warm until I passed out. I dunno, Doc."

The doctor said, "I see. Before you came out of it this morning, you mumbled something about 'hiding'? What does that mean, Phil?"

"Dunno about that either, Doc. Must've been havin' a bad dream. 'Course the whole night is a bad dream to me."

Phil was not telling the whole story but it was truthful enough and told in a manner so that the doctor was inclined to accept it. "Okay, Phil, let's take another look at you." Again, the doctor examined him. In only the few hours since he had last seen him, the frostbite looked much improved. Phil's overall color was almost normal. His vital signs were in the range of normal. He told the doctor that he felt quite warm but still felt like he didn't want to eat anything. He acknowledged his body was very sore and he was exhausted.

"These monks seem to want you to stay here 'til you are back on your feet, Phil. Do you want to do that?" asked the doctor.

"Yeah, Doc. That will be just fine with me. I'll feel okay in a couple of days."

"It may take a little longer than that and, if you take a turn for the worse, you'll need to go to the hospital."

"That's a deal, Doc," Phil answered, knowing that he'd do everything possible to hide any problems that might send him to the Bardstown hospital.

"I'm not leaving for home 'til tomorrow night, Phil. I've ordered an antibiotic for you to help ward off any infection you might have picked up. We'll keep you on vitamins and get lots of liquid into you. I'll check you once more before I leave. I'll let the monks know what else needs to be done for your care after I leave for Paducah."

"You from Paducah, Doc?"

"Yes, do you know Paducah?"

"Naw, just think it's a funny name for a town." Phil was pleased the doctor wasn't heading to Bardstown.

"I'll see you tomorrow, Phil," said the doctor as he left the room.

Phil laid back and thought about his good fortune. In spite of his drunkenness, the sobering events after he left Bessie's Bar allowed him a vivid memory of what happened in the parking lot of the cathedral on the prior night. He believed if he were found out, the consequences might mean his own death. He had the sense that this monastery, or whatever it was, was the perfect place to hide for a while. He wanted to avoid Bardstown and avoid any possibility of being questioned about last night. But if he *was* questioned, the truth that he told the doctor should hold up. He didn't think there were any witnesses to what happened after he left the bar and if there were any, he was sure no one had seen his face close up. Yes, if he was ever put on the spot, he'd stick to a story that led from the bar directly to the ditch on Highway 247.

As his mind churned over all the possibilities and how he must save himself, a sudden thought struck him. *He had brutally killed a man last night.* A flood of remorse and pain once again engulfed him. "How could I? What happened to me? That guy was trying to help me, I think." Phil felt alone, his guilt suffocating. Quietly, he began to sob.

Chapter Four

"John, guess what?" The lab technician was excited. After his visit with Mrs. Maloney, John Sedwick returned to the police station. An urgent phone message had been waiting from Teddy Fry. The detective had wondered what the bald-headed little man might have for him as he returned the call.

"Come on, Teddy, spill it."

"There was a bomb in the car!"

"What?"

"Yeah, John, a pipe bomb. The cops at the scene waited for me to open the trunk of the car in case there was evidence there that couldn't be disturbed. After I did all the blood sampling and print dusting and combed the car, I told 'em to open 'er up. The trunk, that is. In the back of the trunk I noticed a blanket that must be coverin' something so I carefully remove it and there it is, John, a bomb. It scared the shit out of me. Coulda' gone off when I was screwing around in the car."

"What did it look like, Teddy?"

"Just a three-inch iron pipe about a foot and a half long; had a homemade detonator and timing device attached. We moved away pronto and called our bomb squad. Dave Krone defused the damn thing in ten minutes but here's the queer thing, John—it was set to go off at five-thirty *this* evening. Why would that be, John?"

"Dunno, Ted," said the detective. "Anything else?"

"Ain't that enough? I did dust the bomb parts after Krone was done. I didn't get any prints; Dave was careful so I would've got them if the bomber was careless. 'Course, why would he care about prints if the bomb went off? Oh, well, I'll have the whole lab report done first thing in the morning." They hung up.

Sedwick sat back in his chair. He thought about what he'd learned so far. A man by the name of Bobby Swanson was killed in the parking lot of the cathedral overnight. He was from West Virginia and lived in Mrs. Maloney's rooming house. He recently got a driver's license and bought a used car. He had a job. As far as was known, he was a peaceable man and was well liked by those few who knew him. He died from a brutal attack, yet a bomb was set to blow up his car almost a whole day after he was killed.

The police detective made a list of his next steps.

- get the coroner's report and the lab report first thing in the morning
- get the driver's license and produce a picture poster; get it out in Kentucky and West Virginia
- visit Swanson's employer
- talk to the car dealer

John Sedwick's thoughts returned to himself. He had to solve this crime. If he was ever going to move up to deputy chief or chief, he figured this was the case. John and his wife had no children. Work was it. At forty-eight, he knew time was short. This morning after he'd visited Mrs. Maloney, he called his wife Cathy to fill her in. She told him, "John, you can do it. If you get this guy, the whole town will take notice and I bet you'll get a promotion and more money, too."

John had served as a journeyman investigator for ten years. There had been no big cases that allowed him to show his stuff. He demonstrated routine competence on routine robberies and car jackings and domestic complaints. There had been only three murders in Bardstown since he was promoted to investigator, the position for which he called himself *detective*. Two were open and shut and the other was handled by the chief himself, who got all the glory when the murderer was surprisingly discovered on the chief's lucky hunch. Sedwick wanted a big case and this one looked like it could be the it. Chief Richard Rowlands had left a note on his desk while he was out that said, "This is your baby, John. Find the bastard."

The next morning Sedwick was up early. He picked up his local newspaper, *The Kentucky Standard,* and read, **LOCAL NEWCOMER BEATEN AND KILLED NEAR CATHEDRAL.** Nearly the entire first section reported the tragic events of the day before. Beside the messy description of the parking lot scene, there were several articles about local reaction. The city dignitaries were quoted as resolved to leave no stone unturned to find the killer. More noteworthy were the many reactions reported from the town's citizens. One typical quote came from a local dry cleaner. "I hope to hell they catch whoever did this horrible deed. This doesn't happen in Bardstown. If they catch him I want to be there when they fry the SOB." The town was angry. And it would stay that way for months as shown in letters to the editor, editorials, and everyday conversation in all the corners of Bardstown.

Sedwick downed a quick breakfast and headed west thirteen miles to Sheperdsville and the Moore Distillery. The security guard waved him through to the visitor parking. He asked the receptionist to talk with Bobby

Swanson's supervisor. In a few minutes, a professorial looking man of medium height, slight build, and wearing glasses approached. "I'm Clement Smith. I'm the assistant distiller and Mr. Swanson worked for me. I am in shock from what I read in the paper this morning. The receptionist said you are from the police?"

"Yes, Mr. Smith. I'm Detective Sedwick with the Bardstown Police. I need to ask you a few questions about Bobby."

"Certainly, Detective."

"What can you tell me about Bobby Swanson?"

"Well, he seemed like a very nice young man. And talented, too. He'd only been with us a few weeks. He was from West Virginia, I think. Anyway, we are testing some new ideas and young Swanson has or had a real knack for developing some interesting flavors in sour mash whiskey. I didn't press him, but I'm guessing he may have had some good training from, shall I say, some *illegal* experts, if you get my drift?"

"I do, Mr. Smith. What else can you tell me?"

"Really, not much, Detective. People liked him. Even in the short time he was here, he was always offering to do favors for people, like fetching a candy bar for a co-worker or offering to work a Saturday shift for someone who wanted the day off.

"We hoped he liked it here because we're short on his kind of skills in New Product Development. I can't tell you much of any thing about his personal life. He talked of getting a car as soon as he got his driver's license. I'm sorry I just don't know any more, Detective."

Sedwick thanked Smith and started to leave. He turned back. "Did anyone recently come looking for information about Bobby Swanson?"

"No, at least not to my knowledge, Detective."

Sedwick thanked him again and before he returned to his car, he stopped in the payroll department and obtained Swanson's social security number. The detective figured it might lead to the victim's place of origin. When he stopped at the guard gate, he had a thought. He asked the security guard, "Did you know Bobby Swanson?"

"Yes I did!" The guard seemed surprised by the question. "We have lots of employees here but even though he was here only a couple of weeks, I got to know Bobby. Gosh, he was a nice fellow. Did you hear that he's been killed?"

"Yes, I'm Detective Sedwick and I'm investigating the case," he said, showing the guard his badge. "Any chance you might have talked to anyone who came looking for Bobby in the last couple of days?"

"Why yes, Detective. Oh my gosh, I might be in trouble. His uncle drove up a couple of days ago—a real nice guy; friendly like Bobby—said he just came to town and wanted to surprise his nephew. Said that Bobby had always admired his bird gun when they hunted together, and he wanted to make a gift of it to 'im. He asked if he could just slip the gun in Bobby's trunk. Said he would meet up with Bobby that evening and have some fun getting him to discover the gun if he hadn't already. Did I screw up, Detective?"

"What happened next?" said Sedwick, ignoring the question.

"Well, he asked me which car and I told him it was an old '66 or '67 Impala, probably parked over there in the last row near the fence. That was the direction that Bobby headed in each morning since he had the car. The uncle, or whatever he was—never did give his name—drove his car over in that direction and was back in a few minutes. When he came back, he visited for a couple minutes more—a real friendly guy—he told me not to spoil the fun and I told him 'mum's the word' and he left. Golly, I just realized that it's odd that Bobby's uncle had a key to his trunk since Bobby just bought the car. Boy o' boy, do you think that guy wasn't his uncle; that maybe he had somethin' to do with the killin'?" The guard was getting more nervous now.

"I'm not sure. What did he look like?"

"Big guy. Black hair. Had a drinker's nose, you know, big and red. Had some miles on him, probably nearer sixty than fifty."

"When you say 'big,' do you mean fat or tall or both?"

"More fat. He was about six feet but had a big pot on him. Had a big smile, too. But I guess that don't count as part of what he looked like, does it? Detective, am I in trouble?" the guard wanted to know.

"I appreciate your help, uh, I didn't get your name?"

"It's Steven Schumen, Detective."

"Steve, I have no need to get you in trouble. Your information has been very helpful to me. You probably shouldn't let people into the lot and go into employee cars but there is no state law that forbids that to my knowledge. Looks like you may have been duped by the 'uncle.' If the company here has rules that you've violated, you may be in trouble with them. If that happens, let me know and I'll let 'em know how you've cooperated with me. Okay?" The guard nodded and Sedwick headed back to Bardstown. He turned his car around a mile down the road and came back to the guard shack. "Steve, what time did Bobby usually leave work?"

"Oh, around five-fifteen. Why?"

"Doesn't matter. Thanks, Steve. And oh, by the way, I may need you to help us get an artist's sketch of the so-called uncle." Not waiting for an answer, the detective headed back to town a second time. He realized that the 'uncle' must have known when Swanson would be driving his car home.

What an ugly accident that murder could have caused—the pipe bomb surely would have left more dead bodies than Bobby Swanson's. Sedwick wondered if the bomb might have been left in the car as a back up in case the murderer failed in his direct attempt to kill Bobby the night before. Strange, that pipe bomb.

When he arrived back in his office, he called Mrs. Maloney. He checked the description of the "uncle" that he received from Steven Schumen and the woman corroborated it. He asked her, "Did Bobby ever say why he wanted to go out the night he was killed?"

"Let's see. As I think about it, I told him about the fellow who you just asked me about—the man who came to the door saying he owed Bobby some money. Bobby seemed real interested. Asked me to describe him. Asked me to tell him anything I could remember about the short visit I had with the man at the door. It wasn't much. I did mention that the fellow wanted to know where Bobby worked. This really upset him. He said that he needed to find this man before the man found him; called him a rotten ol' bootlegger; told me not to tell the man that Bobby was looking for him if he came back here again. When Bobby left that night, I guessed he was going out to find the fellow. Gee, I guess I shoulda told you all this yesterday huh, Detective? I was really too upset. I just can't get Bobby out of my mind; I guess I think of him like a son, Detective."

"It's okay, Mrs. Maloney. Thanks for your help. I'll let you know if I need more. Maybe I'll have you help us produce a picture of the man we just talked about." He hung up.

The city desk sergeant entered Sedwick's office and said, "Here are the reports you've been lookin' for, John. They came in a half-hour ago."

Sedwick took the files without comment and got right into them. Coroner George Cantrell's pathological report provided no more than was surmised at the scene. It was, however, very detailed in regard to brutal trauma to the victim's head. The report indicated that Swanson's death took place between midnight and one in the morning. Death resulted from repeated blows to the entire head and face area, leaving all features bludgeoned and almost indistinguishable except the right ear. No animal was believed capable of delivering such a focused barrage of blows directly to the head. Bruises were also noted around the throat area. A surprising part of Cantrell's report was the conclusion that the beating "could have been delivered *without* any blunt instrument, with the possible exception of a ring the assailant may have worn that could have had a flesh-tearing effect as the blows were delivered." Given the severity of the injuries to the face, the coroner indicated surprise at not finding more evidence of any weapons such as a pipe or baseball bat.

The toxicology report was clean. No alcohol or chemicals of any kind. However, the coroner performed a court-approved autopsy and found serious cirrhosis of the liver indicating possible abuse of one or both of those substances. Sedwick wondered about a part of Cantrell's report that stated Swanson had less than a year to live. He questioned if that had something to do with all this "love of neighbor" that folks had been reporting about him.

Sedwick was disappointed with Teddy Fry's lab report. He came up with only a few smudged fingerprints at the scene and in Bobby Swanson's room except those of the victim or Mrs. Maloney. All the blood samples collected in the parking lot belonged only to the victim. Teddy had collected many hairs and fibers in and around the car but he reported that none were considered useful unless a match could be made with evidence gathered at a later time.

The detective finished the reports and called the local social security office. After repeating Bobby's number, he asked if they could trace any previous address. Then he left the building, drove to McManus Ford, and asked for the manager. A well-groomed man of about thirty came forward and introduced himself as Jim McManus. He was the son of the founder. Young McManus tried to be helpful but no new leads were offered. He himself had approved the sale to Bobby of a car that one of the firm's salesmen had originated. The manager had also approved the financing on the car after he verified the buyer's employment at Moore's Distillery. He checked his new temporary driver's license and Swanson drove off with the car. The whole process took less than an hour.

When Sedwick returned to the office, he called the social security office and found out that Swanson had applied for the number in *their* office, claiming he'd never had a number before. The detective was perplexed. Another dead end? Could it be this man may not have been officially employed anywhere before? His next call was to the driver's license bureau following up on a call he'd made the day before. He was assured that Swanson's expedited picture ID would be on his desk the first thing the next morning.

And it was. The picture was better than he thought it would be. He had the police photographer blow it up and then touch it up a bit. Then he phoned Mrs. Maloney and Steven Schumen and asked if both would come to the police station that afternoon to work together with an artist to help produce a composite sketch of the "stranger" who might be a suspect or could help in the investigation.

From three in the afternoon until six o'clock and most of the next morning, the two worked along with the artist to develop a likeness of the heavyset man with the dark black hair. Sedwick was satisfied only when both agreed on the finished product. Now he was ready to launch his search.

Working with a local printer, Sedwick developed a poster. The top line in bold letters read: **DO YOU KNOW EITHER OF THESE MEN?** Below the pictures the text ran:

The picture above on the right is taken from a recent driver's license photo. This man lived for less than a month in Bardstown, KY. He was known as BOBBY SWANSON. He was employed by Moore's Distillery in Shepherdsville, KY. Mr. Swanson was murdered late March 5 or early March 6, 1981. His body was found in the parking lot of the Bardstown Cathedral. Efforts to learn more about Mr. Swanson, reportedly from the state of West Virginia, have not been successful.

The man on the left is sought as a material witness in this case. Approach with caution.

If YOU know anything about either man, you are encouraged to report any information to Detective John Sedwick of the Bardstown police. Call 1 800-222-2925.

A reward of $5,000 has been offered by the Bardstown Chamber of Commerce for information leading to the prosecution and conviction of the person or persons responsible for this crime.

The detective had a thousand copies made. He sent one to every state highway patrol in the nation and to several government agencies including the FBI. He mailed a copy to every police station serving a town of one thousand or more people in western Kentucky and all of West Virginia. With each poster Sedwick also included a separate general description of the mysterious man that Mrs. Maloney and Steven Schumen had described. He hoped people in the two-state area might recognize Swanson. If he could find out about Swanson, the description of the stranger might be helpful.

For now, he'd done all he knew how to do. But he was fully committed not to let this case go unsolved. He would run down every lead and talk to anyone who might help him. This was *his* case and he'd find the killer.

Chapter Five

"Well, Phil, you sure look better. How are you feeling today?" Father Abbot was pleased that Phil Johnson was able to get out of bed and walk the length of the long hall outside of the infirmary. It had been only five days since Phil's near death. The abbot knew the emergency care provided by the monks, while saving Phil's life, left him still very weak and malnourished.

"A lot better today, Father. I think I can get outta here in a day or so." Phil still wanted some whiskey.

"You *are* a lot better, Phil, but you need to be a whole lot stronger in order to stay out of bed and travel to wherever you're going. Where will you go, anyway?"

"Not sure, Father. I have a sister in Mississippi. I may go visit and stay with her a while."

The abbot had spent many hours with Phil over the past five days. The priest liked this stranger. He enjoyed Phil's open, enthusiastic way of talking. But he also sensed some deep mystery surrounding his patient. What really happened to him the night he was found in the ditch? Why wouldn't he talk about it? Why was this reference to a sister the first inkling that the man had any family? Why did he avoid any conversation about his past or about his occupations or places he'd been or people he knew? When quizzed, Phil would change the subject or require some immediate medical attention. The abbot kept trying.

"Where in Mississippi, Phil?"

"Uh, I don't really don't know, Father," he answered. "I hope she's still there. But if ever I go, I'll find her."

"Phil, why don't you tell me something about yourself. Who are you? Where is your hometown? Besides your sister, do you have other family?" The abbot was earnest yet kindly.

Phil looked pained. "Father, I uh, I really don't want to talk about me. My life's been a mess. The memories hurt too much. I think I just better get on down the road. Y'all've been swell to me. I ain't got a right to stay on here. Been too much trouble already. So, if you'll just help me find my clothes, Father. . . ."

Phil not only wanted to divert attention away from himself, but he was also worried that the abbot's desire to know more about him could threaten his freedom. He hoped to stay a couple more days to regain some strength but he'd find the energy to flee somewhere if the abbot got too nosy.

"No, son. We don't need to talk about you until and unless you want to. This is a monastery. We keep silence for most of our waking hours in order to be thoughtful and prayerful. As the superior here, I make sure that all who visit us here have a chance to communicate their deepest thoughts to someone. It helps one get focused. It allows a certain kind of cleansing that helps each of us during the silent hours become more reflective. No, you don't need to tell me anything at all if you don't desire. That's our rule here."

Phil was relieved. "Thanks, Father. You know, I'm feeling real tired. I think I'd like to take a nap. Okay?"

"Sure, you need the rest, Phil. I won't press you again to tell me more about yourself. But you know I'm always available to listen if you need me. Do you understand, Phil?"

"Thanks again. I get it, Father. You're here for me."

"Right. Now get some sleep. I'll see you later."

Phil thought, *This may just be the best place in the world to hide after all. These people won't bug me because their religion says they shouldn't. What a deal! I'll just lay low here until I feel real strong; then I'll just slip away some night and get out of the country.* As Phil drifted off to sleep, his feeling of comfort turned once more to guilt and brought on another nightmare. A drunk; a murder; his father; a flight.

March turned to April and Phil was stronger. Brother William had been a big help to Phil throughout his convalescence. It was slow going. For most of a month Phil had been on a healthy diet and exercise program. Brother William was also in charge of his menu and making sure he took the antibiotic along with the handful of vitamins that Doctor Vogel had prescribed. The brother would also chart the exercises the doctor suggested. Each day the combined results of this regimen proved useful and helped Phil feel stronger.

Brother Bill and Phil would eat separately. It gave the two men the chance to visit since the abbot had given the brother permission to speak informally with Phil in order to facilitate his recovery. Bill would regale Phil about his younger days as a circus clown. He explained he joined the Trappists after he recovered from an attack by a tiger that almost killed him. They both enjoyed many visits over supper; the brother would mostly talk and Phil would mostly listen.

With spring now well underway, he took to walking outside, roaming the monastery grounds and buildings. He breathed deeply the fresh smells of the season. He was surprised he actually found himself *noticing* the emergings of spring. Trees showing green amidst recently naked branches. Robins active digging worms. Tulips, in an array of colors, now in bloom.

Besides the monastery itself, several other large and small buildings stood to the north behind a long wall. Phil learned that in these buildings most of the work of the monks took place. There were kitchens, packaging rooms, and a catalog mailing center all used in their food businesses. One large red brick building was a library containing much of the archives of the Trappists of Kentucky. The other buildings housed plumbing and welding shops, maintenance shops, and a variety of other utilitarian occupations. The Trappists were in large part, self-sufficient.

Although much of the monastery and the area behind the long wall was off limits for visitors and, to a large extent also to retreatants, Phil was invited to have free rein of the whole of the Trappist property. He was treated like a guest but one who could make himself at home. He tried to remember if he'd ever been as accepted anywhere as he was here.

He enjoyed watching the brothers at work on the land and in the buildings. He was amazed how they could work and communicate with minimum hand signals. They worked efficiently as a team on each chore, whether it was making a batch of cheese or fixing a broken pipe. He noticed a spirit of togetherness, cooperation, and even good humor prevailed among the monks as they worked. He saw how they worked to maintain their large property that defined their lives as monks. They worked to produce the food products that provided needed income to support themselves. And Phil noticed how they always seemed to work happily.

Phil found himself appreciating their contentment even if their ways didn't make all that much sense to him. As he watched, he would catch himself smiling. But before the pleasant distraction would linger too long, he'd often find himself brought back to that nagging question, *Why can't I just forget what happened? Why can't I just have some peace, like these monks?* He was tortured by the never-ending feelings of guilt and longed for some relief from them. He thought about getting some whiskey to help him forget. He hadn't had a drink since the night he murdered the man in the parking lot. Something told him, however, that if he took a drink and was caught, he'd lose his cover at the monastery. So he struggled to put it out of his mind.

Phil had grown a beard. Many of the monks had beards and it gave him some small sense of belonging. Nor was it lost on him that the beard changed his appearance. Another cover. Was it needed? He wondered.

He'd been surprised that he'd heard no discussion about any murder in Bardstown the few times he could overhear visitors chatting as they arrived before a retreat. Due to his condition, he had been unaware of any news or talk about his crime for the first week or two he was at the monastery. After that, he would stop in the reception area to see if any retreatant might have left a newspaper. One day, two weeks back, he was reading an article about Ronald Reagan's first sixty days in office when his eye caught a small blurb at the bottom of the page. The headline read, **No Leads in Parking Lot Murder.** The article followed:

> Bardstown police have no new leads in the case of the death of Bobby Swanson, a recent new resident of Bardstown. Swanson's body was found in the Cathedral parking lot early on March 6. He was beaten to death with blows to the head. He was not robbed.
>
> Swanson, a boarder at Eleanor Maloney's home at 110 Beall Street, was reported to have moved here from West Virginia, however, efforts to locate his home or family in that state have failed, according to John Sedwick, the police investigator in charge of the case. Citizens are again encouraged to contact Investigator Sedwick at the police station, should they have any information about Mr. Swanson or the details surrounding his death.

This late March report had Phil thinking about it since he'd read it. His victim had a name. That made it more personal. Guilt mixed with fear. Why couldn't the authorities find something about his home in West Virginia? Why didn't the report say more about what the police knew or didn't know? What was this Swanson doing in Bardstown? Unless it had been reported earlier, there was no information about any stranger in town getting drunk in Bessie's Bar or any report about the flight of a man on foot, south on 31E, early that morning.

Phil spent time debating his options with himself these days. He was strong enough to travel now. But he had no money or means of support to get him very far or provide a hiding place if he needed one. He wondered if the police might be close to finding him and so weren't reporting anything in the news. While it felt scary to stay so close to Bardstown, he did see some real advantages in his current set-up. The abbot and other monks seemed to have no interest in prying into his private affairs since that one time the abbot tried to open him up a few days after he arrived. It hadn't even been suggested now that he was healthy he ought to leave. He reasoned that his beard changed his appearance enough that if anyone did remember him from the bar or the highway, there was a good chance he wouldn't be recognized now. On the other hand, sooner or later the monks would have to ask him about his plans. Even *these* nice men couldn't be expected to put him up indefinitely. Little by little Phil had gained enough energy until the day came when both he and the abbot had sensed the need to change the relationship.

One morning in the second week of April, a solution, at least a temporary one, was offered. Father Abbot called Phil into his office. "You seem to be healthy again, Phil."

"Yeah, Father. I've been thinking I'm probably starting to get in the way here."

"Oh no, not at all. We've been happy to play a part in getting you healthy again. In fact, since you haven't talked about a home or any place you are anxious to get to, I was wondering if you might be interested in a job? It would include room and board."

"Well, I. . . ."

"You don't have to decide today; take a day or two to think it over. What I had in mind is a groundskeeper's position. The monks do as well as they can but, as you can see, they are all so busy with their everyday inside and outside work, not to mention the regular schedule of community prayer. The mowing and trimming and snow removal sometimes isn't done to the standard I feel it should be to properly welcome our outside visitors. Do you think you might be interested, Phil?"

Phil tried not to react too positively. The abbot was offering him a hide-out. He thought, *If I can do the job, I could stay until I think it's safe to leave. This might give me the time to find out if the police are on my trail. If they're not, I could take off and find a new life.* On a deeper level, however, there was still a gnawing, painful guilt forcing him to try to understand why he was in this situation at all. He questioned if being in this place would help him forget or would it make him feel all the worse about the night in that parking lot.

He said, "I don't have much experience in that sort of work, Father. I think I'd like to stay, but. . . ."

"Don't be concerned. We'll show you how, Phil. Brother Paul is an excellent groundskeeper; he just doesn't have all the time it takes to do the job properly, because we have him so busy with other things. Paul will train you if you want to try learning the job."

"I'll take it," Phil cried impulsively.

"Aren't you interested in what the pay is or the conditions?"

"Oh sure, I guess so."

"They aren't too difficult but it is important that you understand we have some conditions. You'll have to move out of your infirmary room. There is a cell in the basement of the monastery that we no longer use for retreatants. We'll need to fix it up a bit and put a space heater down there but it should provide adequate shelter for you. You can take your meals in the little room off the kitchen where Brother Bill usually eats after he's done feeding the rest of us. Finally, you must respect the silence of both the monks and the retreatants. You may speak briefly whenever it is necessary to do your work. And because you're not a monk, if you're not doing your assigned work around the monastery, you may come and go as you wish. Of course, you may talk with me at any time you wish when I am in my office alone. One more thing, Phil: You showed up here at the monastery drunk. You won't be able to drink here. I'm not exactly sure if you need any kind of treatment but maybe we can arrange some if necessary."

"Don't worry, Father. I can handle it," said Phil, hoping he was right.

The abbot nodded and added, "Oh, I almost forgot. The pay is only one hundred dollars a week."

"Thanks, Father Abbot. I'll still take the job. Y'all sure been good to me around here. I'll try to do good and keep the rules, too," said Phil respectfully.

Over the next few days, with the help of Brother William, the little cell in the basement of the monastery was put in livable order. Phil had already been given some clothes available in good quantity from the retreatants' unclaimed "lost and found." For the first time in many years, Phil had the feeling of a place of his own.

The days following also brought an unexpected pleasure of their own. Brother Paul looked like the large raw-boned farmer he had been before he joined the Trappists. The shock of unkempt hair seemed in place over his rugged yet kindly face. His large hands betrayed years of manual labor. His skills were in such demand that he had been unable to maintain the grounds of the monastery to his own standard of perfection.

The brother welcomed Phil as a helper. Taking advantage of spring landscaping chores now underway, Brother Paul taught his helper how to carefully run the large mower that would cut the large expanses of lawn surrounding the buildings and gardens. He showed him the tricks of edging and trimming using shears and weedwackers. He explained the flower gardens and what would be proper rotation of plantings throughout the coming growing season. The newcomer learned how to correctly cultivate, water, and fertilize each garden and adjust to weather conditions and the change of seasons. Phil received special instructions about the proper care expected around the two cemeteries in the front of the monastery building. His teacher covered every tool and machine, both as to its use and to its care.

Phil found himself interested in his new job. Both he and Brother Paul were surprised how quickly he adapted and learned. When May arrived, the brother was able to let his "hired hand" take over much of the landscaping chores so he himself could meet demands of the farm and buildings. Phil surprised himself with feelings of pride that he'd long ago lost. He admired the beauty of flower beds he'd planted. He would stare at "his" lawns and smile when he saw no weeds. He would cock his head as he appraised the symmetry of a freshly trimmed shrub. He thrilled to see the results of his labor coupled with the miracles of nature.

"Hey, Father Abbot, did you see them roses?" he giggled one June day as he dropped into the superior's office before supper.

"I have, Phil. They're beautiful. You and God have done a wonderful job with the roses this year."

"Oh, yeah. I almost forgot. Me and God. Nice, huh?"

"Phil, I don't mean to pry and I won't if you ask me not to, but I *have* wondered if you've started to think about God at all since you've been with us these past four months?"

Norton was taken aback by the question. This had been the best time of his life that he could remember. But he hadn't really tried to figure out why. He had truly taken to his new home and job. In spite of the restrictions on talking, he had grown fond of the monks, especially brothers Bill and Paul and the abbot, too. There were parts of days when he even forgot his past and the horror of that night in March. But *thinking about God* hadn't occurred to him. He was aware that these monks spent a lot of time on the subject but that wasn't a subject he felt applied to *him*, especially because it never had. And his life had proved that.

"I guess not, Father," said Phil. "Will I have to do that if I'm gonna stay here?" His question merely sought information. He had not attended any of the religious exercises that were part of the daily routine of the monks. He was curious.

"You're not obligated to think about God, Phil, even by Him. Yet I'd like to invite you to let any questions you might have bubble up to the surface; about God or anything at all. If you ever feel comfortable enough to bring some of the questions around, I'd be glad to tell you how *I* try to understand things."

"Okay, I guess, Father." Phil wasn't sure what to make of all this. He wondered if his good luck of the past few months would end if he didn't make some effort to figure out God. The fear of discovery and its penalty that had never been far out of his mind now took the upper hand again and erased his momentary contentment. He wasn't sure if there was a God, or

One who would care much about Phil Norton. The insecurity rose in his stomach.

"Well, don't worry about it now, Phil. You'll know it if you have questions that you'd like to talk about. In the meantime, take good care of those beautiful roses. Okay?"

Relieved, Phil answered, "You bet," and was gone.

Spring turned to summer and the Trappist monastery grounds bloomed. The walled garden in front of the monastery was Phil's special show place. The garden was used by the monks and retreatants for quiet walks and silent thoughts. He felt it was his job to make it as nice as possible for all who used it. He tended the several varieties of roses. He shaped and trimmed each evergreen and each flower bed every day. He mowed the grass twice a week. He checked each bush and plant as if his own.

One day the abbot found the groundskeeper returning a tractor to the shed. "Phil, Brother Tom who usually drives our van to town is ill today. Do you have a driver's license?"

"No, Father, I'm sorry."

"Well, I guess I could have old Brother Dustin drive into Bardstown, but I need you to go with him then to load the supplies. He's too crippled to do much besides drive."

Quick and sharp came the pain in Phil's stomach. He had not left the monastery since he arrived. His choice would not have been to make Bardstown his first trip away from his new home. He struggled balancing his fear with a certain curiosity about what might be happening there in regard to a murder investigation. He saw no reasonable way of refusing. "Well, okay, Father. I better go change clothes; I've got dirt all over me."

"You do that, Phil; I'll have Brother Dustin pick you up by the front door of the monastery in fifteen minutes."

Phil hurried to his room, changed clothes, and donned a used baseball cap retrieved from the lost and found. He looked in the small mirror on his wall. Yes, his beard was quite full now. The cap helped. He was satisfied that the man going to Bardstown didn't look much at all like the man on the road in March.

Brother Dustin was an old monk; hard to say how old but surely over eighty. His medium stature was shortened by a curved spine common to his age. He had long white hair over a face where pink cheeks and wrinkles coexisted. The brother continued to wear the long robe, or habit, that all the monks wore while at the monastery. He greeted Phil with a chuckle as his rider climbed into the passenger seat. "Hi sonny," he said. "I'm glad to have you along to do the hard work. At my age, I can just sit here nice and pretty in the driver's seat and watch you load all the groceries. It sure is fun to get out once in a while; see what's goin' on; even chat a little."

And chat he did. The old monk was enjoying an outing. On the fifteen minute ride to town, he told Phil about all that had changed at the monastery since he had joined the Trappists almost sixty years ago. How the rule of silence had been even more strict. How the work was tougher years ago without the more modern machinery. How the meals were more sparse, more monastic. How he had been the only monk allowed to drive a motor vehicle until ten years ago when the work of the monks required more mobility. . . .

Phil was only half-listening. He wondered about Bardstown. Soon 31E crossed the Beech Fork River bridge and there they were. Bessie's Bar. The cathedral. The parking lot. His heartbeat quickened. He noticed he was sweating more than normal. He had forced himself to surpress as much of this scene as he could. But even spring to summer and night to day brought it all back. His exit from the bar. The car pulling up to him in the parking lot. His rage at one who would help—not his father. The murder. The flight. Phil thought he might be sick.

Just a block and a half past the cathedral, on Stephen Foster Avenue, they pulled into the Kroger parking lot. Brother Dustin was speaking. "Well here we are, sonny. Here's the list. You go on in there and put all this stuff in a cart or two and have 'em ring it up. Tell 'em it's for the Trappists and they'll send us a bill. Then come on back and load it all in the van. I'll just sit here and wait on ya."

Phil recovered some from his bad memories and tried to focus on his assigned task. He completed the shopping chore in about forty-five minutes; he and a carryout employee each pushed a large-sized grocery cart into the parking lot with Phil leading the way. He returned to the spot where the van was parked and found the vehicle empty. Brother Dustin was not to be seen anywhere near the van. He asked the store carryout clerk to watch the carts as he quickly searched the whole lot. No brother. Phil reasoned that Dustin had become warm and must have entered the store or some nearby place to find relief from the heat. So with the help of the carryout, he quickly loaded the groceries into the van. He ran back into the store and checked all the aisles. Again, no sign of him. Then he set out to find the brother along nearby streets. He wondered if the old monk was a bit daft and prone to just wandering off. He also thought that the man might have become sick and been carried off somewhere. He doubted that the brother was the victim of any crime at this time of day in a busy parking lot. Bottom line: he had to find him.

Phil walked along Fifth Street past Spalding Hall, took a turn to the left and found himself directly in front of the police station. He froze. A quick shiver. Then he thought, *They can't be looking for me. And even if they are, how could they know who I am or what I'm supposed to look like? If I'm gonna find the old brother, this is the place to start.* He took a deep breath and walked into a red brick one-story building that housed both the police and fire departments. A tired-looking uniformed officer sitting behind the glass at the front desk asked, "What can I do for ya?"

"I'm a hired man out at the Trappist monastery. They call it the Abbey at Gethsemani. I came into town with an old brother and left him in the parking lot of the Kroger store around the corner. I was shopping in the store for I don't know how long and when I came out he was gone! I don't know if he just went looking around town or if he's in some kinda trouble."

"Well, you came to the right place. And I do know what they call the monastery. About forty minutes ago, a lady came runnin' in here saying that some old guy was unconscious in a van at Kroger's. She said she'd spotted him and couldn't rouse him. I called the paramedics and they came and got him. Took him to the hospital. Just two minutes ago, I got a call that he had had a heat stroke, whatever that is. Anyhow, they said he was coming out of it and they'd be keepin' him there a while for observation. He'll probably be okay."

Phil was relieved that the brother was found and, with luck, going to recover. He considered the situation and asked if he could call the monastery. Given the phone, he looked blankly at the officer. "I'm sorry, could you tell me the phone number out there? I've never had to call it." The policeman rolled his eyes, looked up the number, and dialed it for Phil. He reached Father Abbot and recounted the events of the afternoon. The abbot told Phil that he already got a call from the hospital; that he would drive their old car to town and bring along Brother Tom to drive the van back to Gethsemani. He told Phil to wait at the police station and he'd be picked up there.

Unnerved a bit, Phil wondered what to do with himself. He thought he'd busy himself by looking at the bulletin board. His eye caught it immediately. A large poster with a banner headline: **DO YOU KNOW EITHER OF THESE MEN?** He was shocked. There on the right was the picture of the young man with light-colored long hair whom Phil encountered in the cathedral parking lot months ago. He was sure of it. Somehow, even in his drunken stupor, the face he had transferred to his father's had been etched in his mind. He scanned the text.

The man had a name. Bobby something. Images of the scene came streaming back into his consciousness. Phil was fascinated and terrified at the same time.

He was about to take a look at the sketch of the man on the left when out of the corner of his eye, Phil saw a man enter the police station, pause, and watch him reading the poster. The man walked over to Phil, put a hand on his shoulder, and asked, "Know either of these guys?"

"No!" Phil almost screamed.

"Oh, I'm sorry to startle you, sir. I'm Detective Sedwick. This is my case. I talk to anyone who might have the slightest information about these two men. You seemed to be reading so intently, I thought just maybe you could help me. I'll tell you this: I'd *love* to get my hands on this guy."

"I uh, I uh, was just waiting here to be picked up. I work at the monastery at Gethsemani. I was in town with an older monk who got sick; he's in your hospital. I'm just waiting for the abbot, he's the boss, to come and pick me up. Detective."

"That's fine, oh, Brother, is it? If you or anyone else can tell me anything about the victim, this Swanson fellow, I need to know it. Sometimes, I think I can see his killer in my sleep. Maybe I get too caught up in it."

Phil hoped the policeman didn't see *him* in his sleep. He said hurriedly, "I understand, Detective. Sorry I can't help you." He decided not to correct the detective about his status at the monastery. "My ride should be here soon and I'll be out of your hair."

Phil left the building to wait for the abbot outside the police station. He felt his heart pounding. He was excited and his breathing was slow to return to normal. A close call? Maybe not. He was right there with the person who was trying to find him. The detective gave no indication that he suspected Phil. If he could come into the police station and talk to his would-be captor about the victim, maybe, just maybe he might be safe. *After all, if no one saw the murder and no one was looking for him in particular, why shouldn't he be safe?*

He pondered this thought as the abbot drove up. Phil got into the car and the abbot drove him and Brother Tom back to the Kroger lot. Brother Tom and Phil drove the van back to the monastery as the abbot went on to the hospital to visit the improving Brother Dustin.

On the way back to the monastery, Brother Tom was silent so Phil found himself wondering about the other man on the poster. He didn't get a good enough look at the sketch to bring to mind anyone he knew. Did the police think this person might be the murderer or did they think he might have seen who really did it? Part of him was pleased that the police might be spending time looking for someone else and part of him worried that, in spite of all he remembered, someone just may have watched the ugly scene that night in the cathedral parking lot. At this point, his worry overpowered any concern he might have that some innocent man may be charged with the murder that he, Phil, had committed.

Chapter Six

By the spring of 1983, Phil Norton (alias Johnson) had become an accomplished groundskeeper. Over the past two years Brother Paul was pleased with how much Phil had learned about maintaining the grounds in all seasons. He saw how Phil had learned to agitate and till the soil for the variety of plantings as well as how to adjust the blade heights of the mowers and lubricate the many types of trimmers. He had showed Phil just once how to sharpen the edgers and the brother was surprised to see him do it right from that point on. Paul had explained how the rose gardens needn't be cultivated if properly mulched in the fall. And how to cultivate the tulip beds that had been planted in the fall. Lately, Phil needed little coaching from Brother Paul, who'd been tickled that *Phil* had designed a scheme and added several varieties of bushes around three of the walls bordering the monastery.

Since his arrival at the monastery, Phil had also taken a correspondence course in basic machinery maintenance. He spent many winter days in the machine shed repairing tractors and mowers and other landscaping machinery. He would assess a needed repair, refer to his school manual and, through trial and error, fix what needed fixing. Then he'd show off his accomplishment to Brother Paul, who seldom needed to correct Phil's efforts.

Father Abbot enjoyed watching Phil when he was working. The handyman seemed truly caught up in his work. But when he wasn't working, the abbot thought Phil seemed preoccupied and distant. The priest was careful not to pry into Phil's deepest thoughts, but he wondered if his groundskeeper might be struggling to bury a troublesome past in favor of his new life. The man worked hard and volunteered for any work that came along and often added effort to any chore to extend the time to finish it. The abbot wondered if Phil might not *want* to always be alone with his thoughts and working had become his escape.

Phil did relish his work and loved the freedom from thoughts of the past that work afforded him. After two and a half years of not hearing anything or even reading anything about the murder, his fear of capture was all but gone . . . but remorse over his crime bothered him even more. Some nights when he couldn't sleep, he wished he could ease his mind with alcohol. He would say to himself, "I can't, I just can't," as he would grit his teeth and muster some new found willpower.

Sometimes even his surroundings made him feel guilty. He saw how the monks were kind to each other and to the retreatants who visited each week. The monks didn't seem to judge him; they didn't act like they suspected him of any wrongdoing. In fact, he sometimes thought they might even forgive him if they did know the whole story. But he wasn't ready to test that. Phil thought, *I'm accepted by these guys, but I'm a killer, they should hate me, if they knew what I did. How in the world could they accept me if they knew?* He tortured himself.

He didn't quite know what to make of their religion, either. If his chores didn't demand his attention, he had little else to do when the monks were in chapel. So Phil would often slip in, sit in the back row, and listen. He enjoyed the rhythmic sounds of the Gregorian Chant even though he didn't understand the Latin. But when the monks prayed out loud in English, the lofty and sometimes flowery words were mostly lost on him. What he liked the best were the sermons at Mass or during retreats when the Trappist priests would preach.

They talked common sense to Phil. They spoke of God as the Creator and referred their listeners to what they saw around them in nature and in human accomplishment—showing how people are God's finest creation. The priests would explain how, even though God's special gift of free will was often turned to evil, human existence would be far less impressive without free will. In their talks, Phil realized these Trappists didn't try to explain mysteries that only God Himself understood. But they did offer a view of God and Jesus as loving, not condemning. Forgiveness was stressed. They showed while hell was possible for those who didn't seek forgiveness, heaven was possible for the worst sinner who did seek it. Phil made special note of that idea.

He heard these themes over and over again. Each preacher had his own twist but the messages were the same. While he found a certain peace in the past year and a half, he did wonder if what these men preached really applied to him. He had never enjoyed work before now; he had never before had friends like these monks had become. Still, there was the ever-present night in Bardstown. Again, he'd ask himself, "Could a murderer like me who murdered a person who was actually trying to help me—a man who did nothing to deserve to be killed—could I be forgiven and find real peace?" He doubted. Then often he'd become obsessed with guilt and remorse.

One evening during supper, Brother William asked Phil a question that hit him like a club in the back of the head.

"Phil, why haven't you ever asked me about how to become a monk?"

"What!"

"Why haven't you asked me what it takes to become one of us?"

"Brother Bill," he cried, "I'm not even a Catholic. I'm not any religion. I'm just the hired man here."

"Haven't you wondered about us? You seem to enjoy living here and working here. I see you even join us many hours in the chapel. Seems to me you might just think about becoming a Trappist."

"I do like it here. I even like some of your chapel services. But I'm not really religious. I don't even know what I believe in, Bill." His reaction was a mix between surprise and curiosity. With his past, the idea of becoming a monk was not something he thought about. And yet even the brother's question seemed intriguing.

"Look, Phil," replied the brother, "I don't know if it's a good idea or not. You'd have to go through a lot to learn what you *do* believe or what you *can* believe and then there would be lots of study just to join the church. After that, if you were still interested in joining our order, you would have to spend a year as a novice before you could take temporary vows. Next, you live our life for three more years before you take final vows, which makes you a Trappist Brother for life. 'Course, if you wanted to be a Trappist Priest, you're talking many more years of study. Really, Phil, I only asked you the question to make sure that if you actually were thinking about any of this, that you felt invited to keep thinking about it and start getting some answers, too."

"I don't know what to say, Bill. I don't know if I'm interested or not. I'm happy being your hired hand. And that's maybe all I wanna be." He hesitated. "I don't even know what I wanna know."

"That's easy, Phil. Make an appointment with the abbot, tell him what we talked about, and he'll take it from there. Or, if you just want to start by learning more about the church, any of us around here would be happy to talk with you and give you some stuff to read if you're interested. In fact, that probably makes more sense anyway; see if you're interested before we take this too far."

"I guess it wouldn't hurt to find a little more about what you guys believe in. Even if I don't buy it, it may help me be a better employee around here."

"Great, Phil. Tonight, I'll slip a pamphlet on Catholic beliefs under your door. When you finish it, ask me or anyone else around here you feel comfortable with for a private meeting. Get your questions answered. No pressure, my friend." The monk moved toward the door.

"Uh, thanks Brother," Phil said as his friend was departing. "I don't know if this makes sense but what you said a minute ago about 'being invited' sounds good to me. I'll give it a shot."

Late that night, Phil finished the pamphlet that Brother William had left. It covered what Catholics believe about the Trinity, the Virgin Birth, Christ's resurrection, confession and forgiveness, heaven and hell, and the seven sacraments. He found it all pretty confusing and wasn't sure he believed any of it. But he was surprised that he didn't out-and-out reject anything. Some of it he'd picked up before in the sermons he heard in the chapel. His biggest doubt focused on how a little piece of bread could become the Body of Christ, but he went to bed figuring that he wasn't going to figure that one out in one night.

For the next several days, Phil went through the motions. His work was satisfactory but he was on "autopilot." His mind went back to the pamphlet. He struggled with what seemed believable and what wasn't. He noticed a certain tension around himself as he thought about what he'd read. At times, he felt exhilarated; at others, he felt unworthy; and at still other moments, he wondered if he was in the right place. He felt like the ball in a ping-pong game. But he kept coming back to Brother William's invitation to ask and learn. He thought about talking to Brother Paul or William himself. But he found himself wanting to go right to the head man, Father Abbot. He had admired the abbot from their first encounter. He figured this man would have the all answers he sought. Phil made up his mind.

"Father, I wonder if I could set up an appointment with you?" he said one morning as he encountered the abbot walking in the garden.

"Of course, Phil. Is there anything troubling you?"

"Well, no not really, Father. I, uh. . . . Well, I'd really like to wait 'til we talk to explain."

"Sure. How 'bout tomorrow morning at nine?"

"Good, I'll be in your office then, Father." Phil hurried away, wondering if he'd done the right thing. The rest of that day and most of the night, he rehearsed his conversation with the abbot. He tried to anticipate how the abbot might react to Phil's inquires about the faith. Would he have to reveal everything that he'd guarded so carefully? Would he have to tell about his past, about his crime, in order to just learn about becoming a Catholic?

Phil was tired when he arrived at the abbot's office the next morning. "Is this a good time, Father? Or should I come back?"

"No, come on in, Phil. Sit down. How can I help you?"

"I don't know where to start. I guess maybe I should tell you that Brother Bill stopped me a week or so ago and surprised me with a question. He asked me if I wanted to become a Trappist monk. Well, I was blown away. Then he said I'd first have to decide if I wanted to become a Catholic. He gave me a booklet." Phil held up the pamphlet to show the abbot. "I read it through many times. I don't know if I wanna become a Catholic, Father. It may not be for me. But I think I'd like to learn more about it. Since you probably know more about it than anyone around here, I was wonderin' if you could teach me?"

The abbot got up from his chair, walked to Phil's chair, took his hand, and pulled him to his feet. A lone tear appeared on his cheek. He gave Phil a bear hug, stood back, and said, "I'd be very pleased to help you, Phil."

Both men were silent for a moment. The abbot spoke first. "Here's what we'll do. I'll assign Father Emmet to spend an hour a day with you to teach you about our religion in detail. Father Emmet is the best theologian in the monastery. He'll explain the principal truths that we follow in our faith and provide insights into why we believe them. In the end, though, you'll have to decide if you believe them. Faith is different than knowledge in that certainty is not proven in this life. If you come to believe, it is a gift from God. Then you can join us."

"I guess that sounds okay. But I was hoping you could teach me, Father."

"You couldn't do better than Father Emmet as the teacher, Phil. My role will be to accept you into the church if and when you're ready. I'll meet with you often to see how you take to what you're learning from Father Emmet. I'll talk to you about how I think we can *live* the faith. If you've already been baptized in some other Christian church, I'll hear your first confession before you make a declaration of faith accepting what we believe as Catholics. Then I'm authorized to confirm you as an adult member of the faith. How does that sound, Phil?"

Phil was relieved he didn't have to spill his whole story here and now. He thought he'd probably have to tell all eventually, but he could first see if this Catholic religion was for him before he risked exposing his horrible past. He didn't understand what baptism had to do with confession; he didn't think he'd been baptized but didn't know for sure. He decided that question could wait for a while. "Sounds good, Father," he said. He walked slowly back to his room.

When he left, he stopped along a long corridor to look out a window that opened onto the walled garden that was the front yard of the main monastery building. The flower beds and plantings were in perfect spring bloom. The multi-colored tulips that Phil had decided to plant last fall (without permission) were brilliant in the late morning sun. He admired it all; this was *Phil's* front yard, the fruit of his labor, this was home. His body felt an involuntary shiver. It was the collision of two emotions, both peace and anxiety, over the journey that awaited him.

Chapter Seven

In these years that Phil Norton was finding shelter and new life at the Trappist Monastery, eight miles north Detective John Sedwick seldom let himself drift far from the hunt for Bobby Swanson's killer.

One morning a week after the Swanson murder when Sedwick had arrived at the station, the desk sergeant told him there was someone waiting for him. He turned and saw the younger man sitting in one of the waiting chairs in the small lobby of the station. He was a short, muscular fellow with dark black hair. "You lookin' for me?" the detective said in the man's direction.

"Are you Detective Sedwick?"

Sedwick nodded and the man said apologetically, "I'm not sure I have any thing important, sir. But I read about the murder the other night, the one at the cathedral, and. . . ."

"Come into my office, son; I'm all ears on this case."

The man followed the detective into his small office. He took the only side chair in the room and said, "My name is Tom Lee, Detective. I'm from Louisville; been the night bartender at Bessie's Bar for the last three months. This may be a long shot but we had a pretty tough customer in the bar late the other night, the night of the murder."

"Tell me about him." Sedwick became very focused.

"Well, this guy was drinking heavy. He was talkin' smart to the other customers. Angry old coot. He ran out of money and expected me to give him one on the house. When I refused, he got ugly. I threw him out. The guy was so mad—he swore and threatened to get us all. Like we did something to him. After I shoved him out the door, I noticed his jacket on the bar stool, tossed it out the door, and yelled for him to come and pick it up. He didn't pay any attention; he just kept walkin' up the highway toward town."

"What'd he look like, Tom, is it?"

"Yes. He was built about like me, fatter though. And older. Hair was lighter but not blond. His face was red like a drinker's face."

Sedwick was disappointed. He pointed to the flyer on his desk and asked if the artist's sketch on the left looked like his tough customer. He also asked if the victim, Bobby Swanson, shown on the poster was in the bar that night. Tom had to say no to both questions. He did not recognize either man on the poster.

"Well, I think your mouthy drunk is just a coincidence, Tom," said the policeman. "We feel pretty sure that this guy here on the poster is our man. But I do appreciate your comin' in. I'll make some notes about your incident the other night and toss it in the file. You never know about these things. Maybe your drunk will get himself in some other trouble, too." He shook the young man's hand and thanked him again. Tom left.

Sedwick did make some brief notes about Tom's story and put them in the Swanson murder file. Then he forgot about it.

By late summer of 1981, the people of Bardstown were still speaking of the murder of Bobby Swanson when they gathered to talk. But some of the intensity of concern and curiosity had abated over time. Any leads that surfaced were long shots and didn't even make the front page of the local newspaper any longer.

John Sedwick was frustrated. He ran down every lead. He accepted every invitation to be interviewed for a newspaper article or a radio show. He even got on two morning TV shows. In all these media opportunities, besides repeating what was known about his chief suspect, he retold what the body of Bobby Swanson looked like when it was found. He thought that the brutality of the murder would keep it in people's minds and so give him a better chance to catch the perpetrator.

Over the course of the next year, Sedwick would follow up every lead no matter how remote. He spent two long spring nights in 1982 on a stakeout in Louisville after he had been sent a photo of a man who resembled the sketch that had blanketed the area. When the man came home to his apartment at five on the second morning, John accosted him at the door, flashed his badge, and said in an unfriendly tone, "I'm Detective Sedwick from Bardstown investigating a murder. I have checked in with the Louisville police, who know I'm here. I wanna talk to you."

The man, startled, replied, "What the heck is all this about?"

Sedwick didn't answer but mused, "Yesss, you do look like our perp; maybe a few pounds lighter but the face is sure right on." Then, more directly, he barked, "What's your name, buddy?"

"I'm not your buddy. What in heaven's name do you want anyway? What authority do you have here?"

"Never you mind, mister. Let's just step into your apartment and I'll give a call to the local police, and while they are on their way, you and I can have a nice little visit." Sedwick exposed the gun under his sport coat. The man hesitated, then opened the door. Sedwick pushed the man through the entry causing him to stumble and hit his head against a vestibule wall.

Inside, with no apologies to the astonished apartment resident, Sedwick made a quick call for a policeman to join him, hung up, turned, and said to the man rubbing his head, "What's your name and what is your occupation?"

"My name is Fenton Taylor. I'm a Peace Corps advisor for the government. I travel on various assignments around the world."

"Oh *sure* you are, and where were you last March fifth and sixth?"

"That's easy. I was in Africa working with a group of volunteers. Of, course you can check that." Mr. Taylor was feeling more confident now. "I think you have made some awful mistake here, Detective, and if I were not a forgiving sort, I might want to make some formal protest here."

"Listen, buddy. You can make all the protests you want. Yeah, you're our killer all right and you'll lie your way out of anything. We're gonna nail you, pal. Look, look here and see." Sedwick pulled out a flyer and showed his suspect.

"Yes, I see some resemblance but I can assure you it is not me, sir."

When the local policeman arrived, a call was made to the regional supervisor of the Peace Corps. The sleepy woman, awakened at her home, verified that Fenton Taylor had indeed been out of the country when Swanson was murdered.

A sheepish and embarrassed John Sedwick did his best to apologize and hoped his "victim," in his kindness, would not be making much out of the detective's mistake.

Mr. Taylor responded, "We all make mistakes, Mr. Sedwick. Perhaps you'll do a bit more checking in the future." Breathing easier, Bardstown's "finest" couldn't get out of there fast enough.

But this setback didn't stop the detective's relentless search for Swanson's killer. If he didn't keep up his quest on his own, the community pressure was enough by itself to provide motivation. Even though the topic was less pervasive than in the first year, for John the people did not let it rest. Whenever Bardstown people ran into him, they'd asked, "How ya comin', John?" He couldn't avoid the people or the question. He was their reminder of how their town had been violated.

For the next couple of years John Sedwick kept the case primary among his other duties. He called the local police every time he heard or read of a West Virginia bootlegger getting in some kind of trouble. He would describe his man and usually be disappointed. On occasion a ray of hope dawned if the description was close. In the end, however, no one ever fit.

Other leads went nowhere. One involved a reported rumor that one of Swanson's co-workers at the distillery had been jealous of Bobby's quick success at work. The detective quickly dismissed this after seeing the man and learning that he had an iron-clad alibi for the night of the murder. Another lead proved worthless that involved a call from Texas from a man who'd seen a poster while traveling through West Virginia on a vacation. The caller was positive he'd seen the suspect working at the front desk of a motel in Charleston. A few phone calls to local authorities quickly eliminated the hotel clerk.

As the months passed, the detective was weary and tempted to give up. He didn't know where else to go with this thing. The passion was still there, though, and he would somehow have to find the energy and inspiration to continue. John Sedwick told himself he was not a quitter.

Chapter Eight

Phil met with Father Emmet for an hour every day from June through October 1983. Phil had not been to school for many years. He didn't like it then but he took to it now. Emmet was a good instructor. He spent the first couple of months taking Phil through the Bible. First they covered the familiar Old Testament stories. The priest would explain the passage like a campfire storyteller; Phil would then read it for himself in the evening. The following day they handled any questions before moving on to the next passage.

Phil enjoyed reading Bible stories. As they progressed, he asked questions about Adam's sin and why God asked Abraham to kill Isaac. He and Emmet talked about why God didn't let Moses lead the Jews into the promised land after he spent forty years getting them to the brink. Phil wondered about the contradiction of God being so good to King David after he'd murdered the fellow who was married to David's lover, Bathsheba.

Mostly Phil asked Emmet his questions, but the one about David he saved for one of his occasional meetings with the abbot. Phil identified with David. Impulsive, explosive, but sometimes soft of heart. He was intrigued with the idea that a murderer like King David might be forgiven. The abbot explained.

"Phil that's what the good news is all about. God is a forgiving God. All He asks is that we want his forgiveness and are resolved not to repeat our sins."

"But murder, Father?"

"Even murder, Phil. This doesn't mean that a murderer might not have to pay a hefty price on this side of the grave but, if the person is contrite, forgiveness is there. Why does that surprise you, Phil?"

"Oh no special reason." Phil wasn't ready to tell his story yet. "Maybe I thought some sins just couldn't be forgiven. Anyhow, I kinda like the Bible stories, Father," he said, changing the subject.

And so it went. Phil studied with Father Emmet and then by himself. As they moved to the New Testament, he found himself interested in details of the life of Christ that he had not considered before. He was surprised at how forgiving Jesus was. From there, they began to discuss the Catholic

Church, going into more detail than was in the little pamphlet Brother Bill had first given to Phil. Emmet covered each of the seven sacraments, the precepts and rules of the church, and the differences between church rules which could change with time and basic precepts Catholics believe to be the law of God Himself.

Phil smiled to himself one day and thought, *Maybe there's something to this.* He couldn't prove the truth of it all but he had no serious doubts. When he mentioned that to the abbot one day, he was a bit startled to hear him say, "That's called faith, Phil. That's the gift from God I told you about."

"Well then, does that mean I can become a Catholic, maybe even a monk?" Phil enthused.

"Well, let's take it a step at a time, Phil. Let's see, it's the middle of October. You go ahead and finish up your studies with Emmet. I'll meet with you early next month and test you a bit on what you believe and what you don't. If that goes well, we can plan for your first confession and baptism."

Oh man, thought Phil. The idea of telling his story and revealing his sin was becoming a reality. He was anxious. Part of him wanted to tell it; the major part was frightened. Then he remembered his question about baptism. "Oh Father, I don't know if I've been baptized. Don't really think I have. What do we do now?"

"We have to try to find out, Phil. See, if you haven't been baptized, you don't need confession. All sin is wiped away with the Sacrament of Baptism. Any serious sin you commit after baptism must be confessed."

"Wow," said Phil. "That's a great deal."

The abbot chuckled. "Yes it is, Phil. The deal comes from God. No strings attached. However, I do recommend that you do tell me about your past life at some point before you accept baptism. It will give me a sense of your conversion and should also give you a sense of peace. Now, how can we find out if you've been baptized?"

Phil thought that if he could somehow reach his older sister, he might find out. "Let me try, Father. Might take a week or so. Can I let you know?"

"Sure, Phil. Then we can finalize just how you can come into the church."

"Okay, Father. I'll let you know."

"Phil, there is one more thing. You have studied hard and learned a great deal. You have even mentioned that you're coming to believe in much of what you are learning. As all this has been happening, have you been praying?" asked the abbot.

Phil was startled. Yes, he *had* been studying and accepting much of what he was learning. He'd heard and read about people of faith praying. He sat in the chapel and heard countless prayers. He was dumbfounded that it had never occurred to him that he, too, might pray. He figured, up to now, his guilt was a barrier to anything resembling direct contact with God. Then as if asking permission, he asked the abbot, "Is that okay—since I'm not accepted yet in your church? And how do I pray?"

"It's easy, Phil. Do you ever talk to yourself?"

Somewhat embarrassed, he answered, "Oh, I suppose I do once in a while."

"Phil, we all do. Most of the time silently; sometimes even out loud; it's normal. Well, praying is something like talking to yourself except Someone is listening. Oh, of course, there are all kinds of formal prayers that we can say or read, but I think the best kind of prayer is just talking to God the Father or Jesus or His mother. Just nice and easy, like you might talk to yourself when you are trying to figure out how to arrange a flower bed. Try it, Phil."

"What should I talk about, Father?"

"Anything. For starters, try Him out on all your studies. Tell Him what you like and what you aren't so sure about. Tell Him what you're afraid of. If you've had a good day, thank Him. A bad day, ask for help."

Phil was becoming curious about the possibility of actually talking to God. Up to now his interest had been mostly intellectual even as he was buying into what he'd been learning. But a personal conversation with God hadn't yet occurred to him. He thought he'd like to try. "I'll give it a go, Father," he said and left to return to his room.

As he lay on his bed that night, he did try. "Don't really know you, God. I've been learning about you, though. You sound pretty good to me. I guess I'd like to ask you something. Can you give me a hand with all this? Thanks, God." Phil slept.

⌒

The information operator had been trying to help Phil for almost twenty minutes. "Her name is Norton. Susan Norton. I'm sure she lives some where around Biloxi."

"I'm sorry, sir. I've looked in a large section of the southern 601 area code. No Susan Norton. But since all of Mississippi is in the 601 area, let me do a state-wide search and call you back. I'll need to charge your phone five dollars for the search, okay?" The woman was trying to be helpful.

"Okay." Phil gave her the number of the monastery and the extension number of his little garden shed. He told her he could be reached at that extension from nine to ten the next morning. As he hung up he made a mental note to tell the brother who kept the monastery books to reduce his pay for any phone charges to his extension.

Phil wondered what he would say if the information operator found her. He hadn't spoken to his sister for nearly twenty years. He didn't think she would be married; as a young woman she fell off a porch roof while helping to paint the house. She was paralyzed from the waist down and confined to a wheelchair. Phil's final blowup with his father happened about a week after the accident. He left and had not returned or had any contact with his family since then. From time to time he did regret not contacting his sister. Two years older than Phil, she had been his only ally, but when he left he wanted no connection with his life or roots in Biloxi, Mississippi.

That night, Phil dreamt about his sister. *He was an eight-year-old and she ten. After a beating by his dad, she found him crying, curled up under the front porch of their farm house. She played a game with him, fantasizing the two of them were on a big ocean liner sailing off to Hawaii. They'd seen some magazine pictures and had decided Hawaii must be the best place in the whole world. Susan would tell of the fine food and the nice people they would encounter on the ship. Phil would ask where they would live in Hawaii and Susan would describe the grass hut. On they would go, with Phil asking questions and Susan painting the glorious pictures of their runaway trip. After their fantasy, Phil felt better and the two would go back in the house to cope another day.* When Phil awoke in his monastery room, he wanted the dream to linger. It felt so good.

The next morning, Phil's heart skipped a beat when the operator called and said she had a number for an S. Norton in rural Jackson. Phil took down the number and, before he could finalize what he'd say, dialed it.

"Yes," a woman answered. Even after all that time, Phil could tell that the woman was not his sister.

"I'm looking for Susan Norton. Is she at this number?"

"There is no Susan Norton here. My name is Sandra. Is this Susan you are looking for from the Jackson area?"

"Not originally. We, I mean she was from Biloxi. I haven't seen her in twenty years, so she may have moved."

"My sister-in-law was from Biloxi. Her name was Susan Norton. Who is this?"

Still cautious, Phil answered, "It doesn't matter. Can you help me find her?"

"Maybe I can but I need to know who I'm talking to?"

"Let's say I'm related to her and would like to see her again."

"Is this Phillip Norton?"

Phil gulped. "Yes," he said quietly. He needed to find his sister.

"Well, hello brother-in-law. I was married to your brother for ten years before he was killed."

"*What?* I don't know what to say . . . Sandra, did you say your name was? What happened to Kenny?" Phil was overcome. His mind raced. He sat.

Sandra Norton gave Phil a quick picture of the family history. Phil's parents were killed in a car accident in 1965. They were returning from a bar late one summer evening and ran off the road near a swamp and drowned. His dad had been drunk. Kenny and Sandra were married in 1967. She spoke of her husband as a caring, loving man who adored her and their daughter, Kerry, now fifteen. The family of three owned and worked a small peach orchard thirty miles north of Biloxi. Kenny was killed in a tractor accident during the harvest in '77. Susan had lived with Kenny after their parents died. She tried life on her own for six months when Kenny was married but it was too difficult. She moved in with Kenny and Sandra and stayed on for a year after Kenny died. Sandra could not manage the orchard operation and sold it. She and her daughter rented a house on a small farm near Jackson; Susan was moved to a nursing facility in Memphis. Sandra used the insurance money and the equity in the farm to support herself and her daughter while she finished college at Jackson State. She had a good job as a social worker for Rankin County. Kerry Norton, Phil's niece, was a popular teenager in her sophomore year at Jefferson, the local high school.

Phil could hardly grasp it all. His parents dead. His brother dead. His sister in a nursing home. Discovering a sister-in-law and a niece who he never knew he had. "Man! Lots has happened since I left. There's much to say, Sandra. But I'm not ready yet. Someday I want to meet you and Kerry. Kenny and I were never close; he was three years younger; Dad was always nice to him and not to me. Or at least that's the way I saw it then. I really do hope we can meet one day and maybe there's a chance for me to have a real family for the first time ever. For now, though, can you tell me how to reach my sister?"

"She isn't well, Phil. Her paralysis is very pronounced. She's having some breathing problems, too. I think you ought to see her as soon as you can." Sandra gave him the address and phone number of the Memphis Manor in Memphis, Tennessee. They signed off with promises to be in touch as soon as Phil felt comfortable with getting acquainted.

Phil had a load to absorb. All the family news made him sad. He felt guilty for not having had a closer relationship with his only brother. He was worried about his sister. He had some sense of joy, however, to know that his brother left a widow and daughter whom he might meet someday. But first, his sister. He called Memphis and found out that visiting hours were every day in the afternoon. He called the abbot, explained that his sister lived in Memphis, and asked if he could have some time off to visit her.

The abbot agreed and two days later Phil was on the early morning bus to Memphis.

An old converted hospital, the Memphis Manor stood three stories high. It was a solid red brick building with two wings that headed straight back from the large rectangular main building. It was built just before the first world war and located on the fringe of downtown Memphis, a neighborhood now in some decay.

Phil asked the receptionist at the main desk for directions to find his sister. He soon found himself in the large general lobby area of the third floor right wing. About forty residents sat around the room. Some watched TV, a few were reading, most sat looking mindlessly into nowhere. One was in the corner trying to sing "Take Me Back To Ol' Virginny" but couldn't get past the first couple of lines before repeating. A nurse's aide pointed out a large, prematurely gray-haired woman sitting looking out the window. Phil approached.

"Susan?"

The woman turned to look at Phil. Her face was not unattractive. There was a small portable oxygen tank attached to the side of her wheelchair, a plastic tube delivering the needed air to her nostrils. She studied his face for what seemed like an entire minute. Suddenly, she opened her eyes wide, sat straighter in her wheelchair, and let out a cry. "Phillip?"

The next couple of minutes were clumsy. They both tried to speak at once, each asking questions and trying to answer what they heard of the other's question. Finally, Phil stopped talking and listened to his sister say, "Phillip, I thought you must be dead."

"Susan, I don't know what to say. I should have tried to contact you before now. I have no excuse except that I was really screwed up. That is, 'til lately. I think I might be getting my life together." Phil spent the next half hour giving his sister an abbreviated version of his life over the last twenty years. He sped through the chronology of his time in the service, his travels, and jobs over the years. He admitted a lack of success in the employment world. He owned up to having been a binge drinker with occasional bouts with the law when he was drunk. He identified his anger as his big problem and shame as the reason he never looked for his family 'til now. He did not tell her about the murder in Bardstown. He did tell her about being found by Brother William and his new life as it had developed since he'd arrived at the monastery.

"As a matter of fact, Susan, I am studying to become a Catholic."

Susan winced slightly. After she had left home and moved in with Kenny and Sandra, she had been befriended by a Baptist minister who had made a call on the family. Under his guidance, she learned about that religion and found much comfort in it. She accepted baptism into that faith and practiced it as best she could within the limits of her disability. She was happy to hear that her brother was "getting religion" but would have preferred that his choice might be more in her comfort zone of the Southern Baptists. She recovered a bit. "Well, that's okay Phillip. I only hope you find what you're looking for there."

"Susan, I think it's for me. I've really given it a lot of thought and I'm real happy there at the monastery. I may even look into stayin' there for good."

"You mean become a priest?"

"No, but maybe a brother. That way I can keep doin' my job. I've really taken to tending the gardens and the grounds. But anyway that's not a decision I need to make now. Don't even know if they'd accept me. For now I just wanna become a Catholic and that's why I've been lookin' for you."

"Why?"

"Because I gotta find out if I was ever baptized in any religion. I don't remember us goin' to church much. A weddin' once in a while. But I thought since you were older, you might remember if I was ever baptized."

"No, Phillip, I'm sure you weren't. None of us were as kids, but I am now. Mom said she believed in God plenty, but didn't think much of any religion. But why would it matter if you were baptized in the past or not?"

"Father Abbot—that's the head guy I told you about—says if I'd been baptized, then the Catholics accept that and I just have to declare that I wanna be a Catholic to become one. I think they call it a declaration of faith. If I ain't been baptized, they do it to me and that makes me one of 'em." Phil left out the part about being able to skip confession if he hadn't been baptized. And he was secretly happy to hear his sister say he hadn't indeed been baptized.

Phil and his sister talked for two hours. He listened to her story. Susan talked slowly, giving herself ample time to breathe. Phil began to see how hard life had been for Susan. Her disability not only limited life's enjoyment greatly, she also suffered some serious respiratory problems from spending so many years confined to a wheelchair. His sister minimized this part of the story as if she didn't want Phil to know the whole story. She also glossed over her existence at Memphis Manor, preferring to take a cheerful outlook on her current situation. She talked more of happier times when she lived with Kenny and his family. She smiled as she recalled her close relationship with their niece Kerry and how she looked forward to visits from Sandra and Kerry. Phil enjoyed listening to his sister. He was put at ease by this woman who had real reason to be very angry with him. She was not feeling sorry for herself, nor was she was taken to scolding her younger brother who, in his mind, deserved it.

When it was time to leave, Phil bent down and kissed his sister on her cheek. He gave her the address of the monastery; both brother and sister promised to be in touch. Phil was happy. He felt forgiveness from his sister for all his years of absence. For her part, she seemed overjoyed to see him again. She had all but given up hope that he was even alive. She hoped to see him again before it was too late, so she made him promise to come back in two months' time.

On the bus ride back to Bardstown, Phil's mood was lightened. He reflected. He had a family. A sister, a sister-in-law, and a niece. And he was finally finishing his studies and looking forward to becoming a Catholic. He'd come a long way since Brother Bill found him in the ditch along the road. His peace was tempered some, however, because guilt, though subdued, never seemed to leave him. And a new delayed sadness over the loss of his only brother also crept into his thoughts. He wondered, *Will peace ever be complete?*

Chapter Nine

The day was set. On Christmas Eve 1983, Phil would be baptized a Catholic. On the morning of December twentieth, Phil was scheduled with Father Abbot for their final meeting prior to the baptism. Phil had completed his studies and was convinced that he could accept what Catholics believed. The abbot, too, believed Phil was ready. This final preparatory meeting would allow Phil to ask any final questions and reveal any of his past life that he wished. Since baptism would be ministered, no confession was required.

"Well Phil, you've come a long way in your preparation. Are you ready?" asked the abbot.

"I think I am, Father."

"Is there any thing you want to talk about?"

Phil took a deep breath. "Father, I guess if I'm gonna join your faith, which I really believe in now, I need to tell you a little more about me."

"Yes, Phil?"

"Even though I don't have to go to confession, I think I'll feel better if I come clean with you. In fact, the secret is killin' me. If I don't get it off my chest, I don't think I can be a very good Catholic, or anything else for that matter."

"Secret?"

"Yeah. But first, tell me again, Father, do you have to keep my secret?"

"Yes, Phil. Although the seal of confession is not an obligation in this case, you can expect the same confidentiality that you would get from a lawyer or a psychologist. That means that only under the gravest of conditions could I reveal anything you tell me. For example, if you told me you were planning to murder Brother William," the abbot chuckled, "I might have an obligation to warn the authorities. But that's an extreme that we couldn't be dealing with here, Phil. So feel free to share anything you'd like."

"What if I tell you something I've already done?"

"Phil, please don't be concerned." The abbot displayed just a whisper of impatience. "If I ever need to tell anything you tell me, I'll discuss it with you first. Okay?"

Another deep breath. "Okay. Father, I've *already* murdered someone!" Phil finally had his secret out of himself.

The abbot blanched. His expression went from shock to sad. He sat silent for several moments. Very serious now, he said quietly, "Tell me, Phil."

"Do you remember about a month ago you came to me with a letter addressed to Phil Norton? You asked if it was for me and I said it was because the return address was from Susan Norton, my sister in Memphis. I didn't lie when I told you I had changed my name to Johnson but I didn't tell you that I just kinda made up the new name right after I came here. I never did change the name legally. That's because I was hiding. Hiding from the law. And I thought that anything, even my name, might lead to me. I was scared and this monastery was perfect for hiding. It wasn't 'til after I was here a while that I found I really wanted to stay here permanently and wanted to be a part of your religion, too. But the guilt of it all has been torturing me every day since it happened."

"But this murder, Phil. When did it happen?" The abbot, fighting disbelief, was struggling with what he was hearing.

"The night before I was found by Brother William."

"Go on."

Phil said, "I'd like to start from the beginning if I can, Father. I want you to have the whole picture. Then if you say I can't become a Catholic, so be it. I gotta get this off my chest now."

The abbot agreed and Phil told his story. He started by describing his home life as a child. The family lived on a very small vegetable farm just outside of the Biloxi city limits. School was discouraged. Work on the farm was demanded. Phil and his sister worked from sunrise to sundown during planting and harvesting. Phil told the abbot that his work as a monastery groundskeeper with all the proper equipment was a real joy compared to the manual labor of digging potatoes or shucking corn.

Phil and his sister went to school in between the heavy work seasons, but they missed lessons and failed several classes. They fell behind and both left school before finishing high school. They both managed to take one thing away from school that stayed with them, however, and that was the ability to read. At Phil's recent reunion with his sister, he realized that they both found common appreciation in reading over the years.

He talked about his very difficult relationship with his father. When his father was drunk in mid-afternoon, he would come home and inspect the progress in the fields; inevitably he'd find fault with Phil's work. Often, he took a belt to his son's backside while Susan would scream for him to stop. Whenever his mother had him to herself, she'd tell Phil to rise above his father, to work hard, to study harder, to be more neat and clean. Always a lecture from his mom. He felt he could never measure up to either parents' expectations of him.

Phil paused. Tears formed in his eyes. He looked up at the abbot and said very quietly, "Father, it was my father I believed I was killing that night." The abbot sat waiting for more but none came. After a minute, Phil composed himself and returned to his story.

He loved his sister because she stood up for him. He tolerated his little brother, Kenny, but resented that Kenny seemed to be treated much better than he. Finally, at seventeen, Phil left home. He joined the Army and spent two tours in Vietnam. He drank and smoked pot to help himself through the horrors of the war. He returned to the States, a discharged addict, in 1966. The Army sponsored some chemical dependency treatment for him soon after he was discharged. It half worked; he was able to shed the use of marijuana, but after a year he was drinking again. He was able to stay sober most of the time, but when he drank, he got drunk and stayed that way for two or three days.

In 1970, he met a young lady in a bar in Chicago. Her name was Mary Fallon. She was different. She wasn't a floozy. She had stopped in the bar with a group of women who worked in a nearby office building. Phil spotted her across the room and thought she was cute. The juke box was on and he asked her to dance. She seemed to like him. And he liked that. At the end of the evening, he asked if he could call her. She agreed and what followed was a six-month romance. Phil was smitten. He was on top of the world. Spending Labor Day weekend with her family at their Lake Geneva summer home, he carried out a plan to give her an engagement ring and ask her to marry him. He had been shocked to hear her say no. She told him that he had not understood her care for him. She liked him a lot and considered him a great friend; she enjoyed being with him, but wasn't interested in marrying anyone until she finished college. He'd known she planned to return to school that very month but he couldn't see why that should prevent their marriage. The rejection was almost too much for Phil to bear. He sought relief in drinking and prostitutes.

And he traveled. From Chicago to Cincinnati to San Francisco and on and on. He would meet someone in a bar, get in a fight, and be lucky only to have it end with bumps and bruises. He was often unemployed and stayed in flop houses or on park benches. He would find jobs, usually low-skill factory or warehouse jobs. The jobs might last for a number of weeks until he'd go on a bender, be absent from work, and then lose the job. He was sullen and most people avoided him. He felt their dislike and didn't like himself. And the emptiness he'd feel after using a prostitute only added to his self loathing. He had few friends when he was sober; none when he was drunk. And if he only had enough cash to have a drink or eat a sandwich, he'd opt for the drink. After about ten years of living like this and hating himself for doing it, Phil ended up in Bardstown in March of 1981.

Phil paused again and looked at the abbot who was listening intently to him. The priest's look was not condemning. He said, "And the murder, Phil?"

Phil told the abbot what he could remember about the murder in the parking lot of the cathedral and his flight along Highway 31. He told how drunk he was and how he thought he was beating his own father in retaliation for the abuse he'd suffered from him. He explained that when he realized what he'd done he had immediate remorse. He said that he didn't really know what he'd done until the man was dead. He also told the abbot what he had discovered about the victim when he went to Bardstown with Father Dustin and found himself in the police station.

Both men sat silent. Father Abbot tried to reconcile what he'd just heard with his image of a different man he thought he knew. Phil wondered what would happen next—a dismissal from his new-found home and life or some form of forgiveness. The abbot spoke first. "This complicates things, Phil."

"Yes, Father?"

"As a priest I feel obligated to suggest that you turn yourself in. We can still proceed with your baptism because I discern that you are sincere about joining our church. And, as you've learned, there is complete forgiveness of sins if you receive the sacrament in good faith. But there is the matter of restitution to society."

Phil interrupted, "But, Father, I didn't know what I was doing. And I'm completely reformed now. I'm not a menace to society anymore. And I've been watching the Bardstown paper that's in the reception area each day. There's been no mention of anyone else being arrested for the murder. What good would it do for me to go to prison? Or even get the chair? If I can be forgiven by God when you baptize me, why can't we just forget it and let me stay here and live a good life?"

"Phil, it just isn't that simple. There is the whole moral issue of the Trappists harboring a fugitive from justice."

"You mean you gotta turn me in?" Phil was near tears. "I've been learning about God being able to forgive any sin as long as the sinner was sorry. And now you tell me I have to go get punished . . . punished by man when I'm gonna be okay with God? I can't believe it, Father." Then he added, "And I suppose you are not gonna honor our confidentiality deal either?"

"Forgiveness doesn't mean there are not still earthly consequences for the sins we commit, Phil. And I *will* honor our agreement. Remember, I just told you that you and I would talk before I would reveal anything you tell me. However, I have to admit I had no idea what a dilemma this visit would bring me."

"Are you gonna turn me in, Father Abbot?" Phil felt betrayed.

The abbot moved his chair closer to Phil's, facing him directly, and took his two hands in his. "Phil, I'm glad you confided in me. It was the right thing to do, especially in light of your forthcoming baptism. I can see how hard this must have been for you. Now, I need to respond in some way. But not today. I need to pray about what to do next. Let's get together late tomorrow afternoon after vespers and continue this. In the meantime, you have my word that I won't do anything that you don't know I'm doing. Okay?"

Phil was scared. "Man, I'm feelin' pretty shaky now. I guess I really didn't expect this. I just felt that if I came clean with you, everything would work out."

"Phil, don't give up on me or on yourself. I can understand why you expected immediate acceptance of your situation. We taught you in such a way that it was a normal expectation. You must understand that I fully do accept *you* and your coming into our faith. And I promise to do everything to help you. So go now and try hard to be peaceful as we work this thing through."

Phil went to his room and threw himself on his cot. "What have I done? Just as my life was really coming together, I'm back in the soup again. I wonder if I should run?" Phil agonized over this question the rest of the day and into the night. He didn't sleep.

Toward morning, he left the monastery building and started walking along Highway 247. His intention was to hide again. About a mile down the road, he stopped. "What am I doing? What have I been learning these past couple of years? If I believed in God yesterday morning, do I still this morning? If I believed in His help then, shouldn't I now? I think the abbot really does want to help me. Maybe I should try out this trust-in-God stuff I've been studying." Phil turned back toward the monastery. He tried to pray as he walked but couldn't.

At the appointed time, Phil was in the abbot's office again. With no sleep and his emotions on a roller coaster, he was limp. He was ready to do whatever the abbot asked him to do. He waited for the priest to speak first. "Phil, here's what I propose. I'll request a meeting with the bishop in Louisville. I'll tell him your story—not identifying you, of course—and get his input. And Phil, I've decided my *goal* will be to allow you to stay here without revealing your crime unless an innocent person may suffer in your place. As I prayed and reflected over all of this last night, I can see no redeeming need now for you to be punished by society. In my view, you are a different person today than the one you described to me before you came here. And if God can forgive you—and He can—I've come to accept that in your specific case, you might be able live out your life without punishment from society.

"But I need some official guidance, Phil. That's why I need the bishop's concurrence in this. So I need your agreement that I can visit with the bishop. Okay?"

"Gee, I don't know, Father. What if he tells you to turn me in? My goose is cooked." Phil wanted to trust the abbot's judgment but was scared.

"I'll try to convince him otherwise. If I can't, I think my conscience would be clear if I informed you I was going to tell the police. In that case, I would hope you would turn yourself in and let us help you with your defense. If you decided to run, that would be your choice but one that could be dangerous, Phil."

Phil exhaled deeply. "Maybe I should just take off now and not put you through all this, Father. I know I'm supposed to trust in God and all that but I don't wanna go to prison or maybe even get the chair. I'm a different man now and not a risk to society. I feel terrible that I killed that poor fellow. I was drunk. I was out of my mind at the time."

"Phil, I can understand your fear. But you've made a great investment in finding yourself and developing a relationship with God. If I can't convince the bishop to allow you permission to remain silent, it might just be God's will that you do face the circumstances and, yes, trust in God."

Phil thought, *This morning I decided to trust a little and return here. I guess this is the acid test for me. Either I believe this stuff or I don't. If I run, I don't believe it. If I stay. . . .* He tightened his lips and said, "Okay, let's give it a shot, Father."

Chapter Ten

"Father Abbot, how glad I am to see you. You fellows out at the monastery are too self-sufficient; we don't get to see you very often. How can I be of service, my friend," said the bishop.

Bishop Hoffman's office was not large but was comfortable. The dark paneled walls and deep leather chairs gave off an aura of both the authority and warmness of the occupant. Daniel Hoffman had been consecrated Bishop of Louisville five years prior to this visit by the abbot. He was in his late fifties, a friendly man, a theologian. Known for his open-mindedness and fairness, the bishop was quick to grasp a situation and his decisions usually came quickly, too.

"Thanks for seeing me, Bishop. I'll get right to the point. I have a tough case I need your help with. If I may, I'd like to give you some background and then get to the problem?"

"Go ahead, Father, I'm yours for an hour and a half," replied the bishop.

Not revealing his friend's identity, the abbot told the bishop about Phil Norton's arrival at the Trappist Monastery. He left out any details of the murder itself. The priest recalled the events that included Phil's return to health, his decision to stay as an employee at the monastery, and his gradual study and acceptance of the Catholic faith. He explained how this live-in employee pursued the whereabouts of his only sister to find out if he'd been baptized. Finding that he had not been, he had come to the big day of baptism scheduled a few days hence. The abbot also recounted the same story of Phil's life that he had heard from the man two days before. He ended with Phil's admission of a murderous act and his own dilemma regarding Phil's debt to society.

When the abbot ended, Bishop Hoffman sat expressionless for a few moments. "Well, this isn't a social call is it, Father Abbot?"

"No, Bishop, unfortunately it isn't. Of course, there is no question about the man being baptized. He is sincere and has completed all the preparatory steps. He seeks the sacrament, and it cannot be denied to him."

"You don't just think he is going through the motions to gain some kind of asylum?"

"No, Bishop, there is no question in my mind about that. He could have stayed with us indefinitely and never mentioned his interest in the church; he was and is a very good employee. He also could have chosen not to tell me about the murder since no confession was mandated, as you know. With the forgiveness that comes with baptism, he could have kept his secret, but I think the seriousness of the situation motivated him to tell me about his sin."

The bishop countered, "But with the knowledge we now have, we must consider our own obligation to protect society and the expectation of restitution that comes with such a crime."

"I know that; that's why I'm here, Bishop," said the abbot not unkindly. "But that obligation is not spelled out in black and white. As I see it, the general obligation to 'do our civic duty' takes judgment. In my mind, and I've had more time to think about this than you, we have a fully reformed man here. Our faith tells us his upcoming baptism frees him from the sin. His reformation has also brought about a brand new person; he is not a drunk, nor a lowlife, nor a murderer today. I firmly believe society has no more to fear from our employee than it does from you or me."

"But shouldn't society decide that?"

"Society is set up to seek blind justice in all cases. Society would have to find against this fellow because having been the man he was before, he would have to be found guilty and punished. It is, again, only because he chose to reveal the murder to us that we are even forced to make some judgment about turning him over to the authorities. And, Bishop, it is my best judgment that we, in this most unusual of circumstances, can remain silent unless, of course, another is ever accused of his crime."

Again the bishop countered, "Because you haven't told me about the murder itself, I can't make any judgment about any extenuating circumstances that may diminish the sinfulness of the crime. On the other hand, we still have a serious obligation of confidentiality here. If this were part of a confession the man made to you, we wouldn't be talking about it today. You might be seeking some sort of generic advice about the pros and cons of withholding absolution. We'd be having a very veiled discussion about the essential facts in the case. But with no confession required in baptism, there is no forgiveness to withhold, is there?"

Bishop Hoffman continued, "No, Father Abbot, I'm not inclined to say what I think is the right thing to do here. However, I am aware of my own serious obligation to maintain confidentiality at this point. You proceed with the man's baptism; he certainly seems right for that. But I want to think about this whole thing for a week or so. Can you call me after Christmas?"

"Certainly, Bishop. Thanks for seeing me and thanks for joining me in this tough decision." The two men shook hands and the abbot departed.

On New Year's Eve afternoon, the abbot called the bishop on his private line. "Hello, Bishop, I bet you weren't lookin' forward much to this call."

"Well, this situation certainly has occupied my mind a lot this past week. I've gone back and forth several times. But I have come to a conclusion, Father."

"Yes?"

"On the one hand, the man is guilty of murder and should face the consequences. On the other hand, we have only come to this knowledge ourselves because this employee of yours has reformed his life, accepted God into his life, and sought some kind of blessing from you before being baptized."

"Right."

"In a sense, he was looking for the consolation that comes when one receives forgiveness in confession. He also figured he would be protected from exposure when he talked to you, is that right?"

"It is, Bishop."

"You also feel quite certain that society is not in future danger resulting from this man's freedom. And I take it you think that society would not be greatly compensated by his incarceration or execution?"

"I definitely feel that way, Bishop," said the abbot.

"It's a tough one, Father, but my best judgment at this time is to let the man be. Even though the case does not come under the seal of confession, the priest/penitent relationship was there and we are held to a very high standard there. If the man is what you tell me he's become, the greater good might be better served by letting the man live out his life in freedom. Finally, there appears to be no person falsely accused here but if that ever happens, you, of course, must convince him to turn himself in."

"I concur, Bishop Hoffman."

"Another thought: even though you say your man is seeking forgiveness, I should think you would instruct him in the idea of *penance*. Without confession, of course, we don't assign a penance to the sinner seeking forgiveness, but perhaps if you teach him about penance, he might do something on his own?"

"Yes, Bishop, I've been thinking about something like that myself."

"One more thing, Father. I think you should also accept some future obligation to keep an eye on this fellow. If you ever become aware that his old habits are returning or if he moves away from the monastery, you'll need to keep track of him. If he goes astray, we have some obligations and I trust you will figure out what to do. In fact, I will send an official letter to you under confidential cover directing you in your future responsibilities in this matter."

"I fully understand, Bishop, and I couldn't agree more. I will watch but I expect no problems. And thank you for your deliberations and your advice, Bishop."

Delayed for two weeks, Phil was baptized a Catholic at the Abbey of Gethsemani on January, 7 1984. All rejoiced.

Chapter Eleven

After his baptism, Phil Norton was on a high. Everything in his world seemed perfect. He'd already become an expert landscaper. He even took to jotting down some of what he learned about the proper care and feeding of flowers and plants. He thought he might like to publish a pamphlet or small book about gardening some day.

When he was outside working, the monks noticed his ferocious pace over the many hours that he put in. It seemed he couldn't work fast enough or effectively enough as he pushed himself to exceed any expectations he had for himself. It wasn't unusual for the monks to see cuts on his hands and arms indicating relentless physical effort. He would tell himself that he must work harder and harder to accomplish a sort of self-imposed penance. He thought this exhausting effort in part might fulfill what the abbot had told him about penance.

Given the time he gained with his efficiency as groundskeeper, Phil had also been recruited to help out during busy shipping seasons for the Trappist enterprises. He enjoyed working alongside the monks in silence as they produced, packaged, and shipped a catalog full of fudges, cheeses, and fruit cakes. He liked the more reasonable pace and the sense of well being that the whole process presented. The monks produced these high quality products as a source of income for the monastery. Their customers would order these delicious foods for their own enjoyment or as gifts for others.

As a new Catholic, Phil participated in all the liturgical exercises that he could. He found himself reading all that he could about the Trappists and the strict Cistercian rules of St. Benedict for living the monastic life. Because the rules of silence among the monks forced Phil to also be quiet most of the time, he had plenty of time to think. If it wasn't for the fading yet ever-lingering memory of his crime that made him feel unworthy, he thought a lot about becoming a monk. He confided his feelings to the abbot and was only encouraged to follow his heart. No hard sell would come forth from abbot.

Three months after his baptism, Phil received a call from his sister-in-law. "Phil, Susan is dying," were her first words.

"What!"

"She's dying, Phil. She won't make it another week or two."

"Oh man." Despite the warm day, a shiver ran through him. "Gee, Sandy," Phil assumed her nickname, "we've been writing back and forth for a couple of years now and she always sounded so cheerful. Did she take a, a sudden turn for the worse?"

"Phil, Susan hasn't been in good health for years, but she really hasn't wanted to worry you. She's been so happy that the two of you have reconnected again. It's really kept her going."

"Oh man," he said again. "You say she won't make it more than a couple of weeks?"

"Yes, her respiratory problems have gone into pneumonia again and the doctors don't think she'll survive this bout. Phil, I think you better make plans to see her as soon as you can. Kerry and I are going up to Memphis to see her this week. You know, although you've been promising, you haven't even met your niece or me yet. A telephone call once or twice a year isn't really enough to get to know one another. It would be nice if you could make it to Memphis this week, too, Phil?"

"I'll leave on Sunday night, Sandy, and be at the Manor on Monday morning." More quietly he said, "I'm sorry I haven't come to Mississippi yet to see you and Kerry. I really don't have any good excuse. Maybe I can do better in the future."

"Okay, Phil. I didn't mean to chastise you. We all need to see Susan soon. And even if the circumstances aren't great, it'll be good for us all to get to know each other, too; we're family, aren't we?"

They hung up after setting plans to meet in Memphis sometime on Monday afternoon.

On the bus ride to Memphis, Phil wondered why he hadn't made more of an effort to see his family. He'd been so happy to discover them. While he often thought about them, he still suffered from a certain kind of shyness in their regard. His past and the shame he felt about it still had its effect on him.

He thought about Susan. She had always been so loyal to him. Not just when they were children, but even later when he was gone. He could have been dead or alive for all she knew. She was the one person who had always loved him. And she was dying. Sadness crept over him—not just at losing her but sad that he hadn't been a better brother to her, especially since they'd been reunited.

The trip to Memphis went quickly as Phil was lost in his thoughts. He reminisced. He regretted. He cried quietly. He found an inexpensive but safe motel near the bus station and on Monday morning he was in a taxi to Memphis Manor.

When he inquired at the receptionist's desk, Phil was directed to the hospice portion of the building. Hospice was a relatively new idea in 1984, and both the dying and those who grieved for them didn't know what to expect.

The hospice section was clearly different than the standard sections of the Manor. Here there was no acute care given to save the lives of those in hospice. Death was expected and planned for. The goal of hospice was the comfort of the dying, not to return them to health.

Phil found Susan in a small private room where she was hooked up to an IV delivering morphine and some nutrition. Oxygen was available nearby but not in use at the moment.

"Hi Susan," he said quietly. He didn't really want to wake her if she was sleeping.

When she opened her eyes and saw Phil, the tears came. She didn't speak for a minute or more as she fought to control her emotions. Finally she said through her tears, "Phillip."

"Susan, I don't know what to say. I shoulda been here before now. It's my fault for not writing more or calling you once in a while. I had no idea that you were this ill. I'm sorry I've let you down." Phil was crying, too.

"Phillip, I'm so happy you are here," she said ignoring his apologies.

For the next two hours Phil and Susan talked. They talked again of the few happy times they had as children. Phil tried to talk about her illness but Susan quickly dismissed the subject as wasting time. She wanted to know all about his life at the monastery and about his life as a Catholic. Phil explained in detail his jobs and the routine at the monastery. He told her about his new religion and the comfort it brought him. He left out any talk about his crime or the lingering concern about it that still haunted him.

Susan seemed to gain new energy from hearing about Phil's life and the happiness he'd seemed to have found. But after a couple of hours the stress of her illness and excitement of their conversation tired her. Phil noticed her fatigue and suggested Susan take a nap, and he promised to return early in the afternoon. She agreed and laid back on her pillow. She was content.

Phil finished his ham sandwich and Coke in the Manor's cafeteria. He wandered down a long corridor to a large general waiting area. He thought he'd read a bit and wait for his first face-to-face meeting with his sister-in-law and his niece. He picked up an old issue of *Sports Illustrated* and tried to interest himself in an article about horse racing. He, too, was tired and soon he dozed off.

He woke with a start when he sensed someone was standing quite near him. "Are you Phil Norton?" asked a handsome woman with dark red hair.

"I am," said Phil. He was still in the daze of first awakening. Recovering, he jumped to his feet exclaiming, "You must be Sandy!" And glancing around, he quickly noticed a slender, attractive young lady with long blond hair standing tentatively several feet away, smiling as if waiting to be introduced. "And Kerry!"

The next few moments were clumsy quick hugs and all trying to talk at once. Greetings, apologies, forgiveness, questions, reactions all came tumbling out at once. They all stopped as if on cue and then laughed. Finally, Sandra took charge and said, "Let's sit down over there in that corner and start over."

Away from the few others in the room, Phil began. "You know, I have so much to say to both of you; I don't know where to begin. I suppose there'll be time later to tell you the whole ugly story of my life, but for now I'd like to just keep it on the past couple of years and, of course, we also gotta talk about Susan. Is that okay?"

Both mother and daughter nodded and Phil gave them a very brief review of his life with the Trappists, including his acceptance of the Catholic faith. He made no mention of the murder. He made it clear that he was happy where he was but hinted that his past hadn't fully allowed him yet to embrace the full peace he was just beginning to understand and enjoy. He said, "I guess I've gotten pretty caught up in my new life. I'm sorry I haven't come to Mississippi yet."

"Phil, we understand," said Sandra, smiling. Kerry nodded approval of her mother's words, not having any wish to make this meeting confrontational. Sandra spent just a few minutes telling of her job as a social worker and then spent more time telling Phil about Kerry's successes as a freshman at Ol' Miss. Mother was proud.

"Oh Mother," Kerry protested after her parent's boast started to embarrass her. "What about Aunt Susan?"

This brought them to the reason for their coming together and Sandra spoke first. "Susan will die soon and we need to do some planning. We need to agree on the arrangements and do the right thing for Susan."

They discussed Susan's social security and Medicare benefits which had been used to provide for her nursing home care. Sandra and Kenny had put away a small amount of money for Susan that might be enough to bury her, if done locally. Phil had saved four thousand dollars as an employee at the monastery and he offered to pay for any funeral expense. Those matters out of the way, the threesome made their way to Susan's room in hospice.

As they entered the room, they saw two hospice nurses on either side of the bed. One motioned to the family to step back outside in the corridor. "I'm Gladys Farrington, the hospice administrator. Susan has taken a bad turn in the last hour. We think she'll pass shortly. You should spend some time with her now; we'll be close by in case we can help."

Though not unexpected, this information still had its effect. The three gathered around Susan's bed. She appeared peaceful. She opened her eyes and smiled at her family. Her breathing was rapid but not strained. Her color was white. She struggled to speak. "I'm so glad you are all here. Take care of each other. I love you all so much," she whispered.

She never spoke again. For the next hour, her breathing became more difficult. She continued to look fondly on her family. She displayed no panic. She closed her eyes and seemed to sleep, the breathing becoming yet more difficult. She opened her eyes quickly and looked at Phil, eyes frozen. Susan Norton was dead.

The next day Sandra and Phil made the arrangements for Susan's funeral and burial. The staff at the Manor helped by providing referrals to a funeral home representative who, in turn, arranged for the family to purchase a vault in a mausoleum at Fairlawn Cemetery just outside Memphis.

On Wednesday morning, the three family members met at the funeral home and viewed the body. As each grieved, whispered goodbye, and supported each other, Phil was moved to offer some prayers for his sister. The casket was closed; then three employees from the funeral home and Phil moved the casket to a hearse. The family was joined by Gladys Farrington from the Manor and four of them entered a car provided by the funeral home. They followed the hearse to the cemetery. Phil said another short prayer and Susan was laid to rest.

After the family and Ms. Farrington returned to the funeral home, Phil and Sandra settled all the bills with the funeral director. Gladys said her goodbyes and offered a few kind words about Susan. Sandra offered to drive Phil to the bus station on her way out of town. The three got into the car and immediately all three began to weep. *How sad it was that such a wonderful woman had so few to mourn for her,* Phil thought.

Phil promised once again that he would visit Kerry and Sandra in Mississippi. In the past three days, in spite of his grief, he was beginning to feel a closeness to these two women, his only remaining family. They, in turn, had shown their own care and concern for him, something he had not known before from his own family, except for his sister. He knew he could not lose touch with Sandra and Kerry.

On the bus ride back to Kentucky, Phil had a good long time to think. As the bus pulled into Bardstown, he had made up his mind. He would ask the abbot tomorrow if he could enter the novitiate and start the process of becoming a Trappist monk.

Chapter Twelve

John Sedwick looked out the window of his office. It was hot. The 1984 version of the Fourth of July parade sounded and looked like all the others he'd seen in Bardstown. The floats and bands started at the football field. They moved past the police station and wound their way along Fifth Street to Stephen Foster Avenue. There they turned east for the few blocks proceeding to the state park where the famous Old Kentucky Home stands. An outdoor production of a song and dance musical featuring the works of the famous American composer always capped the holiday celebration . . . but only after dozens of family picnics, games, and the usual round of the dignitaries' speeches.

Usually Sedwick enjoyed these festive occasions. It gave him a chance to show off a little with the younger children who were still in awe of policemen. But today he wasn't in the mood. The detective had a good record in handling many routine cases for the department, but he'd accomplished little in his investigation of Bobby Swanson's murder. For the past three and one half years, he'd spent untold hours combing through each scrap of data. There had been very little response from all the posters he had circulated around West Virginia and Kentucky except for several mistaken identities and dead-end leads. In the past few months one inquiry that got his juices running came in from Lexington. A man fitting the description was being held on petty robbery in the Lexington jail. Sedwick rushed to interview the suspect only to find and verify that the man was also in jail on the night of the murder in 1981.

He revisited Mrs. Maloney twice since the murder. He had made a second and third trip to the Moore's Distillery and talked to Clement Smith and Steven Schumen to see if he'd missed any little detail. He checked again at McManus Ford and nothing new was learned. Mostly, he spent hours re-reading the lab and coroner's reports. Again, no new information came up that sent him in any new direction.

For yet another time his mind went over what he knew. Swanson came to town in late 1980. He got a job at the distillery and soon after he bought a car and took his driver's test. He lived in Mrs. Maloney's boarding house. His stay there was uneventful. He was a polite and tidy renter. He was

known to be a good Samaritan type, always doing favors for people.
Swanson was valued as a talented distiller at Moore's. People liked him even in the short time he was employed there. Sedwick thought about why this fellow, without any apparent educational credentials, could be so good at making good whiskey. It had been there in the back of his mind all along but he hadn't focused on it in his pursuit of the murderer. Swanson had to have learned his skills on the illegal side of the business. *Swanson must have been a bootlegger or worked for one.* Maybe he worked for the man who murdered him? Sedwick had forgotten but now was recalling that Mrs. Maloney had said that Bobby said the man who was looking for him was a "rotten ol' bootlegger."

Sedwick was suddenly ashamed; he couldn't believe he overlooked this important angle in trying to find the killer. He was realizing that he would have had a better chance to catch the man that the landlady and the parking lot guard identified if he'd publicized the fact that the man he was seeking *was* probably a bootlegger.

The detective had been hoping that if any of the law enforcement agencies could identify Bobby Swanson or the stranger thought to be a bootlegger, he would be able to find the killer. The leads he *had* followed turned out to be duds. He was chastising himself now. Sure he'd been very busy with other cases. But had he been waiting for everything on the *big* case to come to him? Now, he needed to get more proactive. He'd get permission to put his full attention on the Swanson murder. This was *his* case and he was going to solve it. This town, the people in it, his wife, his boss were going to know John Sedwick had it in him. He'd solve it. And soon!

Sedwick began to speculate to himself, "If Swanson was a bootlegger, he was involved in criminal activity. He had to have criminal associates. He had to have some enemies. People who might want him dead.

"But what about his apparent kindness toward others? Hmm." That's why he hadn't pursued the bootlegger angle, Sedwick told himself. "Swanson was dying. Maybe he got religion . . . wanted to go out on good terms with the Man upstairs?"

The detective's juices were running now. He snuffed out his fourth cigarette in the last half hour. He was angry that he'd allowed himself to sit back and wait after he thought he had done all he could. He was mad at himself for not trying to create leads from what he should have figured out a long time ago. Tomorrow he would start.

On the day after the Fourth, John Sedwick was in Chief Rowland's office stating his case. "Dick, I just can't sit around anymore waiting for someone out there to send me information that they recognize Swanson and give me a lead. I gotta create some leads myself. I want to head for West Virginia and get into some of the hill country. Maybe someone there knows Bobby Swanson or the ol' bootlegger who killed him. How 'bout giving me a couple weeks and some travel cash and let me get at it, Dick?"

"Hold on a minute, John. You mean to tell me that you just want to get in a car and head for West Virginny and start looking for folks who knew Swanson or the other guy? Don't you think we would've heard from somebody by now who got your flyer if this Swanson fellow was a known bootlegger in that area?"

"That's what I thought, Chief. But we haven't heard squat. You know how many bulletins *we* get in this business. Maybe the one police station that should have put it up, didn't. Plus the fact, those folks in West Virginia are pretty tight. Wouldn't surprise me if the local authorities might ignore the poster if it was featuring one of their own. I just feel if we're gonna find out something now, we're gonna find it out by getting out and talkin' to folks. Just give me a few hundred bucks—I'll live cheap. Lemme see what I can dig up."

The chief smiled, hesitated, and said, "Okay, John. Things are a little quiet here right now—thank God—so get out there and find us a killer."

The next day the detective got in his Jeep Cherokee and headed east along the Blue Grass Parkway and hooked up to I-64 in Lexington and continued east on the Mountain Parkway. At Salyersville, Kentucky, he ran out of freeway and from there he used several lesser traveled roads on into Williamson, West Virginia. As he drove, he wondered if he should look for a bootlegger who also knew how to make a pipe bomb. But he discarded the thought, figuring that might complicate things and narrow his search too much.

Sedwick believed that Swanson must have come from the western part of that state only because western West Virginia was closer to Bardstown. There were numerous towns nestled among the mountains and hills throughout the state. Moonshining and bootlegging might be informal occupations almost anywhere in the hill country. Sedwick decided to check out as many towns as he could that might have a large enough police or sheriff's department to have taken a look at the poster he'd sent showing Swanson's driver's license photo.

He started with Williamson on the western border along the Big Sandy River. He found the small police station in the center of town and walked in. "My name is John Sedwick," he said to the clerk at the desk. "May I speak with whoever is in charge?"

Before the clerk could answer, a man's voice was heard from behind a half-open door. "Come on in, friend. How can I help ya?"

Sedwick, nodding to the clerk, said, "Guess that means me," and headed into the little office off the small lobby.

The detective introduced himself to Police Chief Elmer Johannsen and was invited to sit down. Johannsen was a man in his early sixties. He was of medium height, with a strong build and short haircut and presented himself as unkempt. Sedwick pretended not to notice the chief's sloppy appearance and handed him a picture of Bobby Swanson. He said, "Chief, I don't know if you remember seeing this picture on a poster we circulated all over this area a few years back?"

"Naw, can't say I do. Why? What's he wanted for?" said the chief.

"Actually, he's dead, Chief. We're lookin' for his killer. The dead man went by the name of Bobby Swanson but he could have been using a phony name. We have a hunch that he was involved in bootlegging. He certainly showed he knew how to make good whiskey at the Moore Distillery near Bardstown. He had told his landlady and others that he hailed from West Virginia, but no one can remember the name of a town that he might have mentioned. So, I'm gonna spend some time looking for any information I can find out about him that might lead us to his killer."

Sedwick went on to describe the main events of the crime as they were known and the investigation that followed. Then he handed the chief a separate photo of the artist's sketch of the suspected killer. "How 'bout this fellow. Do you recognize him?"

"Can't say I know anything about this one either, Detective. Sorry."

Sedwick gave the chief a fresh copy of the poster showing both photos and asked him to display it. He thanked the man and started out the door. He had a thought and turned. "Chief, where would you go next if you were me?"

"Well, Detective, I'm not sure. Like you said there are probably small-time moonshiners and bootleggers hiding all over the hills out there. Maybe you oughta look around some of the hill country that ain't too far from the bigger towns. If a bootlegger was really making good stuff, he'd want to have a good market and that means bigger towns. The bars who'd buy the stuff would use branded bottles but keep fillin' 'em up with the homemade booze. That's the way it works, as far as I know, Detective. Maybe that'll get you started."

"Thanks, Chief," he said and left. Sedwick thought that the sloppy old cop might have something there.

That night he got out his map of West Virginia and plotted out where he would go. He chose smaller towns near larger towns. He figured that the smaller law enforcement agencies were more apt to identify moonshiners who could be selling their merchandise to the bars in the bigger communities.

He decided to visit Logan, Madison, Fayetteville, Summersville, Hamlin, and Wayne, West Virginia. These were all smaller county seats. This route would take him in a large circle in the southwestern part of the state. He planned to interview someone in the sheriff's office in each of these towns. Sedwick calculated that this swing would cover a large area of mountainous country where any number of illegal stills might be operating. Some of them could be supplying unscrupulous bar and lounge owners in Huntington, Charleston, or Beckley.

On Thursday morning he headed into the small town of Logan, West Virginia. He easily found the sheriff's office and was able to talk to the main deputy. Sedwick showed the man both pictures and told the story of the murder and the investigation in Bardstown. The deputy was cooperative and even showed the pictures to the three other deputies who were in the building at the time. No one recognized either of the men. And none of the deputies were forthcoming about illegal alcohol production in the area. They all said they thought there wasn't much of that going on anymore in the hills around Logan.

He left and over the next several days, the detective visited every sheriff's department on the circle. The people he talked to were polite, even amused, but nobody offered any help. He took time between towns to drive up some of the mountains roads to see if he could see evidence of moonshining. He avoided the narrow little trails that branched off the wider dirt roads, seeming to wind their way off to nowhere. Save for a few curls of smoke that might have come from stills, or just as easily come from fireplaces warming a cabin, he could see nothing that proved suspicious. By Tuesday of the second week he decided he'd wasted his time. Sedwick was discouraged and embarrassed. He did not relish reporting back to Bardstown and having nothing to show for it.

He decided to spend his last night in Huntington before heading home. He checked into the Holiday Inn in midtown and, after supper, he decided to treat himself to a drink. The bar was dimly lit and almost empty.

Though his trip had been fruitless, John Sedwick told himself he earned some relaxation. He sat at the bar and ordered a Jack Daniel's on the rocks. He was tired and the whiskey tasted good and felt good, too. He ordered another. He was beat. Also felt sorry for himself. He hadn't noticed the thin, white-haired older gentleman sitting one stool away at the bar. The man spoke, "Had a tough day, partner?"

"Oh, sorry, I didn't see . . . or I wasn't aware you were sitting there. Guess I'm just tired. Tough road trip," he sighed.

"You some kinda salesman," the man asked.

"No, actually a cop. Out trying to find the bad guys." The detective chuckled.

"What kinda bad guys?"

"I'm trying to find a man who is probably a moonshiner or a bootlegger or both. He's a material witness in a crime in Kentucky."

"Why do you think he might be from around these parts, Officer?"

The detective offered his hand. "My name is John Sedwick. I'm a *detective* out of Bardstown, Kentucky." He released the old man's hand. "The fellow I'm lookin' for was in Bardstown at the time a young man was murdered. He came in contact with two of our local citizens when he was attempting to find the man who was killed. Since the victim claimed to be from West Virginia, I decided to come over here to see if I could find the 'needle in the haystack.' Nuts, I suppose." Sedwick figured the folks in Bardstown would agree with that.

The old man said, "Well, you never know. Do you know the man's name?"

"I'm afraid not. If he did use a name I'm sure it was an alias. We know what he looks like, though. We have a composite sketch that the two folks who saw him helped put together. But none of the people I showed it to in the past ten days recognize the guy. It was stupid to think I could find him. West Virginia is a big place when you're trying to find one person without a name. But I hadda try."

"What's he look like?" the man asked, seeming to have little genuine interest.

"Oh, he's a black-haired, overweight fellow. Probably looks like a million others." The two men turned back to their drinks and after a while, they each finished the last of their glasses and drifted off to their rooms.

Sedwick was in the hotel restaurant early and finishing breakfast when the old man he'd met the previous night came into the room. The elder gentleman spotted his drinking partner from the prior evening. He asked, "Can I join you, Detective?"

"Sure, I'm just about to leave but you're welcome to sit down. You know I never did get your name."

"It's Sidney. Sidney Maas. I'm an ol' time 'traveling salesman.' Sell books to school libraries. Been covering the territory for some thirty-four years now. I enjoyed hearing about your hunt last night. I really hope you get your man, Detective Sedwick." Sidney ordered his breakfast as Sedwick finished his. They exchanged some small talk, and when he was done with his last gulp of coffee, the detective gathered his belongings to leave.

Sidney said, offering his hand, "It was sure nice visiting with you, Detective. I wish you the best. By the way, you mentioned you had a sketch of that fellow. I'm from Tennessee and we have a few bootleggers there too, you know."

"Oh, sure. I have a copy of the sketch here in my briefcase. Would you like to see it?"

"Sure," said Sidney, politely interested. Sedwick gave him the copy of the sketch of the black-haired man. Sidney took it in hand showing mild curiosity and looked at sketch. His face turned red. He gulped. He looked quickly at Sedwick. "*This* is the man you're trying to find?" he said, excited now.

"Why yes, Sidney. Do you recognize him?"

"I do. But this man is not from around here; he's from Tennessee. His name is Parton. And you're right. He is a booze runner. A big-time booze runner. And I've seen this here other fella on the poster, too. Don't know him but I've seen him around Washington County."

"You're kidding!" Sedwick's first thought was that Sidney was having some fun with him. They had gotten on well the night before and the detective figured the old gentleman might be teasing him.

"No, no, I'm not kidding. I'm from Johnson County, Tennessee. Anyone who's been in around the bars in the county, and I've been in a few, probably knows about this Parton fellow. He's a notorious seller of illegal spirits. I think he runs a few small 'private' stills, too, if you know what I mean. Or maybe he contracts with them. In fact. . . . You say this guy is wanted for murder? I think he was arrested on a murder charge several years ago in Jonesborough. Don't think it went to trial, though. I kinda forget, Detective."

"You mean to tell me that this Parton, or whatever his name is, is living down there in Tennessee walkin' the streets, sellin' booze, and going around killin' people just as he pleases?" Sedwick sat back down at the table.

Sidney responded, "Well I guess you're right. Seems like the locals just kinda put up with the guy. 'Course, some of the barkeeps are probably making good money off him."

"Sidney, I have a serious question to put to you." Sedwick was almost solemn now. "I need to ask you to promise me *not* to speak to anyone about our visit until all this is over. I will attempt to get your cooperation by legal means, if necessary, and I can do that right now by phone. But my preference is to take your word that you'll be completely quiet. You can understand that if I travel to Tennessee now and start the process to get this Parton behind bars in Kentucky, he may disappear. Seems he may be good at that.

Once I have him behind bars we can both tell folks that you played a big part in bringing this man to justice. In fact, if this all works out, and this Parton is convicted, you'll be getting a five thousand dollar reward. Okay?"

"Wow! I wouldn't turn that down now, would I? And don't worry, Detective. I'm not nuts. I'd probably be the next murder victim if I went around saying you were lookin' for Parton. No sir, I'll not talk to *anyone* about any of this 'til you and I agree on what I can say. Will you look for me when you have Parton buttoned up?"

"I will, Sidney. And I can't thank you enough. You don't know how happy you've just made me." Sedwick took down the old man's address and phone number in Johnson County, Tennessee. He shook hands again, said goodbye, and headed to the phone booth in the hotel lobby.

"Dick, it's John," Sedwick gasped as Chief Rowlands answered his call. "I think I might just have found our man." The detective told his story and explained why his gut told him that Sidney Maas was credible and had no reason to lie to him. He asked the chief if he could travel immediately to Tennessee and work with the local authorities to arrest Parton. Rowlands agreed and promised to get quick action on a requisition for extradition from the governor's office as soon as Sedwick located the suspect.

The long-lost bounce in his step returned as John Sedwick hurried to the parking lot and headed his car south to Johnson County, Tennessee.

Chapter Thirteen

The abbot was busy the day after Phil had returned from his sister's funeral. He told Phil he could see him the following day. This gave Phil another day to plan his approach to the abbot regarding becoming a monk.

The next morning he was in the abbot's office at nine-thirty. "Father Abbot, I wanna talk to you about becoming a Trappist," he blurted.

"How did you decide this, Phil?"

"You know I've been thinkin' about it, Father. I guess my sister dying has something to do with it but I'm not quite sure what. And, what's happened to me in the last three and a half years blows me over when I think about it. My time here has changed me. I really think I'm different now. Since I was baptized, I see that I am happiest when I am working and praying with the monks. I guess I just want to become one of them; one of you, I mean."

"You, of course, understand what this really means?"

"If you mean do I understand that I'll be taking a vow of poverty and that I gotta live your life and follow your rules and can't ever get married, yeah, I understand, Father." The abbot would not know just how hard Phil had thought about giving up intimacy and a certain personal freedom in his life, but today he felt eager to make any sacrifice. And if life in the monastery was "poverty," it was sure better living than he'd ever had.

"It also means a tough couple of years as a novice before taking your temporary vows and then for three more years you renew your vows each year. You can continue making yearly vows for up to six more years. You can make your solemn, perpetual vows anytime after those first three yearly vows depending on how you and your superiors feel about your readiness.

"But during the novitiate, you'll actually have less freedom than even after you take vows. This will be a test to see if our life here is truly for you. You'll live the most strict of the monastic traditions, mostly silence and prayer, some work but less than when you take your vows.

"You'll have your own spiritual director and spend considerable time with him as you develop spiritually. You'll be under the authority of Father Robert who, as you know, is the Master of Novices. You and I will not have as much contact as we've had since you've been our employee."

Phil hadn't considered this. He had become very close to the abbot. The abbot was the one man on earth who knew everything about Phil, including his crime. Phil asked if he would be bound to tell the master of novices about the murder.

"No, you'll not be bound. But you'll need to develop a very open relationship with both the master and your personal spiritual director. After a time, I would not be surprised if you want to tell them, if the relationship is growing properly. But actually, Phil, I might advise against telling them. Not because they couldn't maintain the confidentiality but because of the burden you place on either or both of them when you tell them."

"Burden?"

"Yes. It can be a great burden to know something like this. Keeping it secret is not difficult, but the burden is in allowing the relationship to grow unencumbered with such knowledge in the background."

"Gee, Father, I didn't think that it could be a burden for you or for anyone else who might know. Is it?"

"Of course it's a burden, Phil. But one that I've fully accepted and now carry willingly because I've seen the conversion process take hold and grow in you. And I'm not going to tell you what you should do about sharing your story with anyone at any time. I only ask and advise you to be thoughtful and prayerful about it if you do consider telling anyone else. One more thing on that issue, son: if you ever have some kind of a critical need to discuss it, and you don't want to share it with anyone else, simply ask the master for permission to talk to me. He'll grant permission without questioning why."

"Okay, Father. How do I get started?"

"Well, we will start a new novitiate class August first. Often we have men join us for a while as postulants before they become novices. You've seen them around here wearing their street clothes. They spend time getting a good taste of our life before they actually commit to becoming a novice. Since you've already been exposed to our program for a few years, we can waive that segment of your formation. Between now and August, you can begin detaching yourself from the world. It sounds obvious but avoid TV and newspapers and, pray more, Phil.

"So that's about it. I'm glad you're joining us, son. I've been praying for this for a long time now."

"Another question, Father?"

"Yes?"

"Should I be shootin' for becoming a priest or a brother?"

The abbot laughed. "Phil you should be 'shootin' to become a novice. When you're a novice you'll be working toward *profession*; profession means taking your first vows. When you take your vows, or become professed, you are a brother and will live as a brother. When you take your final vows you will continue to live as a brother and then you can think about studying for the priesthood. I'm sure God and your superiors will help you decide that issue at the time. One thing that you'd have to face is the remedial education level you'd need to reach in order to start the long studies for the priesthood. But again, let's cross that bridge when we get there."

Phil was happy. He had made a commitment and it was accepted. The abbot was helping him get started in bite-size chunks and that made sense to Phil. He saw that he didn't need all the answers now. He also felt some comfort that he wouldn't have to tell his story unless it was something he himself felt compelled to do. He got up and started to leave.

"Oh, one more thing, Phil," said the abbot with a smile. "When you enter the novitiate, you don't get paid any more. In fact, you need to decide what to do with any money you've saved. You can give it away or you can put it in safekeeping with the order in case you bow out of the novitiate. Then it would be returned."

"Gosh, Father, I won't make the big bucks any more, huh?" He pretended to frown, laughed, and was gone.

Chapter Fourteen

"I've found him, Kevin. I've found the guy who murdered Bobby Swanson back in '81. You know, Swanson was the one bludgeoned to death in the cathedral parking lot? Anyway, our guy is right here in the city jail in Johnson City, Tennessee." Kevin Lawton had known John Sedwick for as long as he'd lived in Bardstown, which went back to his fifth grade and John was a young cop. He liked John but never regarded him as a world-class detective. So the Nelson County, Kentucky, district attorney was surprised to hear Sedwick on the line that hot July morning.

"You gotta be kidding, John. I figured we'd never see that guy. Does he look like the sketch on your poster?"

"He *does* look like the sketch on the poster, Kevin. A little older but he's our boy. Now I need you to get the extradition thing going. His name is Danny Parton. He's in jail here on a federal bootlegging conviction—you know, the tax evasion angle. The trial ended last week and he's on his way to a federal prison somewhere in Ohio. Got twelve years, I hear. Even ol' Al Capone only served eight on the same charge.

"They really nailed him, probably because of the size of his operation and how long he's been doin' it. He's a tough SOB; a real brawler. Been charged several times on assault but only did thirty days on two of 'em. Oh, another thing, Kevin. The jailer here told me this Parton guy made some smooth moves a few years back. Got off on a murder charge 'cause he married the main witness. He's a slick one, eh?

"Anyway, he's supposed to be transferred the end of next week, so let's make the feds wait and bring this lousy murderer back to Bardstown."

"Okay, John, I'll contact the governor's office on the extradition this morning. We're lucky. The grand jury is also in session as we speak. I know the case well enough to get an order from the grand jury to *file away* an indictment. This will give us the time we need to get the case on the docket when Parton is back here and we're ready to move. There's no way the grand jury will deny us an indictment. But, John, first tell me more about this Parton guy and how you found him."

The detective and the D.A. talked for another fifteen minutes. Sedwick was happy to regale the lawyer on how he tracked down his long-sought nemesis. He explained in detail how he tirelessly tracked his prey through the mountains of West Virginia. He minimized the luck he had in meeting Sidney Maas, making it sound like he was leaving no stone unturned. He did admit to a bit of good fortune in finding his man in the local jail when he started his search for the bootlegger with a visit to the Johnson City police station.

The two men also went over the immediate details that needed attention to bring Parton to Bardstown. After they hung up, Sedwick called Chief Rowlands and filled him in. The chief was lavish in his praise for his investigator turned "detective." He told John to return home until the Tennessee legal work was completed. Then the policeman could go back and bring his "catch" to Bardstown. John Sedwick felt on top of the world.

Nature did not endow Kevin Lawton with good looks. He was underweight, bald, and wore thick glasses. He looked older than his forty-two years. This D.A. did not lack for talent or brains, however, as proven by his conviction record. On this case as on others, he would move quickly. He prepared an affidavit listing the rationale for his case against Parton. The application was processed in one day. The requisition to extradite Parton along with the affidavit, authenticated by the Kentucky governor's office, were both issued to the governor's office in Tennessee. After the expected approval by the State of Tennessee, it would be up to that state to petition the federal government to stand aside and wait to incarcerate Parton on the bootlegging charge until after the Kentucky murder case was resolved.

Then the D.A. prepared the paperwork needed to obtain the indictment from the tenth circuit grand jury that was currently in session. He scheduled his appearance with that panel for two days later. He was sure the indictment was a foregone conclusion.

Danny Parton was not cooperating. He was brought before a judge in Johnson City and told of the charge against him. He wanted to fight extradition. His court-appointed lawyer, who was already weary of him from his bootlegging trial, begrudgingly but professionally demanded a *writ of habeas corpus* for Parton.

Kevin Lawton's writ was delivered several days later to the presiding judge and found to contain the essential elements. The writ was issued in proper form. The charge was adequate to support extradition. The person being held (Parton) was the same person charged in Kentucky with the crime.

Just one question was raised by the judge. She looked for some proof regarding Parton's previous testimony under oath that he was not in Kentucky at the time of the crime. In the end, Parton could not prove his whereabouts on the night Swanson was killed. The weight of the affidavit, including Mrs. Maloney's and Mr. Beal's sworn testimony to Parton's presence in Kentucky on the day of the night of the murder, was proof enough for the judge. She denied Parton's legal effort to avoid extradition and an official grant of extradition was signed by the governor of Tennessee.

Parton's court-appointed lawyer convinced him that appeal would not change anything. The State of Kentucky agreed to return Danny Parton to the State of Tennessee, if necessary, after any final disposition of the murder charge in Kentucky. Tennessee, in turn, guaranteed the bootlegger's transfer to federal prison, should that state ever get him back.

Ten days after John Sedwick asked Kevin Lawton to request the extradition, he and a uniformed deputy from the Nelson County Sheriff's office returned to the Johnson City jail. They signed the papers and then drove a depressed and shackled Danny Parton to Bardstown, Kentucky.

After the detective delivered his suspect to the Bardstown jail, he went to his office and placed a call to Sidney Maas in Johnson City, Tennessee. "Hello Sidney. This is John Sedwick. We met a few weeks back in Huntington?"

"Oh yes, Detective. I saw in the paper that you found your man?"

"You bet. Got him right here in jail in Bardstown, thanks to you."

"Well good. I hope that justice is served. Glad I could help."

"Do you remember what I told you about a reward if you kept quiet?" said Sedwick.

"I do, but I really wasn't counting on anything."

"Well Sidney, when we get this guy convicted, it will be my pleasure to hand you a check for five thousand bucks. Whatdaya say to that, pal?"

"I can't believe it. I just can't believe it." Sidney hung up the phone and sat down to contemplate his good fortune and how he might spend his money, should the bootlegger be convicted.

Chapter Fifteen

Mike Benson didn't want the job. He'd been public defender in Nelson County for three years. He'd paid his dues and was ready to move on. In fact he had just agreed to join a Bardstown law firm that specialized in insurance law and estate planning. Nice, clean, good paying legal work.

Judge Wyman Fontaine saw it differently. "Mike, you gotta take this case. The new kid, whatshisname, is not ready. Doesn't know his butt from his elbow. If I appoint him in a capital case, I'm asking for a reversal. I don't wanna try him more than once. If we don't give this Parton an adequate defense, we're not doin' our duty. He needs a good defense and only you can do that right now. He can't buy a good lawyer. He blew all his money on high livin' and defending himself on a bootlegging charge just before Sedwick found him in Tennessee."

"But I'm supposed to leave at the end of the month, Judge. This'll never be over by then," objected Benson.

"I'll talk to Scotty Cambridge, your new boss. He owes me a favor anyway." The judge wanted Mike Benson. He knew that Mike, a poor kid from "the wrong side of town" had become a lawyer working forty hours a week while going to law school at night. As PD, Benson did his homework on each case he handled and his skills in the courtroom were widely recognized. In the judge's opinion, Benson's integrity was also unquestioned. The judge continued, "Oh, one other thing, Mike. This Parton was about to be tried for murder back in the seventies in Tennessee. The trial was just underway when they discovered that Parton was married to the main witness. The case fell apart and got dismissed. I hear they're still married but it ain't a love-in. Anyhow, it's common opinion he was guilty as hell on that one. However, we'll keep it out of this trial, so don't worry about that."

"Oh, brother. This guy is a peach. Okay, Judge, but this is it, my last PD assignment, right?"

"Yep, now let's get on with it. Get over to the jail and talk to your client. The indictment is in order and yesterday we set bail so he won't be going anywhere. The charge is first degree murder. And today I just assigned a public defender, you, right? By the way, and I don't like 'em, and it's my call, but if you want a preliminary hearing, it will be two weeks from yesterday. Let me know by the weekend." The judge was done.

Mike Benson looked like the high school jock that he'd been: six feet tall, black wavy hair, dark complexion, a solid build. That afternoon, he made his way to the Nelson County Jail at Stephen Foster Avenue and Fourth Avenue in Bardstown. The jail was re-built in 1874 on the site of an earlier jail built in the early 1800s. It had been remodeled from time to time but was still functional. He checked in with the jailer and proceeded to what served as the conference room, a small lockup with a table and three chairs. It was soundproof.

Parton was brought in and the door was shut and locked behind him. He said, "So you're the lawyer they picked out for me, eh?"

"I'm Mike Benson," said the attorney standing and extending his hand. "Sit down and let's get started."

"Just a minute, Mike or Benson or whatever you wanna be called. I want you to look me straight in the eye."

Mike was taken aback a bit but sat down and complied. Parton sat and stared for a moment at the lawyer. Then he said, "Mr. Benson, I want you to know I did not kill Bobby Collins."

The lawyer had heard this kind of talk before and wondered why this time should be something different. Something in his client struck him, though. Maybe it was the deadly serious intensity in his eyes. Usually it was his practice not to question the client about guilt or innocence; he generally would lead the accused through a series of questions which would provide a set of facts that would help build a plausible defense. He figured most of his clients were guilty but that was not his concern. As a good defense attorney, the question was not if his client was guilty, but if the state could prove it beyond reasonable doubt. Mike hesitated then asked, "Do you want to tell me about it?"

"Yes I do. Now, I understand whatever I tell you is confidential, right?"

"Of course."

"Well, Mr. Benson, or can I call you Mike?" The attorney nodded. "Mike, I really did *want* to kill Bobby Collins. I even came to this town to do the job back in '81." Mike shifted in his seat. Parton said, "Now don't squirm, just let me tell you about it.

"I'm a moonshiner, a bootlegger, and a damn good one. I can duplicate almost any whiskey taste you'd want. I've made lots of money makin' and sellin' booze all across my little corner of Tennessee, Kentucky, and Georgia. The barkeeps in the area would buy my stuff and put it in empty branded bottles. Everyone enjoyed a nice little profit. 'Course you probably heard that I'm supposed to be doin' time right now on the bootlegging charge. Guess my days as a businessman are over."

"What about Swanson or Collins or whatever his name was?" interrupted the lawyer.

"I'm comin' to that. Bobby Collins was my right-hand man. Taught him everything I knew; treated him like a son. He could even do better than me on some batches of high-priced hooch. Well, one day he got religion or something. Said he was tired of the business and was gonna leave. Wouldn't say where. And he did leave.

"I didn't trust him. Figured he'd either start up somewhere nearby and try to get my customers or, if he did want to quit, that he might squeal on me. He'd been a big drinker himself and wasn't very stable. The way I saw it, he had enough stuff to put me away or out of business. He said he just wanted to move away and start a new life but I didn't believe him. If he was alive and out there someplace where I couldn't keep him under my thumb, he was a threat. I had to protect myself, right? I wanted to eliminate that threat."

"Sounds like a confession coming here, Mr. Parton," mused Mike Benson.

"No way. That's my *problem*, Mike. I'll tell you the truth. I did want to kill him and came here to do it. Even set the bomb in his car. But he had to be killed by somebody else the night before the bomb was supposed to go off. Even the cops here know he was supposed to die the next evening. But they figured I just found him and did 'im in the night before. They probably think I planted the bomb as some kinda backup. I can't prove otherwise 'cause nobody saw me during the night he was killed 'cause I took the back roads home. Didn't figure I'd need an alibi that night, though, 'cause the bomb was not set 'til the next night. I stayed out of sight 'til the next night when the bomb was set to blow. Figured that was the smart thing to do. When I got a chance, I went to a library near home and went through the newspapers from all around. I finally saw a piece that told of Bobby being beat up and killed in a parking lot. Mentioned they were looking for someone that sounded like me. I was worried because that meant they probably found the bomb and might tie it to me."

"Didn't you think that they might be looking for you anyway? I've been told that folks here identified you as looking for the victim for a day or two before the murder."

"Well I thought that if I acted friendly like, people wouldn't put me in the picture with a bomb that went off a day or two *after* I was asking about him. And I was seen back in Tennessee when the bomb was *set* to blow. I figured that was a good alibi if the bomb exploded but maybe it'll work against me now 'cause they found it before hand."

"Yeah, Danny. It's Danny right?" Parton grunted an acknowledgment.

"Yes, that won't help us," said the lawyer. "And of course, I must tell you *trying* to murder someone is a very serious crime by itself regardless of whether you got the job done or not."

"Are you on my side or not, Mr. Lawyer!" retorted a quickly angry Parton.

"I *am* on your side, Danny. I'll do my very best to defend you. You have that coming as a citizen. But I don't have to like what you did or, rather, planned to do. Now let's calm down and get on with the work of preparing your defense, okay?"

Danny Parton and his lawyer spent the rest of the afternoon going over the case with the lawyer looking for the best possible way to defend his client. Benson was finding himself believing Parton's story. Mike wrestled with the conflict. Should he have his client admit to the lesser crime of attempting to commit murder in order to prove Parton's innocence in the actual murder? Parton, for his part, was hoping for some magic that would allow him to walk in this trial. They didn't reach a conclusion that day. Mike promised to return in a day or two.

On the following Monday morning, Mike Benson and his client were back in the small conference room at the jail. Mike said, "Danny, I have to let the judge know today if we want a preliminary hearing. This means we force the prosecution to show us what they have in the way of evidence. I think, in your case, it might be smart to avoid a jury trial in this community, which is what happens if we can convince the judge that the evidence isn't strong enough. However, if we lose in the prelim, it doesn't hurt us too badly, at least legally."

"I wanna do everything I can to prove I didn't do this murder, Mike," Danny responded. He knew he could get the death penalty if he was convicted of the murder. He was scared.

"In order to convince the judge, Danny, I think we gotta tell your story just the way you told me. This means you are gonna face some consequences, probably you'll have to plea to attempted murder. If so, we'll try and use your admission and the circumstantial nature of the evidence to get a reasonable sentence, maybe something concurrent with the time you're gonna do for bootlegging."

Danny took his time to consider his lawyer's words. "Can you guarantee something like that, Mike?"

"I think you know the answer to that, Danny. We'll give it a hell of a shot. But no guarantees. Danny, even though it is not my practice to say this, I want you to know that I've been listening carefully to you and I believe your story. Don't get me wrong; you are guilty of a damn serious felony, but I'm convinced it is not the crime you're charged with."

"That's good enough for me, Mike. Let's give this hearing thing a try. Oh, I forgot to tell you about a little problem I had back home several years ago. See, I was arrested for murdering a local fella. . . ." Danny told Mike about his aborted trial years before in Tennessee.

"Forget it. The prosecutor may bring it up at the preliminary hearing but we'll fuss and they won't be able to use it at trial." Danny relaxed a little hearing this. Then Mike asked, "Is there anything else that I should know, Danny? I can't be surprised in the courtroom or we're both dead meat."

Parton explained that as a young man he had been arrested several times for assault. He explained that he had a bad temper and whenever he was drinking he got into fights and, most often, did some damage to his fighting partner. Danny said, "I did two or three thirty-day sprints in the local workhouse for assault and got probation a time or two."

"How old were you, Danny?"

"Early twenties, I guess. I'm sure any little problems I had as a teenager were taken off the record."

"I'm glad you told me, but these prior convictions might be a problem later on, Danny. We're just gonna have to work hard to keep you from being convicted."

The defendant and his lawyer discussed details for another hour, and then Mike was off to schedule the preliminary hearing with the judge.

This case had received enough notoriety that D.A. Kevin Lawton wanted to handle the hearing himself.

On the early October morning the hearing was set to begin, Judge Fontaine was spending considerable time with the two attorneys redundantly reviewing the purposes for a preliminary hearing. It was the place where it would be determined if there was enough evidence to show that there was probable cause to believe that the defendant committed the offense charged in the case. If there was, the matter would proceed to trial. The actual guilt or innocence of the defendant need not be proven in the preliminary hearing; that would be left to the trial. The hearing was also the forum where the admissibility of any and all evidence would be determined.

The judge reminded the attorneys that the prosecution must proceed first to show what evidence it has and to show that such evidence indicates probable cause. The defendant then has the right to challenge the evidence and therefore any indications of probable cause. Judge Fontaine also reminded the parties that guilty pleas or pleas to lesser charges could be made anytime before the court ruled on the issues presented.

Kevin Lawton revealed to the judge and to Mike Benson that he was prepared during the hearing to enter police and court records from Washington County, Tennessee. These records would document several assault convictions on the part of the defendant. Benson objected to the judge that these matters were irrelevant and should not be presented or considered in the hearing or in any trial.

"I'm in agreement with that, Mike. I don't think I would let that old stuff into the trial so we don't need to hear it in this proceeding, if Kevin doesn't insist. But if there is a conviction later, it could come up in sentencing," said the judge. Both attorneys nodded. Mike didn't like this answer, however. It meant that the judge was anticipating that the D.A. would go for the death penalty.

When the judge and the two attorneys finished their conference in chambers, they moved into the court-room for the hearing. Waiting there were a bailiff, the court reporter, and a police deputy who had Danny Parton in his custody. Not surprisingly, there was also a full gallery of local citizens. They had not lost interest in Bardstown's most remembered crime.

After the usual initial administrative proceedings were completed, the judge asked Prosecutor Lawton to proceed with the evidentiary presentation.

Kevin Lawton was an articulate and convincing presenter. "Your Honor, the state will show that the defendant here present is the only man alive who might have committed that awful murder in our cathedral parking lot back in March of 1981. We intend to call several witnesses who will show, when all their testimony is heard, that there is no likelihood any other human could have committed this crime. The first witness I would like to call is Inspector John Sedwick of the Bardstown police department."

The detective was sworn in and, responding to questions from the prosecuting attorney, told his story. He replayed the finding of Bobby Collins' (Swanson's) body and the discoveries made in the next days following. He explained the ugly details of how Bobby had died. Sedwick also revealed that a live bomb, set to blow up later the day Bobby's body was discovered, was found in the trunk of the victim's car. The fact that no prints were found on the bomb was explained away by the detective as proof of a careful professional. He talked about his visits with Mrs. Maloney and Steven Schumen who described the defendant and together conferred with the artist on the composite sketch that ultimately led to his arrest in Tennessee. Recent evidence gathered in Tennessee also confirmed that Parton and Collins knew each other and were suspected of working together in the illegal manufacture and sale of spirits.

Next the coroner, George Cantrell, was called to the stand. He repeated most of what was in his pathology report, emphasizing the brutal nature of the wounds that Bobby Collins suffered. The citizens reacted with gasps and groans as the D.A. set up his questions to draw attention to the grossness of the murder scene. Mike Benson objected, but the judge allowed the prosecutor to proceed. When the coroner was excused the din in the courtroom swelled, causing the judge to restore order.

Following the testimony of the coroner, Mrs. Maloney and Steven Schumen testified. Mrs. Maloney described how Parton was looking for Collins, and Steven Schumen told how the accused had access to the victim's car. In spite of the passage of time, they also both identified the man sitting in the courtroom as the man they spoke of in their separate testimonies.

Then Kevin Lawton called a Wendell Carson from Jonesborough, Tennessee, to testify. After the swearing in and establishing his domicile, the prosecutor said, "Mr. Carson, are you familiar with the defendant, Mr. Parton?"

"Yes sir," said Wendell, breathing heavily, and his ample stomach expanded and contracted. He was clearly not happy to be in the courtroom that morning.

"How are you acquainted with Mr. Parton?"

"I worked for him for a few years."

"When?"

"Late 70s—early 80s."

"Were you acquainted with a Bobby Collins, sometimes called Bobby Swanson?"

"Yeah, I mean yes, sir. Bobby worked for Danny Parton, too."

"What was the business that Mr. Parton was engaged in when you and Bobby were employed by him?"

"We made and sold a little booze. I guess it wasn't legal. But I didn't know much about that. I was just making deliveries for Danny."

"I see. Do you recall when Bobby Collins decided to leave Tennessee and how Mr. Parton felt about that?"

"Yes sir. Danny, Mr. Parton, was really mad when Bobby said he was leaving. Bobby wouldn't say where he was going. Said he just wanted out of the business before it was too late."

"What did that mean?" said the prosecutor.

"I think Bobby was scared of gettin' caught. He told me one time he didn't wanna go to jail for Danny."

"What else?"

"Well, I think Bobby was gettin' religion or something. The last couple of months before he took off, he was sayin' he felt, like guilty, for all the bad things he'd done. He quit drinkin' and changed, kinda."

"What do you mean, Wendell?"

"Well, he got real nice, kinda. Started doin' favors for people. Even did some favors for me."

"Like what?"

"Like, he'd buy my lunch if I forgot mine and didn't want any payback. One time, I was late 'cause my car broke down. Bobby came and got me and then stuck up for me when Danny chewed me out."

"I see, and what did Mr. Parton think about all this, Wendell?" asked Kevin Lawton.

"He was gettin' madder and madder. He told me he thought Bobby was gonna leave and go into competition with him. He thought that Bobby was a big fraud with the no drinkin' and all the nice stuff."

"Was Mr. Parton concerned about anything else?"

"I think so. Danny told me that he thought if Bobby *was* for real, with his big change and all, he might squeal on us. And that got Danny really pissed, oops, I mean mad."

"Okay, Wendell. What kind of other things did Danny Parton say when he talked to you about being mad at Bobby Collins?"

"Objection!" cried the defender, Benson. "Leading and suggestive. Calls for speculation by the witness."

"I think I'll allow it," said the judge. "We'll see if the answer should be heard or stricken. You may answer, Mr. Carson."

"What was the question again?" asked Wendell.

"What other things did Mr. Parton say to you about being mad at Bobby Collins?" said Kevin Lawton.

"Nothing much 'til Bobby left."

"What did he say after Bobby left?"

Wendell squirmed in his seat. He glanced at Danny Parton. Then back to the prosecutor. "Well I don't know if he meant it but. . . ."

Lawton quickly interrupted, "Wendell, no opinions now; just tell us what he said."

"Well, he said he was gonna find Bobby and shut him up."

"Did he say what 'shut him up' meant? Like did he mean he'd just talk to Bobby or threaten him? Or did he mean something more serious?"

"Objection, leading the witness and calls for speculation." Mike Benson didn't like where this was going.

"Sustained; can you rephrase your question?" the judge asked Lawton.

"What exactly did Danny Parton say about Bobby Collins after saying he was going to find him and shut him up?"

Wendell was speaking very softly now. "I uh, I think he said somethin' like that if he found Bobby, nobody'd have to worry about him talking to anybody about our business. Somethin' like that."

"Did you take that to mean that Mr. Parton wanted to kill Bobby Collins?"

"Objection. Calls for a conclusion by the witness!"

"Sustained."

"Did Mr. Parton ever say anything to you directly about killing Mr. Collins?" said Lawton.

"No but. . . ."

"But what?"

"One day after Danny got back from a trip somewhere, he said somethin' like we didn't to have to worry about Bobby screwin' up our business any more."

"Your witness," Lawton, said nodding to Mike Benson.

"Mr. Carson, did Danny Parton ever tell you or *anyone* else to your knowledge, that he was going to kill Bobby Collins?"

"No sir, never."

"Did he ever tell you that he *had* killed Bobby Collins?"

"No sir."

"Did anyone else ever tell you that he or she had knowledge that Mr. Parton killed Mr. Collins?"

"No."

"So you have no way of really knowing if Mr. Parton did indeed kill Mr. Collins?"

"No."

"Thank you, Mr. Carson. I have no more questions at this time. Your Honor, I would request a recess at this time. I would also request a meeting with you and the district attorney in your chambers."

"Very well," said Judge Fontaine. "You may step down Mr. Carson. We'll recess 'til tomorrow morning at nine o'clock." He tapped the gavel, and the two lawyers followed him into chambers.

"What do you wanna propose, Mike? The evidence looks pretty bad for your guy," said the judge. "We've got two eyewitnesses who will identify Parton as looking for Collins or his car during the day the night before he was killed. We have this Wendell's testimony that sure sounds like Parton was planning a murder."

"It's all circumstantial, Judge; I'm convinced that the prosecution will not be able to show undisputed evidence that will convict this guy.

Remember that bomb was set for the day *after* Collins was killed. There is no evidence that it was Parton in the lot that night. And there is no forensic evidence that links Parton to the murder. There's reasonable doubt, very reasonable doubt, Your Honor."

Kevin Lawton interrupted, "Mike, come on. The circumstantial evidence, as you call it, is so damn strong, any jury will convict. There is no plausible hint of *any* other killer. The guy's guilty as hell."

Fontaine raised his hand. "Okay, boys. We're not trying the case here in my chambers. Do you have something in mind, Mike?"

"Yeah. My client has told me that he did want to kill that fella but that he was on the road back to Tennessee when Collins was killed. For that reason, he's willing to plea to an attempted murder charge. That's all he's guilty of, and we'll ask for a reasonable sentence since he's willing to admit what he *did* do. He is not trying to cop a plea to a lesser charge than the crime he *did* commit."

"Pretty slick, Mike," said Lawton. "I think we have a cold-blooded murderer here and I think a jury will agree."

"Kevin, not so fast," said the judge. "I don't know if this Parton is guilty or not but the evidence is not yet bulletproof. I know this town has wanted to solve this crime for years and Parton does *look* guilty. But if Mike can convince a jury that the evidence is not foolproof, reasonable doubt etc., the guy walks for a crime he *did* plan."

The three men debated for another twenty minutes until the judge called a halt to it. The district attorney agreed to sleep on it and get back to the judge and the defense attorney at eight-thirty the next morning.

The next morning the judge and two lawyers got together again in the judge's chambers. The judge spoke first. "Well, Kevin, what do you think of Mike's offer to plead Parton guilty to attempted murder?"

"I wish I could count the calls I got last night. Some identified themselves and just tried to offer some friendly advice. Others didn't say who they were and were belligerent as hell. This town wants this guy tried for first degree murder and the vast majority want the death sentence. We haven't had anyone die in the chair in Kentucky since capital punishment came back in '76, and the people see this as a bellwether case."

Mike Benson protested that he wanted no part of any railroad job that the D.A. seemed to be promoting. He suggested that Lawton's motives might not be pure and that politics was playing a big part in the prosecutor's decision making. The D.A. was insulted and the two lawyers traded barbs until Judge Fontaine called a halt to it. "Okay, boys, this is getting us nowhere. Have either of you got more you wanna do in this hearing?"

Mike Benson responded, "Hell no. If Kevin won't buy a plea that is right on the money with what Parton *is* guilty of, I'm done here. I will ask you to find no probable cause, Judge, based on the lack of hard evidence. I think you should rule that way."

"Mike, there's enough here under the law for *probable cause*, maybe not for conviction, but for probable cause. You guys are gonna have to try it."

Mike looked disgusted; Kevin looked pleased; Judge Fontaine looked disappointed. They proceeded to the court room where the preliminary hearing was brought to a close with the ruling that the evidence bore the weight of probable cause that a murder had taken place and Danny Parton was responsible.

As the news hit the streets, the citizens of Bardstown rejoiced and smacked their collective lips for the trial.

The next morning, the judge, the D.A., and the public defender were back in judge's chambers again. At the close of the hearing the day before, Mike Benson had moved for a change of venue for the trial. His logic was simple. The community had taken such a biased interest in the case that there was little possibility of a fair trial. Mike had detailed all the news reports about the case and the local reaction to it. He pointed out the circus-like atmosphere around Bardstown. The people wanted blood.

"Mike, I've been thinking about the venue thing myself for three weeks now. I've noticed what's happening in the community, too. The whole issue of the fair trial for me is in jury selection. I've lived in Bardstown all my life and I know the people of this community. We can find enough jurors in Nelson County who will carefully weigh the evidence and make an honest judgment about what they hear. That's all we could expect from any jury in the country. I'm gonna deny your motion, Mike. Be ready to work hard on jury selection."

The meeting ended. Mike Benson wondered if Judge Fontaine had reasons of his own for not granting the change of venue. He had always felt that the judge was the most objective and most honest judge on the circuit bench. Benson also started to second guess himself. Why couldn't he seem to get a break in this case?

He shook off these thoughts and resolved to out work Kevin Lawton and win at trial.

Chapter Sixteen

On August 1, 1984, more three years since he came to the monastery as a near-death vagrant, Phil Norton entered the Trappist Novitiate in the Abbey of Gethsemani. Novices would not become real monks until they took their vows but they did take a religious name. He asked to keep his own name and became *Brother* Phillip. Last names were rarely used among the monks.

The regimen was not easy. Up each morning at 3:15 for forty-five minutes of prayer. Back up at 5:45 for another twenty-five minutes praying the psalms of sacred office. Then Mass. This gathering for prayer was repeated at several specific times throughout the day. During the long periods between, the novices read and studied in the manner of monks for centuries past. Sometimes, at these unscheduled times, individual conferences were scheduled between the novice and his spiritual director.

However, what the novice enjoyed most was his study of the Trappists. He found that this order of monks, known as Cistercians, comes closest to following the original rule of St. Benedict. Phil had already heard about the deep tradition of *his* monastery, the Abbey of Gethsemani—the first Trappist monastery in America, founded there in Kentucky in 1848. Phil learned that the Trappists traced their beginnings back to 1098 at Citeaux in France. They expanded rapidly throughout the Middle Ages, building many monasteries. Among these was the Abbey of La Trappe, the scene of a significant seventeenth century reform, hence came the order's more familiar name, the Trappists. Phil read how the order grew when certain of their monasteries would send out a few monks to sponsor the foundation of new communities of Trappists who would multiply themselves by recruiting new vocations. The novice took pride learning the Trappists were currently spread throughout much of the world and that they are recognized as one of the most strict yet admired of all religious orders.

Each afternoon, the novices were assigned chores that took about an hour and a half. Meals were served in the refectory three times each day. The monks and novices all gathered one last time at 7:30 P.M. for night prayer, and they could retire at will after that.

The master of novices met regularly with each novice and separately with their spiritual directors to monitor their progress. The master observed how each novice was maturing and experiencing his spiritual life. The monks were concerned with helping each novice discern for himself his own level of acceptance of the monastic way of life. They expected the novices to conform to the regimen and to make progress in spirituality. Yet there was no effort to force the novices to complete the program and no disappointment or negative reactions shown if novices dropped out. This way of life was not for everyone, and the Trappists did not try to communicate that it was.

Phil took to the routine and enjoyed its discipline. He grew to appreciate and respect the wisdom that was shared by his assigned spiritual director, Father Bart. The priest had been in the navy during World War II before joining the Trappists in 1946. It became clear to Phil that Father Bart had lived a full life as a sailor with all the stereotypical wanderings and bravado for which the occupation is famous. He'd been a *rounder.*

Father Bart's earthy navy experience, along with almost forty years of living and growing in the monastic life, became the perfect mix of credibility that matched Phil's needs for guidance. He studied the Scripture and other holy books. He learned about both the inner and outward life of a Trappist. He enjoyed the study and the learning. But he still struggled with praying. Over time he came to understand that each step led to another; he began to see that he'd never fully arrive as a monk.

Phil thought his two years as a novice were the best of his life. He'd been almost entirely shut off from the outside world. No newspapers or TV. He was allowed to receive mail, so he corresponded several times each year with Sandy and Kerry. Their letters to each other were upbeat. He sensed his family supported his decision to become a Trappist monk.

During these two years in which he was protected from distraction, Phil tried but could not quite forget about his crime. He was starting to believe, however, that he'd actually been forgiven by God. He was comforted that these two years away from the outside world changed him. With no knowledge to the contrary, Phil assumed that no one else had been accused of his crime. He felt sure the abbot would let him know if that happened. However, unlike the other monks, the abbot was expected to keep a general eye on national and local news so *The Kentucky Standard,* the Bardstown newspaper, was delivered to his office three times a week. What Phil didn't know is that the abbot had learned about the apprehension of one Danny Parton for the murder in the cathedral parking lot. Justifying his action on the knowledge that Parton would have been otherwise incarcerated for other crimes, and with much prayer and soul searching, the abbot had made the tough personal decision to defer telling Phil about Parton until sometime after he took his vows.

As the day approached, Father Robert and Father Bart conferred and agreed that Phil was ready to make his first vows. The abbot approved their recommendation.

On the second Sunday morning in July 1986, the whole assembly of Trappists gathered within the stark white walls of their long chapel with its high ceiling. Special chairs were set for the monks in the sanctuary facing the altar. Each monk wore the standard white cassock under a long black scapular that covered all but the arms of the cassock. Father Abbot was the main celebrant at the Mass at which the novices would profess their first vows. The strong male voices of the monks rang out in grand accompaniment for the special liturgy.

In the congregation Phil's only living relatives, Sandy and Kerry, smiled proudly. They were awed by the beauty and pageantry of the ceremony. Later they would enjoy a picnic with Phil on the monastery grounds.

At the solemn moment during the Mass, Phil Norton made his vows and he became known as Brother Phillip, a Trappist monk.

Chapter Seventeen

Mike Benson had been frustrated at the outcome of the preliminary hearing in 1984. In the spring of the following year, he'd still been convinced that his strategy of having his client agree to a lesser crime couldn't fail. Besides, Mike had come to *believe* that attempted murder was the crime Danny Parton had committed against the victim, Collins.

Since the hearing, the public defender had made several overtures to Kevin Lawton to allow Parton to plea to the lesser charge. Lawton was civil but refused. Mike appealed to the judge to try to convince Lawton to accept the plea of attempted murder. The judge said that at this point it was Lawton's call.

After several meetings with Judge Fontaine and Kevin Lawton, an exasperated Mike Benson reminded the judge at one of their meetings that he had agreed to take this case as a favor to "his honor." This didn't sit too well with Fontaine. "I can't believe you said that, Mike. You've always been the lawyer who worked with a sense of duty, even if it wasn't convenient. Scotty Cambridge has assured me they'll wait for you over at the law firm. Besides, you know the law here. Kevin can go for broke if he wants to. Even if I agreed that Kevin oughta let your client plea to a lesser charge, I'm not gonna force him."

Kevin Lawton smiled. "Mike, I think we can get a conviction on first degree here. Especially with Wendell's testimony."

"Yeah, Kevin," Mike said, annoyed. "You got lucky finding that character. But his whole testimony doesn't prove murder any more than it suggests attempted murder. Remember, if I beat ya, Parton goes free."

"I'll take my chances, Mike," the D.A. fired back.

Benson indicated that he might make a motion for a *lesser included* charge at the end of the trial. That would allow the jury to find the defendant guilty of the charge of attempted murder if the charge of murder was not proven at trial. The *lesser included* charge would have to meet certain criteria in order to be entered. Specifically, the elements of the major charge must include the elements of the lesser charge. Therefore, the greater charge of murder would, by definition, include the lesser charge of attempted murder.

"Go ahead make your motion for *lesser included*, Mike," said Lawton. "That'll be up to the judge at the time."

"Are you goin' for the death penalty?" asked Benson, more annoyed now.

"Maybe."

"Oh, jeez, Judge, are you gonna let him make a circus out a this?" Mike pleaded.

Wyman Fontaine replied, "Okay boys, I've heard enough of this over the last couple of months. This is the end of November; I'm setting trial for April second. Kevin can stay with the murder-only charge if he wants. It's his call. Mike, defend your client." The meeting was over.

The community had taken a strong and biased interest in this case. Bardstown wanted its pound of flesh. It was the topic of conversation at church socials, Little League Games, in bars. The murder had been a major local event three years previous but had fallen to the back burner as time passed. Now, with the capture of Danny Parton, the case had taken on a new life of its own. Those faded memories were restored with an array of new suppositions and new and stronger cries for justice.

Stories were invented, told, and retold about Bobby and his kindness to people. He couldn't have run so many errands, babysat so many kids, given so many rides, and given away so many dollars had he lived ten years in Bardstown. If he'd survived, even with only three weeks at Moore's, there was no question he'd have been the employee of the year. Guaranteed. Bobby Swanson was a hometown hero now; no, more of a local icon, and he didn't deserve to die. The fact that his real name was Collins and he lived most all his life in Tennessee was lost on the populous of Bardstown. Bobby's death would be vindicated. They'd see to it.

Details of his horrible death were made even more gruesome, if that were possible. And the story of the never-give-up "detective," John Sedwick, also grew in great detail. The policeman's hunt was no less a success than if he'd climbed Everest in a t-shirt. And John Sedwick did little to dispel any exaggeration. "After all," he told himself, "I persevered when others would have quit."

The people of Bardstown were a God-fearing, hard-working lot. They stood for the tried and true American values, and some amount of emotional exacerbation could be expected in this community.

It was into this hotbed of excitement and desire for "justice" that Mike Benson had to defend his client. He felt boxed in. He couldn't understand why Judge Fontaine had denied his motion for change of venue. With the trial about to start, he had no new strategy other than to hammer away on the circumstantial nature of the evidence. No one had seen Danny kill Bobby. And it was clear the bomb was set to go off when Collins would be returning from work the day *after* he was slain in the parking lot. Would that lead a jury to have reasonable doubt? What Mike needed and didn't have was a plausible alternative: a person or event that might have caused Collins's death. When the trial started, he was ready to use what little he had to do the best he could. Mike Benson wished he could be more optimistic.

On Tuesday, April 2, 1985, the overcast day matched the serious mood of all assembled in the courtroom. Judge Fontaine tapped his gavel and the trial was underway. The first four days were taken up with preliminary motions and impaneling the jury. An initial pool of fifty potential jurors was available to both sides. Mike Benson did the best he could to detect prejudice among prospective jurors. He could identify only two who were *obvious* trouble, both of whom the prosecution excused, perhaps trying to demonstrate their objectivity to the judge and other prospective jurors. People wanted to serve on this jury. They wanted to be part of local history. Most were careful to appear unbiased. Only three in the initial pool said they could not vote for the death penalty and were excused quickly by the prosecution.

Mike used numerous preemptory challenges, trying his best to sort through and pick the most *logical* among the group . . . people who appeared likely to think rationally rather that emotionally. At any hint of a prospective juror's bias against his client, Mike challenged, and the person was excused. He figured the thinking types might buy an admission of attempted murder in favor of having to find proof of murder in the first degree. He challenged any who said they disapproved of the use of alcohol, figuring they'd be against Parton from the outset. He also challenged one woman simply because she was employed at the Moore Distillery and another who was a close friend and neighbor of Mrs. Maloney, a key witness for the prosecution. By Friday evening, after starting on a second pool of possible jurors and considering over seventy-five citizens, twelve were picked to hear the evidence.

Monday dawned a cold spring day in Bardstown. On his way into the courthouse, Mike Benson considered that the weather might be an apt reflection of what he was facing in this trial.

Opening statements were predictable. D.A. Lawton recounted the evidence that certainly would point to Parton. The public defender asked the jury to notice the circumstantial nature of all the evidence they would hear. The following day witnesses were called by the prosecution. Clement Smith, Bobby's supervisor, was called and made the case for his being an exemplary employee. Three other witnesses were the same as those used at the preliminary hearing: John Sedwick the investigator, Mrs. Maloney, and Stephen Schumen who talked to Danny Parton. The state also called George Cantrell, the coroner, and Teddy Fry, the lab technician, who participated in the investigation at the crime scene and afterwards.

The public defender spent considerable time with each of these witnesses in cross examination. With each of the witnesses, Mike carefully sought and received a begrudged acknowledgment that their testimony did not prove by itself that Danny Parton killed Bobby Collins. Benson was very tough on the coroner and the lab tech. He hammered away at the fact that what they found in no way, forensic or pathological, led directly to the defendant. Both of these men were not happy with Benson's candid and logical dismissal of their evidence as nothing more than sensational information given to incense jurors. He received a mumbled "no" from each when he asked if any of their testimony indicated *who* killed Bobby Collins. Mike felt he gained some ground with his cross examinations. He was breathing a bit easier.

A crowning blow, however, came when Wendell Carson, Collins's fellow employee in Parton's business, was called as the state's final witness. It happened when he answered the last question from the D.A. When Lawton asked if there was any additional reason for Wendell to believe that Parton could kill Collins, the big man said, "Well, if he killed the guy back home after he took the gun. . . ."

"Objection!" cried Mike Benson.

"Sustained!" rejoined the judge. "The jury will disregard the last statement by Mr. Carson. And Mr. Lawton, I warn you not to lead your witness in that direction again." The judge was angry.

"Yes, Your Honor. I have no more questions. The state rests."

Mike Benson's head dropped. He knew the damage was done. He knew that Kevin probably asked his question knowingly but would protest otherwise. He knew Kevin might expect Wendell's answer if he asked the right question. He also knew he could do nothing about it. As he had done with the other witnesses, he cross examined Wendell Carson.

During the cross examination, Mike tried to clarify that none of Wendell's testimony provided any proof that Parton killed Bobby Collins. Wendell didn't disagree. But Mike felt himself losing ground with the jury now.

The following day, after hearing Wendell's testimony, Mike decided to open his defense by calling Danny Parton himself to the stand. He had told Danny that he had hoped not to have to call him if it appeared that the jury was buying the idea that there was no direct proof that he murdered Collins. Mike felt the jury was now ready to find Danny guilty. He would have Danny admit to attempted murder and maybe even get the judge to accept a motion for a *lesser included* charge at the end of the trial.

After the swearing in, Mike got down to business. "Mr. Parton, did you murder one Bobby Collins, known in Bardstown as Bobby Swanson?"

"No sir, I did not," said Danny, almost too emphatically.

"You have heard witnesses come forth and testify that you were looking for him and that you entered the trunk of his car during the daytime preceding the night he was murdered?"

"Yeah, I heard 'em."

"You heard Mr. Carson testify that you told him that there would be no reason to be 'concerned about Bobby Collins' after you returned from a trip around the time that Collins was killed?"

"Yeah, I heard the sumbitch say that," bellowed Parton.

"Mr. Parton," thundered the judge, "you will be found in contempt if you don't answer the questions in a clear and composed manner. Do you understand, sir?"

Quieter now, "Yes, I understand, Your Honor," said the chastised defendant.

Mike Benson added his assurances that Danny would behave. Then he asked the defendant, "Mr. Parton, you also heard testimony that an armed bomb was found in Collins's car the morning after he was murdered?"

"Yes."

"How do you suppose that bomb was put in the trunk, Mr. Parton?"

"I put it there."

There was an immediate outbreak of noise in the spectator seats. "Did you hear that?" "The guy did it!" "This baby's wrapped up!" "Give 'im the chair!" The judge pounded his gavel, causing a quick silence. No one wanted to miss what would follow.

"Explain," said the public defender.

"Well, I did come to town to find and kill Collins. I found his car at the distillery and set 'er in the trunk. I rigged it to go off the next evening when the fella should be drivin' home."

"Mr. Parton, why did you want to kill Mr. Collins?"

"Because I thought he was gonna take away some of my business. Or, if not and this 'do-gooder' act of his was for real, I figured he might turn on me and testify against me for sellin' booze without a license."

"And what happened after you put the bomb in Collins car?"

"Nothin'. I went home. Took the back roads 'cause I wanted to stay out of sight 'til I got home."

"Why didn't you establish an alibi for the night that Collins was murdered?" offered the lawyer.

"Didn't think I'd need one. Besides, I didn't wanna be seen anywhere 'til I got home."

"What you are saying, Mr. Parton, is that you came to Bardstown to kill Bobby Collins and then left. And that you did not see or kill him in the parking lot the night of March fifth or the early morning of March sixth of 1981. Is that correct?"

"That's what I'm saying. I was long gone when Collins was killed that night. Not that I was sorry to hear about it at the time but it weren't me who did him in."

"Thank you, Mr. Parton. Your witness," said Benson, looking at Kevin Lawton.

Kevin had not quite anticipated that Benson would put Parton on the stand and admit to attempted murder. This would call for some solid cross examination of his own. He began, "Mr. Parton, before you were brought to Bardstown to face charges for the murder of Bobby Collins, where were you located?"

"Uh, the Johnson City Jail."

"Objection. Irrelevant," said the public defender.

"Overruled for now. Let's see what direction this is going," replied the judge.

"Thank you, Your Honor," gushed the D.A. "Mr. Parton, what were you doing in the Johnson City Jail?"

"Objection!"

"Overruled, Mr. Benson. Let the district attorney proceed."

"Approach the bench, Your Honor?" said Mike.

The judge beckoned the lawyers to come forward and they huddled out of earshot of the jury and spectators.

"How can you let Parton's pending incarceration get into *this* trial, Your Honor?" pleaded the defender.

The judge looked at Lawton, who said, "What I'm trying to show is this guy won't do much more jail time if he's convicted on an attempted murder charge. He can probably get leniency in sentencing on attempted murder after he does a bunch of years for bootlegging. He's trying to save his life— avoid the death penalty. In other words, he hasn't got a lot to lose if he is found guilty of the lesser charge. We think he murdered Collins and we don't want him to end up doing a couple of extra years in some prison or another and get off on murder one."

Benson responded, "Judge, if you let all this stuff in about his past, that will only help convince the jury that he's a bad apple and more likely guilty of murder. I agree with Kevin on his point that Parton is trying to save his life. But that's because he's *not* guilty of murder one."

"I guess I'm inclined to let Kevin proceed. I think the jury, in the end, is going to have to decide if he killed Collins or not. Go ahead, Kevin." The judge waved the two lawyers back to their places.

Lawton started again, "Mr. Parton, what were you doing in the Johnson City Jail?"

Parton looked at Benson, then at Judge Fontaine. The Judge said, "You may answer, Mr. Parton."

"I was waitin' to be sent to some joint in Ohio."

"You mean to a federal prison?" said Lawton.

"I guess so."

Ignoring the defendant's less than perfect cooperation, Lawton asked, "And why would you be going there?"

"I guess for sellin' a little booze."

"I see, and how much time did you expect to spend in Ohio?"

"Uh, I guess the judge said somethin' about fifteen years. But I think I woulda done less than that."

Ignoring the last statement, Kevin said, "And don't you also think that, if you were to do that much time in Ohio and if you were convicted of attempted murder to which you've just admitted, you just might be able to get off rather easy—maybe just a couple more years?"

Benson was on his feet. "Judge, I strongly object! This is not only leading the witness, but it is also attributing motives to the defendant that have no basis or foundation in fact."

"Sustained. The jury will disregard and give no weight to the district attorney's last question."

Benson was demoralized. Again, the D.A. was able to seed ideas in the minds of the jurors with nothing more that a sustained objection from the judge. Lawton's cross examination was over and the lawyers would give their final arguments the next day.

Both lawyers' final arguments were much the same as their opening statements. Each was eloquent in making his points. Lawton made a strong case that, while the evidence might be seen as circumstantial, such evidence was like pieces of a patchwork quilt. Each piece by itself may not prove the guilt of the defendant, but when taken as a whole, the mere preponderance of the evidence produced a blanket of facts that could only point to one Danny Parton. Lawton added the logical point that the defendant was only trying to save his skin with his admission to attempted murder. He asked the jury to do its duty and find the defendant guilty of first degree murder.

The public defender gave a worthy rebuttal using the classical doctrine of *reasonable doubt*. He again argued that none of the evidence in the actual killing led directly to Parton. He reminded the jurors of his client's willingness to admit to trying to kill Bobby Collins, which would explain the circumstantial nature of the evidence. Mike was especially hard on the professionals in the case: the police inspector, the coroner, the lab tech. He challenged the jury to find one piece of evidence presented by this group that pointed right at Danny Parton. He played on the guilt that the jurors might feel should they condemn an innocent man. His final words were, "If you cannot be absolutely sure, you cannot convict."

After both sides completed their final arguments, Mike Benson asked for a short meeting in chambers with the court reporter present. He made a formal motion to the judge to allow the lesser charge of attempted murder be included. This would allow the jury to find the defendant guilty of attempted murder if they could not find him guilty of murdering Bobby Collins. Kevin Lawton argued that he was confident that the prosecution had proved beyond a reasonable doubt that Danny Parton was guilty of murder. He asked the judge to deny Benson's motion. As the people's advocate, Lawton wanted a conviction on the charge of murder only.

The judge hesitated just for a few seconds. He flashed a quick, pained expression. He had anticipated this and had already searched his conscience many times for what he felt was the proper ruling. He had settled in his own mind that even his own upcoming re-election as district judge in Bardstown was not influencing his decision. "Motion denied," said the judge.

Later, in the presence of the jurors, the judge said, "Ladies and gentlemen, it is important that you understand that when you deliberate, you can only find the defendant guilty or innocent of the charge of murder in the first degree. If you are not fully convinced that the prosecution has adequately proved murder in the first degree in this trial, you have no back-off position other than finding the defendant innocent. You cannot find him guilty of any other charge."

The judge gave the jury explicit instructions as to their mandate. He explained again the definition of murder in the first degree and the jury's charge to find its verdict only on that charge. A few more details were completed and the jury had the case.

Chapter Eighteen

"I think you all know what we are called to do here. It is our job to dispatch justice to this Parton fella. We've probably heard enough so I suggest we take a vote to see if we need to spend much more time on this thing." Thus, Tommy Kendrick, the jury foreman, called the jury members of seven women and five men to the business at hand. Tommy, short and thin as a pencil, lived in the nearby rural town of Loretto, Kentucky. During the trial he kept thinking about the Bible. He struggled to remain objective, but his mind always came back to an eye for an eye sense of justice. Tommy had pretty well made up his mind that Danny Parton was guilty.

Sara Winkel, a gray-haired grandma from Bardstown spoke. "Don't we need to at least discuss this some? Shouldn't we look at the evidence and all that to make sure we're doin' our job?"

A few heads nodded but Tommy retorted, "Let's just see where we are. Then if we gotta talk about it, we can do that." With that he passed out ballots and asked the panel to make their marks and return their ballots, folded, to him.

Tommy counted the ballots and was surprised to find the tally nine to three in favor of conviction. "Oh, man, how can it be that a few folks aren't sure, or even wanna let this killer go free? This guy's guilty as sin!"

Norm Page, another local juror who looked like the typical linebacker he'd been, said, "Yeah, let's get this over with. He's guilty. Let's find him guilty and then get on with the real stuff, whether he gets the chair or not."

"Whoa, we ain't no lynch mob here!" yelled another juror. The whole group was talking now. Back and forth went the opinions, warnings, and attempts at peacemaking. It was a full five minutes before Tommy Kendrick was able to call the group back to some semblance of order.

"Well, I guess we do need to talk about this. Let's go over the evidence one more time on our own and then vote again." Tommy was a better facilitator than he'd first appeared. Through a series of his questions, the panel walked through the evidence, step by step. General debate ensued about the nature of the evidence and which of the two lawyers' arguments about circumstantial evidence made the most sense in the case before them. The issue of Parton's alibi one night but not the next, was brought up but soon dismissed as proving nothing. Ms. Peters brought up the fact that Parton had *admitted* to attempted murder, but she was quickly rebuffed. Most jurors loudly supported the D.A.'s argument that Parton admitted attempted murder to save his hide.

Kendrick reminded the jury, "We have only one choice here. Guilty in the first degree or not."

Peters persisted, "We *can* consider both possibilities and if we come to believe that Parton is guilty only of attempted murder, we don't convict him."

A lull in the conversation occurred. Each member gradually fell silent processing his or her own thoughts. After a few minutes, the foreman quietly suggested another vote. The result, eleven in favor of conviction.

There was another outburst of questions and comments among the group. People demanded to know who the holdout was. Tommy said he was disappointed but the "holdout" need not identify oneself. Sara Winkel spoke up. "I'm not convinced Parton is guilty. Why would he set up a bomb and then kill Collins in the parking lot the night before it was gonna go off?"

"Maybe, that was his plan all along. Maybe he was looking for Collins so he could personally kill him 'cause he hated him so. Maybe the bomb was only a backup," said Norm Page.

Sara admitted she hadn't thought about that. The jury debated that point for another hour and a half. After more talk to reinforce Norm's backup theory and considerable discussion about circumstantial evidence, the jurors voted once more. The verdict was unanimous. On Wednesday at two in the afternoon, just two and a half days into the trial, the jury returned to the courtroom.

When the foreman read the verdict, guilty in the first degree, there was an outburst of hurrahs and applause in the court. Danny buried his head in his hands; Mike's head sunk to his chest. The judge banged the gavel and reminded the jury that they were to return on the following day to immediately begin deliberations on the appropriate sentence for Danny Parton. They were warned that they must continue not to discuss the case or expose themselves to media reports about the case.

That night the topic of conversation in every bar, public place, and in most homes was about the trial. There was exhilaration in the air. Bardstown and all of Nelson County could feel proud again. An evil deed had been done and justice would be delivered. And now speculation ran amok with theories about the sentence. This had always been in the back of their minds, but now with the conviction a done deed, the real issue of justice was on the table.

After a few days, as some of the excitement would wear off, the community would become split on the subject. Some would see Parton only deserving the death sentence. There was a certain thrill about it. A rotten murderer gets the chair. Others would feel that the evidence was not *absolutely* pure, so life in prison would be best. Still others would be opposed to capital punishment on any grounds and were not specific about what alternative sentence might be suited to the crime. The topic would churn daily in Bardstown.

Detective John Sedwick did not go to the bars that evening. He came home and slumped into his easy chair. He asked his wife to pour him a drink. She had been much more solicitous since John brought Danny Parton back to Bardstown. In fact the whole town was paying him the respect he'd felt he deserved all along. He enjoyed it. After supper he called Sidney Maas and made arrangements to send him a five thousand dollar check that the Chamber of Commerce had approved as the reward for the arrest and conviction of Bobby's murderer.

The twelve jurors reassembled in the courtroom the day after the trial ended. Kevin Lawton asked for the death sentence. He reviewed all the evidence and testimony that was brought out in the trial. He emphasized the details of Bobby Collins's painful death. He reminded the jurors that Parton had full intent in this murder; it was not just some act of momentary passion. He also asked the jury to remember that in their own deliberations, they had found the defendant guilty of this heinous act without reservation, and such a crime not only allowed but "indeed called for the death sentence."

Lawton then placed in evidence the documents from Tennessee that showed Danny Parton as a convicted criminal on several assault charges. Benson objected and the judge overruled him.

Mike called three witnesses when it was his turn. One was a psychologist who had examined Parton in the time since the trial. His name was Doctor Wesley DeSoto, a handsome, middle-aged man. He had a positive reputation as an expert witness on both sides in criminal trials. After the swearing in and the establishment of the doctor's credentials, Benson asked the witness, "Have you examined the witness, Doctor?"

"I have."

"And what did you find?"

"Mr. Parton has a rather normal profile. While he may have a propensity to anger, today he generally seems to be in control of his emotions. He also has average intelligence and does not seem to suffer from mental illness."

"In your opinion, Doctor," the public defender continued, "is there any thing in Mr. Parton's personality that would lead you to believe that he could or could not have committed the crime for which he was convicted?"

"No."

There was a general stirring in the courtroom. The jurors, the prosecutor, the judge, and the spectators all wondered why Mike Benson had this expert on the stand. He didn't seem to be helping his cause.

Benson went on, "Is there anything at all that struck you about the defendant in relation to this crime?"

"Yes there is. I am convinced that Mr. Parton did not lie to me during our three visits. Let me clarify. In my experience with clients accused of criminal activity, there is a good deal of delusional or contrived statements of falsehood, especially in the early stages of our visits."

"Objection. This is going toward the matter of guilt or innocence, which was already settled in the trial," said Kevin Lawton.

The judge mused, "I'll allow it for now. Let's see where this is going."

"Go on, Doctor DeSoto," said Benson.

"Well, as the defendant and I reviewed his life and his experiences, he was very forthcoming with the highs and lows of his life. He didn't seem to alibi for mistakes he made in the past. He was also very adamant about *not* committing the crime of which he was accused."

"Objection. We are not trying this case. We're here for sentencing," cried Lawton.

"Approach the bench." The judge signaled for the two lawyers.

"Where are you going with this, Mike?" asked the judge.

"Your Honor, we were shut out of allowing the jury to consider attempted murder at the trial. I didn't use him at trial 'cause I was convinced we'd get the lesser charge included. We're only trying to show that a recognized expert witness, respected by both prosecutors and defense lawyers, has found Parton to be truthful. He'll talk about psychological tests he gave him to verify his own impressions that the man was telling the truth. Frankly, I want to give the jury a chance to consider in the sentencing what they could not consider in the trial. If they have doubts, they can give him a sentence we can live with, like life with some chance for parole at some time off in the future."

"That's nuts, Judge." Kevin Lawton wanted to stop this approach right now. "We tried the case. We went for broke. The jury convicted him on the murder charge. They ought to be allowed to finish the job without this unfair distraction. Mike, you know court procedure. You're outta line here."

"I'm sorry, Mike. As a matter of law I have to agree with Kevin here," said the judge.

Benson reacted. "You mean if the witness can convince the jury that the man is not lying, that's not okay? But if he makes up something about Parton being loony, that's okay?"

"Now, Mr. Benson, I didn't say your expert witness could make up anything." The judge was not happy with this last exchange. "Now, you can either use the witness appropriately or dismiss him."

Mike returned to his seat and the judge gave the jury the legal argument why they were to disregard part of what the psychologist had said. The public defender fumed, asked the witness a couple more innocuous questions, and said he was finished. The D.A. did not cross examine the witness.

Benson brought two more witnesses. One was an old neighbor of Parton's who gave a glowing character reference for the defendant. It had little effect on the jury. The final witness was a guard at the Bardstown jail where Parton had been a resident for more than six months. The guard talked of Parton as a model prisoner during his stay there. This, too, did not impress the jury.

Both lawyers made final appeals to the jury. Both were convincing in telling their story. Mike Benson was careful, yet skillful, in once again suggesting to the jury if any lingering doubt existed, they could address it with a lighter sentence than the D.A. was asking for. Judge Fontaine spent an hour explaining the obligations of the jurors in recommending the sentence for Danny Parton. He explained that their formal recommendation to the court would carry the greatest weight in the sentence that would be dealt to Danny. He described each of the alternatives: a limited sentence, life in prison with or without chance of parole, or the death sentence by the electric chair to be carried out at the state penitentiary at Eddyville, Kentucky.

The judge elaborated in regard to the death sentence. "Under Kentucky law you must consider certain aggravating and mitigating circumstances that have been made known to you in these proceedings. I have determined that there are no mitigating circumstances among those available by law that you should consider. There are, however, two aggravating circumstances that you will need to consider. Should you find that there are no aggravating circumstances between the two I'll lay out for you, you cannot find for the death penalty.

The first aggravating circumstance is this. Did Mr. Parton have a substantial history of serious assaultive criminal convictions? The second aggravation in this case runs to motive for the crime. If you determine that there was a *monetary* motive on the part of the defendant, you can deem that motive as an aggravation."

The jurors were somber as they assembled in the jury room. There had been a sense of closure when they had come in with the guilty verdict. Today seemed more serious. Any comfort they felt after the trial was gone. The reality of deciding a man's life was sinking in.

Tommy Kendrick spoke first. "Well, this is a little tougher, isn't it? Maybe we should talk first before we start takin' any ballots. What does anyone have to say?"

There was an uncomfortable silence until Winnie Jones, a black woman with a motherly face, spoke up. "I think we have enough violence in our society. Let's just punish the man by putting him in prison 'til he dies there."

This sparked a reaction. Norm Page said, "The way I look at it, we all agreed that Parton killed Collins. It was one of the most brutal murders ever reported anywhere. Collins suffered, suffered a lot. If we believe the man could do such a thing and that he *did* do it, we should vote for death, not just to punish him but to be true to ourselves."

Sara Winkel replied, "I don't think it is any less proper for us to put the man away for life like Winnie says. We are just as true to ourselves that way as to kill him. Killin' him doesn't prove anything in my mind."

Another juror raised a question about Mike Benson's final argument. "How solid are we that this wasn't attempted murder all along?" he asked. Several jurors shouted him down. They didn't have the mind or the will to go back to that issue. They would live with their guilty verdict.

On went the discussion. Sometimes polite, sometimes confrontational. All of the reasons for or against capital punishment were debated and then debated again. One juror recommended that the jury tell the judge that they couldn't decide and let the judge render the sentence on his own. This felt pretty good until the group re-found its sense of duty and kept on deliberating.

Tommy Kendrick said, "Maybe if we take up this aggravation thing, we can get somewhere. The judge wrote down all that stuff he said about it.

Let's see: 'history of serious assaultive convictions.' Ain't no question about that one, is there?"

The group agreed quickly that the previous assault convictions were adequate legal aggravations. The second item was not as easy. Tommy read, "'For the purpose of receiving money or any other thing of monetary value or for profit.' Do we think Parton had any thing of value to gain here or was this just revenge?" asked Tommy.

"Why sure he had something to gain. He was paranoid, this Parton was," said Manny Colletta, an overweight, older juror and one of the quieter ones. He went on, "Parton thought this Collins fellow, or whatever his name was, was gonna give away his secrets for making moonshine. He was even more afraid that the kid would go back to Tennessee and steal his business. If that ain't 'monetary value' what is?"

Heads nodded. The group had at least found quick agreement on the two possible legally acceptable aggravating circumstances outlined by the judge for their consideration. This seemed to give the jury some motivation and energy to move on.

At the end of the first day one straw poll showed seven for the death penalty, but there was no passionate support voiced for anyone's position. Deciding one's death left the group in a somber mood. The next morning, Tommy Kendrick asked the judge for a copy of the coroner's pathology report that was submitted following the murder of Bobby Swanson. He chose an introductory sub-section of the report written soon after the coroner finished viewing the body of Bobby in the parking lot. He read it to the jurors:

> On arriving at the scene, I approached the body so I could get a good look at the victim. I rolled him on his back and could not believe what I saw. The victim's face was virtually gone. Both eyes were pulled from the man's head. His nose was broken so badly that it made a ninety-degree angle as it protruded from his face. All of his front teeth were gone and several were located lying near the body. Blood had poured from every orifice in his face including his left ear, resulting in massive disfigurement and dried blood. The trauma to the victim's head is unparalleled in any photos on file in my office. Our professional opinion is the man did not die instantly but suffered greatly as he was beaten by his attacker.

The group listened and no one broke their silence until the foreman said quietly, "I've prayed about this and I think the man deserves to die." More silence.

Charlie Murphy, a wisp of a man who had not participated much in each of the open debates, said, "Let's take a vote." They did.

⌒⌒

On the following morning the courtroom was overflowing. The three hundred spectators who could not get in packed the corridor outside the courtroom. Speculation was loud. Those in the courtroom fell silent when the judge entered. The crowd remained quiet as the judge ordered the convicted man brought into the court. All eyes were on Danny Parton as he took his seat. Kevin Lawton was stonefaced. Mike Benson fidgeted.

Judge Fontaine turned toward the jury. "Has the jury reached its conclusion regarding its recommendation for sentencing Daniel Parton following his conviction of first degree murder in the death of one Bobby Collins?"

"We have, Your Honor," said Tommy Kendrick.

"Will the bailiff please collect the jury's written findings and deliver them to the court?" said the judge.

The note was passed to the bailiff and quickly brought to the judge, who read it and returned it to the bailiff. The judge asked the bailiff to read the contents of the note.

He read, "We the jury, deliberating in the matter of a sentence for Daniel Parton following his conviction of murder in the first degree in the death of one Bobby Collins, including our affirmative finding in regard to two possible aggravating circumstances available under the law, one under the serious assault standard and the other under the monetary motivation standard, find and recommend that Mr. Parton be put to death by electrocution as full and fitting recompense for the crime committed."

Silence for a moment as reality sunk in. Then, murmurs. No outbursts or high fives. The murmurs grew in volume until the judge pounded his gavel and asked for order. Mike Benson had not moved. He stood and said, "Your Honor, I move that the court disregard the jury's recommendation and consider a lesser sentence of incarceration."

Again, the judge had prepared for all possible jury recommendations and any motions that would follow. He said, "In light of the solemn effort that this jury undertook to reach this recommendation, and following my own deliberations in this matter, I accept the jury's recommendation for sentencing and do hearby sentence you, Daniel Parton, to death in the electric chair at the State Penitentiary located at Eddyville, Kentucky. The time and date for this punishment to be rendered will be set in due course." Then turning to Mike Benson, he said gravely, "It is with regret but firm resolve that I deny your motion, Mr. Benson." Then he turned back to Danny

Parton. "Do you have any comments, Mr. Parton?"

"Yeah, this jury screwed up and so did you, Judge. I admit I wanted to kill Collins but I didn't do it. I was framed by this whole town. People wanted someone to pay for Collins' murder and it was gonna be me no matter what anyone said. You ain't heard the end of this, Judge."

"Very well, will the bailiff notify the sheriff for the transfer of Mr. Parton to Eddyville?" Judge Fontaine chose not to respond to Parton's comments. He concluded, "I would like to offer my sincere gratitude for the very difficult work that each of you on the jury contributed to this difficult process. I thank you most deeply on behalf of this entire community for your service on this panel. If there are no further motions, this court is adjourned."

Danny Parton was led from the courtroom by a sheriff's deputy. The jurors mingled with the spectators as the mood lightened. Kevin Lawton received the congratulations of well-wishers. Mike Benson did not move from his chair until the courtroom was almost empty. Then he slipped out through a back door and went home.

Chapter Nineteen

Summer in central Kentucky is hot. That first summer after Brother Phillip made his vows, he was given two assignments. One was to reprise his old duties at the abbey before becoming a monk. He was placed in charge of all outside maintenance. He would have the help of other monks for large projects and the help of pre-novice postulants for routine work around the grounds. But he would also have plenty of time to work quietly on his own. He enjoyed the combination of hard work and solitude.

His second assignment was to be on-call three half-days a week to provide spiritual guidance to any who might drop into the monastery for counsel. Brother Phillip had somehow been able to bring together a new understanding of his life's experiences with the intense religious training he'd just completed in the novitiate. Without knowing its origins, his superiors in the novitiate had noticed Brother Philip's deep philosophical and spiritual insights. They felt he should be sharing those insights with visitors who might come to the abbey seeking spiritual guidance. Phil was surprised to find himself good at counseling. And even more surprised that he liked doing it. But he was most surprised that the people who came to see him really seemed appreciative. "I'm a real monk," he laughed to himself one day. Not only that; while he would always carry the guilt of his crime, he now felt forgiven by God and was able to find peace in his own soul. For the first time, perhaps in his life, Phil Norton thought, Yes! I am a happy man.

On the day after Labor Day, Brother Phillip and the whole Trappist community was shocked by the death of Father Abbot Conrad. The abbot died of a swift and an apparent painless heart attack in his sleep. Father Robert, the Master of Novices, was elected to replace him as temporary abbot and would later be confirmed as the permanent leader.

The news hit Phil like a locomotive. He could hardly stop weeping those first few days after he'd heard his friend, the abbot, was gone. Even prayer was little consolation to him. He debated remaining at the monastery after such a loss. He felt abandoned and confused. But after a time, he slowly came to realize that, if what he'd learned as a novice and now believed to be true, the abbot was in a better place . . . that Conrad had reached the ultimate goal of all mankind . . . that a certain and even logical joy was really called for from the monk at this otherwise sad time. *Easier said than done*, thought Phil. But he would try.

After Phil made his vows, Father Conrad had been planning on telling the new monk about Danny Parton's trial and conviction. The abbot had figured he could wait a few months until the new monk was secure in his new vocation. Again, he had rationalized that he had plenty of time because Parton would be sitting in prison on the bootlegging charge anyway. He knew it would be years before the actual execution date would draw near. But the abbot also knew he had an obligation and decided to arrange another meeting with the bishop. He hoped he might somehow arrange some understanding with the bishop that would allow Phil to remain a Trappist—at least for a while. Two days before he died, Father Conrad called and made an appointment to see Bishop Hoffman during the following week. When the bishop heard of the abbot's death, he wondered what the priest might have wanted but dismissed it as out of his hands.

For Phil's part, the new monk had no knowledge that there was a man sitting in the penitentiary for a murder that he himself had committed. And with the sensationalism of the trial and sentence now a year old, there was little or no lingering news that the brother would notice. Besides, after two years in the isolation of the novitiate, he had little interest or occasion even now to read newspapers or watch TV.

A week after the abbot's death, Father Robert stopped by Brother Phillip's room to deliver an envelope. He told the brother that it was found among the abbot's personal effects. The envelope read, "TO BE DELIVERED TO PHILLIP NORTON IN THE EVENT OF MY DEATH."

After the abbot left, Brother Phil opened the envelope. It contained a note from Father Conrad written two and a half years before, along with another sealed envelope. The note read,

> Phil, you must know how proud I am of you. You have changed your life and I have been blessed to bear witness to the change. I have complete faith that you will continue to grow in your walk with God. However, all of us bear some responsibility for past sins. Since you are reading this after my death, I would ask you now to read this letter from the bishop. From it you can discern your obligations from this point in your life until you join me in heaven.

It was signed, "Conrad, Abbot."
The brother opened the second envelope. It was in Bishop Hoffman's own handwriting. It said,

Dear Abbot Conrad: January 3, 1984

This letter confirms our conversation three days ago in regard to the ongoing responsibility you have in regard to the newly converted and baptized man, not identified to me, now living at the Trappist Monastery. You are convinced of his remorse and the very strong likelihood that he will never commit the grave sin of murder again.

We have agreed that, given the exemplary life he now leads, after careful and prayerful deliberation, we have determined that he need not now turn himself over to the proper authorities. However, should it be discovered that any other person is accused of the crime that your friend has committed, both you and he have a moral obligation to come forward and prevent any punishment that might be levied on an innocent person.

                    The Right Reverend Daniel Hoffman
                    Bishop of Louisville, Kentucky

Brother Phillip sat silently for a few moments. He recalled a fleeting thought he'd had when he first heard of the abbot's death . . . that he alone now held his secret. His grieving overcame any sense of safety at the time. The brother sat resisting any temptation to let all the old guilt and remorse overtake him. He rationally accepted the obligation he would have if someone were being punished for his crime. He reasoned that at the present moment he did not need to tell anyone else in the monastery about the murder in the parking lot. He told himself he'd been forgiven and rehabilitated. With the absence of any knowledge there actually was a man imprisoned for his crime, the brother would now finish mourning his mentor and then concentrate on living his new life.

But first he must add a third note to the two letters that he had just read. He figured that he would've found out from the abbot by now if someone had been falsely accused of his crime, but he was worried that one might be charged with the crime after he died. Phil recalled from seeing the poster in the police station five years ago that the man he'd killed was named Bobby Swanson. And so he wrote,

After my death should any person be accused of the murder of one Bobby Swanson in Bardstown, Kentucky, in March of 1981, please know that I, Phillip Norton, am the true murderer. I have been forgiven of this crime by God and have been given permission by my superiors to remain silent regarding my guilt unless another is accused. The two letters enclosed should prove this confession.

Phil signed and dated the note and put it in the same envelope with the two messages confirming his guilt and silence. The envelope went into his desk where it would only be disturbed in the event of his death.

Chapter Twenty

Danny had been bored on the ride from Bardstown. He was unmoved by the news he'd received that morning that his wife had finally filed for divorce. He knew he'd used the woman but, despite wishing he could, he felt no remorse. He had abandoned her years before and knew he'd never see her again. Maybe she'd get a break in life someday, he thought. "I guess she deserves that," he said to himself.

As the sheriff's car left the Bluegrass Parkway and turned onto I-24 then quickly onto Highway 93 to Eddyville, the prisoner began to get antsy. They passed a recreational area and a horse farm that looked pleasant enough. And when they turned off 93 onto a road where a small sign indicated the penitentiary lay ahead, his heart began to pound. The small homes and trailers along the road looked middle class with the exception of a few newer houses that appeared more expensive. Danny hoped somehow this look of everyday Americana might carry over to the prison. As they rounded a curve to a descending hill, his heart dropped to his stomach.

From the top of the hill, the penitentiary looked like a modern version of an ancient fortress. Built in the 1870s by Italian stone masons using local limestone, the original building stood cold and gray on a rounded peninsula surrounded by Lake Barkley.

As the sheriff's car descended and began to circle behind the prison complex, Danny got a close-up view of the high double fences topped with razor wire that enclosed the large open area to the rear and hillside of the main building. Inside the fences stood several smaller buildings one or two stories high. He could see at least two guard towers as they proceeded along the curve of the road. As the car approached the end of the peninsula, Danny noticed a low, white, free-standing building on his left outside the fence. The sign said it was a museum of some kind. He wondered if the prison was making some kind of horror show out of his new home that summertime tourists could come and gloat over.

On his right, he saw huge concrete rectangular additions that butted up against the main limestone building matching it in height. It must be a series of cell blocks, he reasoned. The car turned right as it came to the lake and proceeded around to the main entrance. To the left the lake was lined with pleasant-looking white cottages that Danny figured must be homes for employees of the institution. To the right, the main entrance area appeared foreboding. Approachable by a two-flight concrete stairway running parallel to the building, the door itself was sheltered by an open porch-like structure. The entrance area stood in the middle of the limestone building, the focal point of that original section as it jutted outward several times to its tower-like prominence.

The car passed the entrance and took a U-turn up a ramp-like driveway to the concrete stairway. A deputy opened the car door for Danny and cuffed him to himself. They walked up the steps and turned left and into the front door. Danny was nervous but said nothing. Inside the door there was a small vestibule, immediately confronting those entering with ivory-colored bars and a sliding gate. The warden, Adam Caufield, was called and in less than a minute appeared inside the bars. He directed the guard on duty to open the gate. Danny swallowed hard as he and the deputy passed through the gates. The reality of his situation was sinking in. He felt an involuntary shudder. The warden welcomed him in a professional, not unkind manner. The deputy and Danny Parton were disengaged and a guard was called to escort the new prisoner to his cell on death row.

Death row at Eddyville was not plush but was better than most of this prison's other cell blocks. Twenty-two cells were arranged eight on each side and six at one end of the larger common area. The cells had the standard penitentiary layout with a bed, a chair set at a small desk built into the wall, and a toilet in the back corner. At the other end of the common area were three doors, one leading in from a corridor in the main building, one leading to the execution area, and the third opening to a soundproof conference room large enough for five or six people. The conference room had no window but had two video monitors that covered the entire room. There was no audio monitor in the room.

The common area was furnished with several fifties-style lounge chairs, a large TV, two three-by-six tables holding several ashtrays, two bookcases with a selection of current books and periodicals, and a ping-pong table off to one side. A stationary bike was in one corner. The inmates were allowed to spend several hours each day in the common area. The meals were served there as well, three times a day unless a fracas of some kind brought disciplinary action that forced them to eat in their cells for some period of time.

The inmates were confined to death row and did not mingle with the rest of the prison population. They were, however, allowed access to recreation outside twice a week.

There were only seven men on death row when Danny joined the group. He stayed in his cell for the first week, not joining the others even for meals in the common area. He suffered a mix of feelings. He was very angry. He was depressed, often on the verge of weeping. He felt alone, without the support of any other person.

Eventually, Danny ventured into the common area. There were four white and two black men, all of whom kept to themselves and did little more than grunt a welcome to Danny. A third black man, a friendly fellow by the name of Shorty Greenfield, laughed often and tried to be friendly with the newcomer. Within a few weeks, Danny and Shorty did become friends. Shorty amused Danny enough to help him survive the boring days.

The death penalty was not all that common in Kentucky and there had not been an execution there since the death penalty had been restored in 1976. Each of the convicts' cases were in various stages of appeal with only Shorty Greenfield holding a scheduled execution date in 1988.

Eventually, prison life became routine for Danny Parton. His first year passed slowly on death row. He had hoped that a mandatory review of the death sentence by the Supreme Court of the Commonwealth of Kentucky would reverse his sentence. By law, the Supreme Court had received the complete transcript of the trial along with other required documents within ten days of the close of the trial. The job of the court in the review process was to determine whether the sentence of death was imposed under the influence of passion, prejudice, or any other arbitrary factor. They were also to rule if the evidence supported the jury or the judge's findings of statutory aggravating circumstances in the sentencing were adequate under the law. Finally, the Supreme Court would judge if the sentence was excessive or disproportionate to the penalty imposed in similar cases.

When a *direct appeal* of the conviction itself was also to be made to the court, however, Kentucky law provided that both the appeal and the sentencing review would be handled as one process. This law forced the long delays that are commonplace in appeals related to capital cases.

As a matter of routine, Mike Benson had filed the direct appeal but also petitioned the court to assign a public defender to represent Danny Parton through the appeal process. Mike was both too committed to his new job and too burned out by Danny's trial to take on the appeal. Besides, both the massive legal preparations and the heavy court calendar could delay a decision on the appeal by the Supreme Court for years. Mike had felt he needed to move on.

So, Danny Parton would sit. He'd become too bored to be scared. His second year at Eddyville dragged on like the first. The date for his execution had not been set, pending the appeal.

Chapter Twenty-one

For the first few years after the trial, Mike Benson did try to forget Danny Parton's case. After the trial, Mike had lost himself in his work as a private lawyer in the Cambridge law firm. He performed well as a defense lawyer for the local upper class who occasionally found themselves the targets of civil law suits or white collar crime. His income also increased handsomely. He was enjoying the fruits of his labor.

But Danny Parton never really left him. Mike couldn't rid himself of his belief that his client was not guilty of the crime for which he was convicted and awaiting execution. After trying to ignore the case, Mike decided to visit Danny in prison.

"Hi Danny, remember me?" said the lawyer as Parton joined him in the tiny visitor's room off death row.

"Yeah, Mike. I kinda wondered why I ain't heard from ya. 'Course, I guess I understand. Nobody likes to think about losing."

Mike was a bit embarrassed. "Sorry I haven't come to visit you before. Real busy with the new job, you know."

"Yeah. I ain't been so busy. Just waiting to have 'em fry me."

"Well, we hope that doesn't happen, Danny. Hopefully the Kentucky Supreme Court will see the light and change the verdict and the sentence."

"I don't have much faith in any court, Mike. Things take forever."

"Has anyone been assigned to represent you yet, Danny?"

"Yeah. I never saw an attorney for the first couple of years here. Guess they don't give ya one until the appeal looks like it's gonna get scheduled. She's a woman by the name of Cynthia. Nolan, I think is her last name. Some judge gave her the job about a year ago. She is a public defender. About twenty-five years old I'd say. Real busy lady. I've talked to her only a few times. She says she's working on the appeal but she tells me it don't look so hot for me, Mike."

"Danny, if I could find a little time to help out on the appeal, how would you feel about it?"

"Really?" Parton smiled for the first time in a long time. "I'm sure you could help me a hell of a lot more than the girl. She's just gettin' started in the lawyering business. She doesn't seem real happy to have me as a client either. Are you serious, Mike? Would you really help me, Mike?"

Mike Benson didn't know where he would steal the time but he knew this was something he must do. He wouldn't turn his back on Danny again. He would see him through to the end, whatever that might mean.

"Danny, have you got Ms. Nolan's telephone number? I'll call her and offer to help her pro bono and see what happens."

"Pro bono?"

"For *free*, Danny." The attorney and his old client exchanged a few more words as Mike promised to be in touch soon. Then he headed back to Bardstown.

Mike Benson was welcome help to Cynthia Nolan. Like all new public defenders, she was overwhelmed with cases. Cynthia was short and thin. She wore horn-rim glasses. Her short, straight, brown hair did not flatter her face. She had studied the process for appealing a capital case before the Supreme Court of Kentucky. She even made a trip to the capitol in Frankfort to observe the appeal process firsthand. But the process was one thing; the facts in this case another. Mike knew about the case and the trial, and it was clear he could help.

Mike coached Cynthia on how to understand and tell Danny's story. His early criminal history. His desire to murder Bobby Collins. His failure to do so. His apprehension in Tennessee. The failure of the judge to allow a change of venue. Parton's willingness to admit to attempted murder with the prosecutor's unwillingness to let him do it. The judge's rulings favoring the D.A. The circumstantial nature of the evidence.

Benson emphasized that the thrust of the appeal should show error on the part of the trial judge. So the telling of the facts of the case could only be done briefly and only to support alleged errors in the judge's rulings.

After several meetings, Mike saw that Cynthia Nolan was coming to share his belief that Danny Parton was not guilty of the crime he was sentenced to die for. She stopped her complaints about her heavy workload. She began to think and talk like one who was involved in saving someone. A victim. Danny Parton.

The appeal was scheduled to be heard in July of 1989. With the help of Mike Benson, the rookie public defender told herself she would be ready to argue before the Supreme Court that her client was wrongfully convicted and sentenced for a crime he planned, but did not commit.

In the meantime, Danny himself got some good news as he waited on death row. His friend, Shorty Greenfield, was granted another stay of execution pending more legal maneuvers in the long, grim process.

Chapter Twenty-two

One hot summer morning in 1989, Phil received what was to him a surprising request from Father Robert, now the permanent abbot at the Trappist monastery. The abbot knocked on the brother's door after the monks had completed their morning prayer in the chapel. "Can I disturb you for a minute, Phil?"

Over the past two years, Phil's life had become almost blessed in its routine. In spite of the sad loss of his friend and mentor, Abbot Conrad, 1987 had been most significant for Brother Phillip. He'd completed his first full year as a Trappist monk. The grounds and gardens at the abbey had never looked better. The brother also had enjoyed working in the monastery, whether in the candy kitchen, cheese factory, or packaging department. He remembered how it amused him to see the plethora of hand signals and facial expressions he and the brothers used to communicate with barely a word spoken. He had come to *appreciate* working that way and the extra time it gave him to think and pray.

But most of all he had relished his job as an on-call counselor during that first year. He'd been pleased to have played some part in saving a few marriages. He also recalled with a bit of surprise that he'd witnessed ways in which some people found God in their lives again after years of ignoring Him. But he was most tickled that year about two young men who decided to join the Trappists at least partially inspired from their visits with him.

While 1988 flew by much the way the year before did, Phil thrived on the continual work and the pace of it. That year, Michael Jordan was MVP. Bush beat Dukakis to become president of the United States. The monk took little notice. Even the terrorism of Pan Am Flight 103 brought little but prayers from Brother Phil. The sameness and solitude of his life became both the goal and the joy of his life. The remote news about the appeal process of one Danny Parton was relegated to the back pages of the newspaper and never seen by the monk. He cared little for what the rest of the world seemed interested in knowing.

Brother Phillip stood to let the abbot into his room. All of the monks' rooms in the monastery were similar. The rooms, called cells, stretched on both sides of the long corridors of the main monastery building. The cells measured ten feet by twelve feet. Each cell contained a table, two chairs, a wardrobe closet, a bookcase, and a wooden bed frame holding either a straw or standard mattress. The latter was one of the modernizing options afforded to the monks since the seventies.

Father Abbot took a seat at Phil's desk. "Phil, I'll be brief. I want you to think about something. I've had the privilege of observing you closely as a novice and, since then, I have been inspired by how you've taken to our life here. I am especially pleased by what seems to be your vocation to counsel people who come here seeking spiritual comfort. Of course, I don't know the private things you tell people, but I do hear many positive comments these people make. I also hear third-hand comments from the other monks who have heard people tell of being helped by you. You're blessed, Phil."

The brother squirmed in his chair but said nothing. The abbot went on. "Now Phil, one thing you must know is that when people seek spiritual guidance, they also often seek forgiveness for sin in their lives. You've probably experienced some of the folks you've counseled asking to make a confession to you seeking absolution. You, of course, must tell them that you are not a priest and refer them to one of the monks who is ordained." Brother Phil nodded.

"So this is what I want you to think about," said the abbot. "I want you to consider becoming a Trappist priest."

Phil's head jerked around. "Father Abbot, I'm not worthy of that. Nor am I an educated man. And the time for me to study and qualify to be ordained would take so very long. I uh, I can't believe you would ask me to do that. I feel so happy just to be a Trappist brother. I just don't know what to. . . ."

"Calm down, Phil. I don't need an answer right now. You need to think and pray about it. You might want to know that our order has been granted a special privilege by Rome in certain cases. The privilege allows us to make use of an accelerated program leading to ordination, where a monk like you can pursue a course of study that takes about three years. You'll learn all you need to know in order to function as a priest but not all the general education that is expected of clergy who live and work in the secular world. It makes sense for monastics like us, but not for parish priests. If you think you could better serve God and the people who visit our abbey by being a priest, Phil, we'd make use of that 'short path' to ordination. Will you think it over?"

Phil was slow to answer. "I'm overwhelmed, Father Abbot. This is such a surprise. I don't know how I feel about it. But I will do as you say and think and pray about it. When do you need to know?"

"We don't have deadlines about such decisions here, Phil. You'll tell me one way or the other when you're ready." The abbot gave Phil his blessing and left the little cell on the third floor.

Chapter Twenty-three

On Monday, July 10, Cynthia Nolan woke up in her Frankfort motel room at one in the morning. In fact, she wasn't sure she had slept at all. She had spent most of the last few days and nights rehearsing the argument she would make today before the Supreme Court of the Commonwealth. The court had received all the necessary briefs and documents that supported her appeal requesting the court to set aside both the conviction and the sentence in the Danny Parton case. It was her job to make the oral argument persuading the justices that the verdicts should be reversed as well as answering any questions the justices might have about the case.

She finally got out of bed, put on her bathrobe, and delivered her argument out loud to the mirror in her bathroom. Not bad, she thought. At four A.M. she laid back down on top of her bedspread and closed her eyes. Though not a religious person, she somehow felt like saying to the ceiling, "If there is a God out there, I could use some help today." She dozed off for twenty minutes and woke with a start. She checked the clock, got up, put on her best dark blue suit accented with a discreet off-white scarf, and headed for her car and an early breakfast with Mike Benson.

The two went over the main points of the presentation one more time. Mike made few suggestions; he was impressed at the young woman's preparation.

At nine A.M., they were both seated at their two-chair counsel table in one of the modern courtrooms of the building that housed the Supreme Court of the Commonwealth of Kentucky. To their left was a large podium centered in the room directly facing the seven-chair arched bench at the front of the room. To the left of the podium was the two-chair table occupied by the attorneys for the state. Behind the counsel tables at the back of the room were two rows of benches for spectators. The room's walls were paneled in rich maple wood. The floor was inlaid blue tile and the ceiling a white plaster dome with two very large skylights positioned symmetrically over the bench.

A few minutes after nine, three robed justices of the Supreme Court took the middle seats behind the high wooden bench at the front of the courtroom. After the preliminary administrative matters were dispatched, the justice seated in the center asked which lawyer for the defense was to deliver the oral argument. Cynthia Nolan stood and identified herself. She was told to proceed and, after a deep breath, she began.

"Your Honors. You are familiar with the briefs and therefore the facts in this case. I cannot add more factual detail to what you have already read. And the defense understands that the facts presented at trial themselves are not open to appeal. What the court can consider on appeal is 'error' on the part of the judge hearing the case, and that is the basis of the defendant's appeal. In order to demonstrate this 'error,' some restating of the facts will be necessary to show the defense's logic in asking you to set aside both the conviction and by definition, the sentence.

"But before doing that, I would ask the court to note our contention of an early error by Judge Fontaine in disallowing the defense's request for a change of venue for the trial. In the briefs submitted, you can see many examples of news stories and letters to the editor that demonstrated the virtual frenzy that existed among Bardstown residents for a conviction for the murder of Bobby Collins. The town's people simply made it known to one and all that only a conviction with the death penalty would be acceptable to the local population. It is the defense's position that any citizen serving on the jury could not help but feel the pressure to convict Danny Parton. Therefore, please keep in mind, Your Honors, the environment in which this trial took place as we now get to the main contention of our appeal.

"In order to decide the merits of the defendant's appeal, I'd ask you accept our position momentarily *as if* it were the truth. In other words, as you think about this case one more time, accept the *possibility* that our statement of what we believe to be the true facts, indeed could be the truth. It is our hope that when you listen to the whole story in that light, it will convince this court that actions taken at trial prevented fair consideration of reasonable doubt in this case.

"The first fact is not in dispute. Danny Parton intended to murder Bobby Collins and came to Bardstown, Kentucky, to find him and murder him. The testimony of witnesses who talked to Danny Parton the day before the murder is also not challenged by the defense.

"Further, there is no dispute that Mr. Parton confided incriminating statements to one or more people in his home area of Washington County, Tennessee. Clearly and shamefully, Mr. Parton wanted to kill his one-time protégé and friend, Bobby Collins. And he did go so far as to plant a bomb in Mr. Collins's automobile that was set to explode when Mr. Collins was most likely to be driving it the evening after he was actually killed.

"Your Honors, we ask you now to listen to a narrative of what we believe truly happened: after planting the bomb in Collins's car, Danny Parton leaves Bardstown on March 5, 1981. He chooses an obscure route back to Tennessee. He does this for no other reason than this is his normal mode of operation. As a moonshiner and bootlegger, he is most comfortable traveling the hills and valleys of the countryside rather than the major highways. So, as a result of his veiled trip home, there are no witnesses who can put him elsewhere at the time of the murder. Of course, and this is the point: he feels no *need* of witnesses until late the following day when the bomb is set to explode.

"When he returns home late the next morning, he feels he has already put into motion the process by which Mr. Collins would be killed that afternoon. He feels satisfaction with his plan and its execution so he brags to Wendell Carson that there would be no more, and I quote from the transcript, 'worry about Bobby screwin' up our business any more.'

"Apparently, news from Bardstown, Kentucky, didn't readily reach the hills and hollows of southeastern Tennessee. It was not until the defendant, Danny Parton, was apprehended in Washington County, Tennessee, years later, that he learned that his intended victim, Bobby Collins, was killed in a cathedral parking lot the night *before* the bomb was set to kill him. It is difficult to believe, we acknowledge, but Mr. Parton was so sure his plan would work, he did not bother to verify that his bomb had done its work." Cynthia took a drink of water and continued.

"As despicable as his intentions were, Mr. Parton did not kill Mr. Bobby Collins. While intent was proven, the murder of Bobby Collins in the parking lot by Parton was not proven at trial beyond any reasonable doubt by the prosecution. In fact the logic of Mr. Parton committing that brutal murder, when he'd taken great pains to do the deed in a remote fashion the following day, is clearly the fodder of reasonable doubt. It renders all incriminating evidence as circumstantial and, if you will, *weak* circumstantial evidence.

"And that points to our belief of serious 'error' at trial on the part of the judge. The defense repeatedly made motions and arguments to the judge to allow Mr. Parton to plea to attempted murder or to allow a lesser included charge to be considered by the jury if they could not find murder in the first degree. In every incidence the judge allowed the prosecution's desire to limit the charge to first degree murder only. The jury, therefore, was hamstrung. It had no flexibility to consider a lesser charge or even the logic of the facts in the case that pointed to attempted murder. This, by itself, had the effect of also limiting the jury's free consideration of reasonable doubt. Their choice was to convict on first degree murder or to set free a man whom the defense admitted was guilty of a very serious crime. It is our contention in this appeal, Your Honors, that the trial judge's refusal to grant consideration of the crime that Mr. Parton did commit has deprived both the state and the defense of obtaining justice in this case. We respectfully request that the court find the 'error' of the trial judge and reverse the verdicts of the jury."

Cynthia paused for a moment and looked straight at Judge Vass. She was ready to go for broke. "In support of our request for such reversal, the defense will not ask this high court to grant a retrial due to the judge's failure to grant a change of venue. Nor will the defense ask this court to review the aggravating circumstances that the jury offered and the judge approved in support of the death penalty. The defense believes that to do so would only weaken the central logic of this appeal. That logic is that the trial judge failed to allow any consideration of the crime that Mr. Parton did commit, which was attempted murder. Thank you, Your Honors."

Judge Vass, a heavy, white-haired justice asked, "Counsel, would you just have us put this Mr. Parton back on the street?"

"It is my understanding, Your Honor, that any action by this court in overturning the jury verdicts will not preclude an indictment against our client for other crimes alleged."

The judge seemed embarrassed to have asked the question and did not follow up. He invited the state to rebut. The state was represented by an assistant D.A. from Nelson county. He presented in detail the arguments also made at the trial: 1) The motive was clearly established and not disputed by the defense; 2) accepted in court for centuries, evidence that is *circumstantial* in nature but clearly points to one with proved motive, is valid; 3) admission to a lesser crime is often the method defendants use to effect a lesser punishment—it is often the sign of a guilty person, and not an innocent one; and 4) a trial judge has no obligation to allow consideration of a lesser included charge if the prosecution desires to make its case on the capital charge alone. In a word, the assistant D.A. emphasized that Judge Fontaine made no "error" at trial.

Judge Vass asked if the defense wanted a ten-minute rebuttal. Cynthia had only one comment. "If the prosecution was so sure of its case of first degree murder, what harm would there have been to allow the jury the option to *consider* attempted murder? And, would not the judge be assuring fairness by at least allowing consideration of attempted murder in a case that weighed so heavily on circumstantial evidence? And is not *fairness* the first obligation of the bench?"

Judge Vass, as is protocol in the higher court, made no response to the parties. He thanked them and promised their ruling on the appeal in the normal time frame. The session was concluded.

Mike had high praise for Cynthia's performance. "If they can't get this one right, there truly is no justice, kiddo. You did a great job." They promised to be in touch as they awaited the Supreme Court's ruling. This day was done and both headed home.

The hot months of summer were unsettling for Brother Phil. He tried to drown himself in his work but his mind always came back to the request of the abbot to consider ordination to the priesthood. As he mowed lawns and watered the gardens and weeded the perennials, he would talk to himself. "I can't do this. I'm not smart enough. And I sure ain't holy enough. Man! I'm a murderer, reformed, but still a murderer. What would the abbot say if he knew that? Maybe I should tell him and see what he says?"

Then he'd force himself to think about his work or some of his other duties as a brother. The next day, he'd go through it all again and look at the other side of his dilemma. "Well, maybe this is a sign from God? I do find I am able to help some folks. And it would be nice to be able to hear confessions when people ask." Then he'd answer himself, "But saying Mass? I don't deserve to do that!"

Phil waffled for the entire summer and into the fall. During the World Series in October, San Francisco suffered a serious earthquake where many were killed. Stories of suffering and heroics led the news for weeks. Brother Phillip had no knowledge of the event because he had spent much of the month in a private retreat. He decided to spend this time trying to calmly look at his situation, weighing the pros and cons and, banking on some help from Upstairs, make up his mind.

One morning during retreat the subject of his reflection was *forgiveness*. He was thinking that he was pretty well versed in that topic since he had worked so hard to accept that he'd been forgiven of his past sins. He also had helped convince people he'd counseled that they could be forgiven if they sought forgiveness. Then it hit him: forgiveness is a two-way street. And in his heart, he had never forgiven his father. At first, this terrified him. How could he have let this pain in his soul go untreated? With the help of the retreat master and much time in the chapel, he was able to work through it and, before the retreat ended he made a formal, silent declaration of forgiveness to his father. Then he prayed the soul of his father might forgive *him*. That evening, Phil slept peacefully.

When he emerged from the retreat, he had made his decision. He reported to the abbot, Father Robert, that he would accept the call to the priesthood and begin the course of study at any time the abbot suggested.

After much thought, he chose to keep his secret, as he had no knowledge that anyone was being held for his crime. Phil reasoned that he should finally trust that he'd been forgiven and live out his new life to the fullest. He had a higher mission and purpose in life now. Later, if circumstances demanded, he would admit his guilt; but for now, he accepted and concentrated on his new opportunity to grow in his life as a Trappist monk.

Before Christmas that year, Brother Phillip had immersed himself in a daily routine that consumed some eighteen hours each day. He poured hours into manual labor and the chapel calls for prayer, along with many hours of study to prepare himself for ordination to the priesthood. Phil began the first two years of study by concentrating on philosophy and theology. Although most priests spend some five to six years covering these two subjects, Phil was allowed to cover the basics in just two years to prepare him for his focused ministry at the monastery. His third year would be taken up with learning how to function as a priest, performing the sacramental services and other duties of the ordained.

Scholarly study did not come easily for Phil. He had never learned how to study and understanding of the material dawned slowly. While several Trappist priests at the monastery tutored him, he still struggled and often questioned his decision to become a priest. With the encouragement of all who were assigned to help him, Phil made enough progress to stay in the program but not without suffering long periods of exhaustion. By the end of the first year, however, the brother began to catch on and looked more positively on the prospect of completing the program on time.

Chapter Twenty-four

On Friday February 2, 1990, Mike Benson was about to leave his office for the day when his phone rang.

"Mike?"

"Yes."

"This is Cynthia Nolan. I have some bad news, Mike."

"Oh, damn. I hope you're not gonna tell me that we lost the appeal, Cindy." Mike slipped to the nickname.

"We did, Mike. I feel terrible . . . awful. Where did we blow it? Can't these old men at the Supreme Court see that Danny was screwed when you weren't allowed to make the case for a failed murder attempt? I'm pissed, Mike—excuse my French—and I wanna keep this fight going. Do you wanna help me?"

"Of course, Cindy. What've ya got in mind?"

"Cindy, eh?" said the woman, now hearing the moniker. "I guess 'Cindy' is fine. That's what my dad always calls me. And you're kind of a father figure," laughed the lawyer. "Anyway, I want to take it to federal court, Mike. Some judge has got to be smart enough to see that Danny Parton might be a bad actor but his story should be believed."

"What did the ol' bastards of the Commonwealth say about our appeal?"

"They basically upheld all the rulings made by Judge Fontaine at trial. They saw it the way he did on allowing the prosecution to limit the charge to murder in the first. The old guys backed the contention that the circumstantial evidence entered at trial rose to the level of meeting 'reasonable doubt' standards. Of course, they gave no consideration to my request for a mistrial due to Fontaine's refusal to grant a change of venue. And naturally, they went ahead and reviewed the aggravating circumstances anyway because it's S.O.P. They found that the judge and jury were correct on *everything* they did at trial. I guess our big gamble didn't pay off, Mike.

"You know, I have a feeling that because Kentucky hasn't used the death penalty since it was restored in '76, that the judiciary may be hankering to see a case go all the way. I'm really getting the feeling we could lose Danny and I think that would be the worst miscarriage of justice since the old lynching days."

"Okay, Cindy, take it easy. We're a long way from the electric chair. I read somewhere that last year there were between two and three thousand inmates on death row in the U.S. And I think only fifteen or sixteen were executed. We have more battles to fight and I'll find the time somehow to lend a hand. As a matter of fact, I have kinda wondered if we should have made some effort to challenge the 'aggravations' that were approved at trial. I'm not sure, but maybe there is some relief for us up that alley. I'll take a look at that, if you'd like, Cindy."

Cindy agreed and began feeling a little better. The two lawyers figured out procedures for the filing process in federal court and agreed to be in touch in a week or two to get the new appeal underway.

In April the following year, Cindy would receive word that the Federal District Court in Louisville would grant a stay of execution and would hear another appeal. A date was set for the following January to set the parameters of the court's review of Danny Parton's case. In the meantime, Danny waited on death row in Eddyville.

Chapter Twenty-five

On Easter Sunday 1991, the abbot asked Brother Phillip to stop by his room after breakfast. After the brother arrived and sat down, the abbot said, "Phil, I've been keeping an eye on you and you look tired. You are working hard and making good progress, so I want you to get some rest and a little change of pace. This is highly unusual, but I'm going to grant you permission to take a week off and go visit your family. I know it's been a while since you've seen them and it'll be good for you to let your mind think of something else for a while."

"I *am* tired, Father, but I shouldn't be taking off; I've got to keep studying so I'm ready for ordination at the end of next year."

"Phil, if you don't take some time to relax a bit, you may not make it to ordination. You'll burn out. Now, let me say in the kindest way that this permission I'm granting you is not at your option. I have trouble believing I'm saying this—in fact some of the old Trappists are probably rolling in their graves right now—but as your superior, I am directing you to go have some fun for a week or so. The study can wait. Okay?"

Phil sat back in his chair, perplexed for a moment, then smiled. "Gee, Father Abbot, I guess I do need a break. I would love to see Sandy and Kerry again." He chuckled and asked, "When can I leave?"

"Not before tomorrow morning," said the abbot. "We want you here for the rest of today to enjoy our celebration of Easter but you can make your phone calls and travel plans and leave whenever you can arrange it all. And, Phil, I think the Trappists can spring for an airplane ticket this time. You need to have as much time with your family as possible, not riding a bus, so get on with it and let me know what you work out."

Phil was both dumbfounded and happy. He was quickly warming to this chance to visit Kenny's wife and daughter and to have a change of scenery, as well. Before nightfall he had called Sandy and made a plane reservation. He would leave on Tuesday morning. He smiled to himself and thought, *Not bad. I must be one of the first Trappists ever to get an off-campus vacation. Don't question it; enjoy it, Brother.*

Wearing the black suit of a cleric, Brother Phillip walked briskly up the TWA jetway into the Jackson airport. When he saw no familiar face in the gate area, he wondered if he should wait there or go to the baggage area to retrieve his suitcase. As he thought about this, two women rounded the corner, out of breath, smiling and laughing and calling to Phil. Hugs all around and then standing back, Phil and his family took a good look at each other.

They all began talking at once and finally Sandy was able to say, "Phil it's just been too long. A letter once every couple of months just doesn't do it. We're so glad you're here."

Kerry, now a beautiful young woman, piped in, "That goes for me too, Uncle Phil. You look great!"

Phil couldn't answer right away. He swallowed and brushed back a tear. He hadn't realized how much having a family could mean to him. Finally he said, "I'm really, really so glad to see you both."

After a few more false starts, the conversation settled down and the threesome moved on to get Phil's luggage.

In the car on the way home, Kerry said, "Uncle Phil, tell us all about life in a monastery. What it's like to be a monk?"

Though Phil wasn't used to open conversation, he tried his best. "Well, our life is pretty organized. Each day is scheduled. We get up early to pray— three in the morning, actually. Then we eat some breakfast, do some more prayin', and then have Mass. About eight o'clock we go to our jobs. My job is keeping up the grounds and doing general maintenance work. Nowadays, I spend the rest of the day, except for prayer calls and meals, studying for ordination." He went on to explain his special program of preparation and why the abbot had asked him to become a priest. They listened intently as he described his studies and why he accepted the abbot's call to become a priest.

Kerry asked Phil how he could live without talking. "Well, Kerry, silence is one of the best parts of living the life of a Trappist monk. Do you realize how much time is wasted each day in talkin' about nothing important?"

Sandy enjoyed listening to Phil and Kerry visit. Kerry said, "But Uncle Phil, don't you go crazy being so quiet all the time? And all that prayin'— how can you think of all that much to say to God?" Religion was not a big part of their lives, but both mother and daughter knew it was now something special for Phil.

"Well for me, Kerry, praying is a lot like talking to yourself. You take both sides of the conversation. You say your part to yourself and then you listen. Then when some kind of an answer pops into your mind, you put it into words, think of those words as God's words, and then say *those words* to yourself. 'Course when God's words don't make much sense, you keep talking to yourself until they do make some sense. You'd be surprised how often you get good answers praying that way. And who's to say God's not a part of that?"

"That's too deep for me, Uncle Phil, but I'll take your word for it."

Both women could quickly understand, though, Phil's desire to help people. They understood well the need people have for the help and direction a close counseling relationship provides. When Phil finally dropped into bed sometime after midnight that first night, he felt good. He realized that being forced to talk about it, he further defined for himself what he'd been about these past few years.

Most of the week turned into one long visit. All the while the threesome sat in the park, took long walks, or ate together, they talked. Phil responded to all their questions and asked as many of his own. He learned about Sandy's promotion to head the entire social services division in Rankin County. And Kerry, recently graduated from Ol' Miss, had enrolled in law school. He made them tell him about their lives as he relished every detail.

The women told Phil they were surprised how out of touch he was in the monastery. They couldn't believe how little he knew about the Gulf War that had just ended. As they visited they would amuse themselves about Phil's lack of knowledge of world events and Phil enjoyed the teasing, comfortable in his isolation.

On the night before Phil was to return to Kentucky, Sandy told him she wanted to tell him some family news. Kerry was not home that evening, so after supper she said, "Phil, would you have any bad feelings if I told you that I am seriously considering getting married again?"

"Why no, Sandy," Phil was surprised. "Tell me about it."

"Well, I met a great guy at work about two years ago. We found we enjoyed a lot of the same things and one thing led to another and a month ago, he asked me to marry him."

"And?"

"Well, I told him I'd let him know soon. I am fond of him. His name is George Carron. But I'm a little old-fashioned and I wonder if it would dishonor Kenny if I married him. And I'm not sure Kerry will be comfortable with it. What do you think, Phil?"

"Sandy, I am not any kind of expert on marriage or romance. I have talked with people who are wrestling with some of the issues you are, and it seems that in the end most people have the answer to their own questions. I don't know if you're into praying but if you are, that might help a bit."

"That seems so simple, Phil. I don't want to lose George, and yet I don't feel entirely comfortable just jumping into this."

Phil laughed. "Sandy, if you can just be patient and relax about it, I know the answers will come. I have a hunch Kerry will support your decision and my own reaction to any concern about dishonoring Kenny is unnecessary."

"Thanks, Phillip. I do see some of the same logic in you that I always saw in Kenny. I'll let it rest for a while."

The following morning, Phil kissed Kerry goodbye as she left for school. Sandy dropped him at the airport on her way to work. Both promised to write more often and Sandy said she and Kerry and maybe George would come to Kentucky for Phil's ordination. As his plane leveled off at thirty thousand feet, Phil sat back and gave thanks for the week he'd just experienced. He felt more committed than ever to his future as a Trappist and this week had provided him an enjoyable yet confirming break in his pursuit of the priesthood.

Brother Phillip arrived home to the monastery to spend the next year and a half in final preparation for his ordination. He worked hard, studied, and progressed toward his goal. When he thought of it, he marveled at how at peace with himself he'd become in these last few years.

~

In January 1992, the court's review of Danny Parton's case was delayed for eight months due to the nebulous excuse of a busy court calendar. When the court met in August, Wilfred Barnes, a federal district judge in Louisville who would hear the appeal, limited the upcoming hearing to the trial court's rulings in regard to "aggravating circumstances." The court date was set for April 1993.

Danny had mixed emotions about the news. Though happy about the delay, he was also beginning to realize that the long delays added more pain to that of waiting for the gruesome event. Yet there was room for optimism. Shorty Greenfield had recently received news that his sentence was reduced to life in prison without chance of parole. Although Danny missed Shorty as a cellmate, it gave him some hope for himself. That hope, however, was considerably diminished when he remembered that the alternative was spending another twenty years or more locked up for a crime he did not commit.

Chapter Twenty-six

At noon on Sunday, January 24, 1993, the long white chapel at the Trappist Monastery glistened. The abbot had arranged with Bishop Hoffman to have Brother Phillip's ordination in the monastery rather than at the cathedral in Louisville. Other than on special feast days, flowers were a rare display in this chapel. On this day, however, dozens of roses and potted ferns dotted the sanctuary and main aisle of the chapel. The monks had taken their places in the pews that faced each other in the sanctuary. Before the ceremony began, the brothers chanted Latin hymns of joy to signal the special event that was about to take place.

Brother Phillip was the only one ordained that day. Sandra and her fiancé, George Carron, and Kerry were settled into the first of the horizontal pews set farther back in the chapel. Some retreatants and others whom Phil had served as counselor were also seated in the back pews. At the front of the sanctuary, the bishop, the abbot, and five Trappist priests who had helped Phil in his studies waited facing the back of the chapel. Brother Phillip Norton processed reverently from the rear of the chapel to the sanctuary as the ceremony began.

The High Mass was interrupted throughout with solemn rubrics that dealt specifically with the ordination. There were special prayers for Phil and for the church and its priests and ministers. The brother laid prostrate on the floor at the beginning of the ceremony signifying his unworthiness to receive the sacrament of Holy Orders. He was then asked by the bishop several questions, including one that sought Phil's promise of obedience to the bishop. A brief thought crossed Phil's mind as he said, "I do." He knew this was the man who already had required his obedience should another ever be accused of his crime. He also knew that the bishop had no knowledge that he was ordaining the reformed murderer. The thought passed quickly as Phil long ago had learned how to release most of the old guilt and worry about that night in the parking lot.

Brother Phillip became a priest when the bishop prayed over him with the words, "Hear us, Lord our God, and pour out upon this servant of yours the blessing of the Holy Spirit and the grace and power of the priesthood. In your sight we offer this man for ordination: support him with your love.

We ask this through Christ our Lord. Amen." Then the bishop placed his hands on Phil's head and prayed silently. Brother Phillip Norton was now Father Phillip Norton, a Trappist priest. Then all the priests present, coming forward one by one, also laid hands on his head, giving their brother priest their individual blessings. The rest of the High Mass proceeded with all the trappings of incense, music, and ornate ceremony.

At the special reception afterward, Kerry could hardly contain herself. Unabashed, she ran up to her uncle and planted a big kiss on his cheek as she wrapped him in a bear hug. "Oh, Uncle Phil, I'm so proud of you. I loved the ceremony and oooh . . . the singing was like from heaven. Maybe I'll become a Catholic. Do you think I should, Uncle Phil?"

His fellow monks enjoyed this scene while the new priest, a bit embarrassed, chuckled back a response, "Well, Kerry, I guess I'm supposed to say 'you bet' but that's the short answer. You and I can talk about it someday if you'd like but for now, I'm just so pleased you and your mom are here. And I want to meet George, too."

Sandy and George arrived at that moment and after introductions were made, Sandy said, "Well, Phil, you met your goal. Congratulations. I'm really happy for you. And guess what. George and I will be married in Jackson in May. Maybe you could come?"

"Congratulations to you two, as well," said Phil, hugging Sandy and shaking hands with George. "I don't know what my life will be like for a while but if it works out and I can get the abbot to go along, I'd love to come and be a part of it."

Each person at the reception came forward and offered best wishes to Phil. Many asked for his first priestly blessing and he was happy to oblige. Laughter and cheerful conversation filled the large parlor in the main monastery. When it was over and all the guests and Phil's family had left, he walked alone back to the chapel.

It was dark, illuminated only by small ambient lights. He knelt in the back pew and sighed deeply. He said softly yet out loud, "Today I am more happy than I've ever been in my life. Thank you, Lord."

Chapter Twenty-seven

In April the appeal hearing was held in a district courtroom in Louisville for purposes of making it officially public, yet only the judge, two lawyers for each side, and a court reporter attended. The courtroom was seventies vintage modern; it lacked the fine wood and grace of older halls of justice. The hearing was the next step in Danny Parton's appeal and the first on the federal level. At the earlier meeting, Judge Barnes agreed only to hear arguments regarding the mandated aggravating circumstances recommended by the jury and approved by the judge in the original trial.

With Mike Benson at her side, Cindy Nolan made the opening statement. "Your Honor, while the jury had technical reasons in recommending two allowable aggravating circumstances under the Kentucky requirement for the death penalty, the weight of both do not rise to the level of true aggravating circumstances. First let's examine the aggravation of 'serious assaultive convictions.' When writing this provision as an acceptable aggravation to a capital crime, the legislators put the words 'serious' and 'conviction' in the law. It is true that Mr. Parton was a fighter as well as a bootlegger—such talents often run together, if I may add a side comment.

"Indeed, Mr. Parton was charged several times for his bellicose ways. But only twice was he convicted of assault. Once he broke the nose of a 'competitor' when he heard the man had sold some bootleg whiskey to one of Mr. Parton's customers. And second, he beat up one of his 'salesmen' for losing an 'account.' Due to the nature of their businesses, the complaints in both these cases were somewhat veiled and brought by the victim's spouses. Mr. Parton served thirty days in jail for each of those convictions.

"The defense will move that two convictions totaling two months of jail time, while representing very negative and regrettable behavior on the part of defendant, are not *serious* assaults in the sense of qualifying as aggravating circumstances in a capital crime."

Cindy took a drink of water and continued, "The second aggravation offered by the jury and approved by the judge at trial is that of one committing a crime 'for the purpose of receiving money or any other thing of monetary value, or for profit.' We believe the jury's logic in offering this aggravation was based on some theory, not an actual fact, that Mr. Parton was motivated to kill Bobby Collins to protect his future illegal sales. The defense contends that such circuitous logic cannot be allowed to send a man to his death."

The rest of the session followed predictably. Cindy Nolan added more support to her arguments. In her summary, when she alluded to the defense's contention that discussion of aggravating circumstances should be moot based on their position that Parton did not commit the murder, the judge quickly cut her off. "Ms. Nolan, you know that position of the defense is not a matter of appeal in this court. Counsel for the Commonwealth of Kentucky may now proceed."

In a five-minute presentation, Kevin Lawton, for the Commonwealth, made the argument that the provision for aggravating circumstances did not include a definition of the standard of seriousness in assault convictions. In fact, any assault that does bodily harm is serious. Lawton also rebutted the defense's point that Parton's action was not motivated by money. He read testimony from the trial transcripts showing Parton's concern that Bobby Collins would steal business from him.

Cindy had only one comment in her final rebuttal. "Your Honor, while certain provisions of the law may not always be specific, for example the lack of standards in defining the word 'serious,' the defense must rely on the fairness of this court in making such a judgment in the absence of such a standard." She sat.

As they left the courtroom, Mike Benson encouraged her as he'd done in the past. They agreed to talk soon.

Danny Parton accepted the news of the court proceedings passively. Until he heard actual good news, he would not allow himself any attitude adjustment. Most hours of most days he sat in his cell and read. He read about the bombing at the World Trade Center. He read Pat Nixon died. He read about drug lord Escobar getting shot down in a Columbia airport. Reading helped the boredom, but everyday life for Danny Parton was a long mix of fear, depression, anger, and hopelessness.

In January 1994, Cindy Nolan received word that Judge Wilfred Barnes of the Federal District Court in Louisville denied Danny Parton's appeal and lifted the stay of execution. She called Mike Benson and gave him the news.

Mike responded, "Cindy, you can't fault anything you've done on this case. We just can't give up on Danny or on ourselves. Tell you what, I see a little space in my calendar. Why don't I contact the Sixth Circuit Court in Cincinnati? We'll see if they'll hear an appeal on the district's ruling and in the meantime grant us another stay."

"Mike, I'd really appreciate your doing that. I'm sure you know that my calendar as the PD is really packed now. If you can get it going and then let me know what you want me to do, I'll pitch in." She thanked him and signed off.

Mike called the clerk of the appeals court and went over the requirements for the next appeal. His first step was to submit briefs providing the basis for the appeal and to request another stay of execution. Over the next week, he and an assistant wrote and sent the brief. In March, Mike received word that the appeals court would hear the appeal based only on any alleged errors in the processes or rulings of prior courts in the case. The Sixth Circuit Court would hear the oral arguments on the appeal in the fall of 1995 and rule after that. All written briefs would need to be delivered by January of next year. Although a new execution date had not yet been set, an indefinite stay was also granted pending the outcome of the appeal.

When Mike called Danny to let him know the news, he was surprised by his angry reaction. "Mike, I don't much give a damn anymore. I'm tired of all the bullshit. I didn't kill Collins and they're gonna fry me for it anyway. Let's get it done. I can't stand the waiting!"

"Danny, stay with us on this. You've got a couple of lawyers who want to keep working for you, not for money, but because we believe you *are* innocent. Do you know over fifty people who've been on death row since '76 have been later found not guilty and released?" Mike paused for a moment. "So don't give up, okay, Danny?"

Calmer now, Danny said, "Okay, but Mike you don't know what it's like sittin' here waitin' to die."

"Danny, you're right, I don't live in your shoes so I can't appreciate how tough it is on you, but you gotta hang in there and have a little faith, okay, buddy?"

"Yeah, okay Mike; I'll be good. When you comin' over?"

Mike promised to make a trip in the next month and hung up. He wondered if they really had a chance to win in the circuit court after all the setbacks so far, but he knew he and Cindy had to do their best to save Danny.

Over the years, Mike Benson had spent considerable time writing and submitting briefs in behalf of Danny. There was nothing new about what he wrote. He highlighted all the rulings by Judge Fontaine and each of the justices who heard appeals. He wasn't offering fresh arguments, but he was clear and logical in putting forth their case. Again he pounded at the stubbornness of the court in not allowing the lesser included charge of "attempted murder" to be considered when the direct evidence was so circumstantial. The venue of the first trial was challenged once more. Mike designated certain allowable testimony as "sensationalized" and "out of context." The skinny strength of the "aggravating circumstances" that authenticated the death sentence was hammered at again and again.

On September 25, 1994, Cindy Nolan accompanied Mike Benson. Watching and listening, she thought he made an eloquent summary of the briefs. She felt his emotional appeal that the justices consider carefully each and every point offered by the defense, and she thought him particularly eloquent when he reminded them of the horror of sending an innocent man to his death. When Mike was finished, Cindy could not believe that not a single question was asked by the justices.

After two and a half months, the Sixth Circuit sustained the original verdict and sentence in the Danny Parton case. The Commonwealth of Kentucky then reset Danny's execution date for August 6 of 1996.

Chapter Twenty-eight

The biggest story in the small world of the Kentucky Trappists was the growing fame of one Father Phillip Norton. His reputation as a counselor and confessor grew every month. He also began a ministry delivering sermons at the group conferences during the multi-day religious retreats held at the monastery. Every week, one or two of these live-in retreats were sponsored for men and women from every walk of life. The person speaking at the conferences was called the retreat master. In 1995, Father Phil had been assigned as the retreat master one or two times each month.

His simple message that God was always loving and forgiving brought great comfort and encouragement to all his listeners. Even as his reputation spread among people who visited the monastery, he was not well known beyond that group. The Trappist way was generally not to publicize individual monks to the outside world; the holiness of the community itself was to serve as an inspiration to the world at large.

Just before Christmas, Father Phil and Father Robert sat in the abbot's office at his annual ministerial review. Phil was reassuring the abbot that he felt great fulfillment in his role as a counselor and retreat master. He said, "If I were to complain at all it is that so many of the people I meet and serve here in the monastery seem closer to God than I. Sometimes I wish I had a real sinner so I could help turn his life around," he joked.

The abbot laughed but then said, "You know, Phil, if you are serious, I might have something for you. The bishop called me last week and asked if the Trappists might start a new ministry among the imprisoned. He explained that he got a call from a senior person at the department of corrections asking for some help. Some official said something about not having enough chaplains for solid one-on-one spiritual work with male inmates. Especially the hardened guys who are doing long sentences. The bishop asked me if I thought the Trappists might expand their mission to take on visiting some of these hard-nosed criminals who might be softened enough to consider a little religion in their lives."

"What did you tell him, Father Abbot?" Phil said enthusiastically.

"I haven't replied yet, Phil. This kind of work has not been our traditional mission. We are monastics. We serve by helping those who visit us in the monastery and by offering prayers for those living in the outside world. That's clearly what Trappists had in mind in the seventeenth century when our branch of the Benedictines decided to follow the early Cistercians in living our strict monastic life. But, you know . . . " mused the abbot, "We have begun to relax just a few of our rules a bit lately. Our charter has been to serve the outside world only when they come to us here in the monastery. But what of those who can't come here? Maybe we could experiment some by going to minister to prison inmates who might be open to us. What do you think?"

"Well, I hadn't thought until now, Father. But it seems to me that it isn't much different than the spiritual counseling and direction we give to the people who come to the monastery. The only difference is we have to go to them rather than having them come to us. 'Course, the people themselves might be a lot different than the folks who visit us here. Or would they be that different. . . ?" Phil's voice trailed off.

"They just might not be that different, Phil," answered the abbot. "Their sins might be greater and they may have neglected God longer, but they're humans in need of some connection with the Almighty, just like all the rest of us. I'm beginning to think I'd like to try something here, Phil. Are you interested in giving it a go?"

Phil *was* enthusiastic. He responded without further thought. "If you wanna do this, Father, I'm your man. I'd love to see if we could help." Somewhere in the recesses of his mind, he grasped a connection. He'd be serving his own kind.

The abbot agreed to get more details and get back to Phil right after the Christmas holy days.

During the first week in January the abbot invited Father Phil to a meeting in his office. "Phil, I talked directly with Anthony Kendall, the head man at the department of corrections. He is delighted we're interested in helping out at the prisons. We agreed it would be a pilot test for both the Trappists and his department. And, Phil, I committed you as our guinea pig, if you'll excuse the expression."

"Great," answered Phil. "And you can call me anything you want, Father Abbot. You should *hear* some of the names I've been called."

"That won't be necessary, Phil," said the abbot, laughing. "Mr. Kendall and I agreed to your spending two days a month at the Eddyville Penitentiary. You'll spend time with anyone who signs up to talk to you and if there is time left over, the warden will direct you to some hard cases where he thinks you might be able crack their shells."

Phil said, "Do you have any advice for me, Abbot?"

"Yes, Phil, I'd start out slowly. Get their confidence first. Don't be judgmental. Listen a lot."

"Sounds like what I try to do here."

"Right. They're people, however hardened. If someone is looking for some help, even if he doesn't know he's looking for it, it'll happen."

"When do I start?"

"Next Tuesday. Take the monastery car and drive over to Eddyville early and ask for Mr. Kendall when you arrive."

"I'm ready!" Phil left to think and pray about his upcoming assignment. It would be an adventure.

Eddyville, Kentucky, is about a hundred and ninety miles southeast of the Abbey of Gethsemani at Trappist, Kentucky. Each time Phil would make the one-day trip, he left the monastery early in the morning and traveled by way of the Western Kentucky Parkway, making the trip in less than three hours. Arriving about nine in the morning at the old gray prison, Phil met with the non-denominational chaplain over coffee and donuts and got his assignments for the day. Usually he was assigned about six to eight inmates, then he offered a mass for anyone who wanted to attend. He was on his way home by four in the afternoon and, with a quick supper stop, he'd be back at the monastery at about seven.

Father Phil enjoyed his prison ministry once the men on death row had put him through an "initiation" of sorts. The first couple of weeks he heard a number of catcalls and insults as he moved among the inmates, introducing himself and making small talk. Gradually, the banter diminished when the men realized they weren't getting to him. His first "clients" were mostly curiosity seekers—men who were looking for some diversion in their boring routine. These early visitors provided Phil with a clear picture of life in the "big house." They talked of the crimes that their fellow inmates had committed. They spoke of the quiet but degrading crimes that took place every day within the prison walls. Eventually, some of the men shared their own stories and the regret that came attached.

During these more serious visits, Phil would try to channel the inmate's remorse toward some type of repentance and a relationship with God. When the word got around that the Trappist priest was a good guy, listened well, and offered helpful advice, other inmates also started to request time with Phil. After a few months, the abbot approved the request from the prison officials to allow Phil to make a weekly trip. Phil was happy to oblige. He felt he was getting more than he gave in his work with the inmates. Several told him he was making a difference in the way they looked at things. When he could assure a repentant inmate that his sins could be forgiven, he could sense the relief and even joy that the prisoner was experiencing.

Most of Phil's clients were in the general prison population, but he was most touched by the experience he had with an inmate on death row at Eddyville. The man, Joey Anderson, was a five-and-a-half-foot square, bull of a man. His olive complexion softened his homely pock-marked face. Joey was a hardened criminal who had raped and murdered six young women. He had no remorse and seemed not to care if he lived or died. Joey was one inmate whom Phil *asked* to see. There had been no interest on the part of the prisoner himself. Joey agreed to see the priest, if only to allow himself a change in his monotonous routine.

In the first visit, the Trappist asked Joey about his life: what kind of music he enjoyed, favorite foods, interest in sports, movies, and other mundane topics. No religious topics. No mention of crime. Joey apparently found Phil a good listener, so the inmate opened up more than he expected. When the monk left, Joey asked to be put on the schedule again.

In subsequent visits, Joey slowly began to share his story. He talked about the poverty he lived in as a child. His mother died when Joey was six. There was no father in the picture. He was adopted by a neighbor who showed little interest in the boy. He explained how he got started stealing fruit from the small grocery stores that displayed their products along the sidewalks in front of their stores. At first he stole to eat. But soon he realized he enjoyed the thrill of getting away with it. To feed his excitement as he got older, his crimes accelerated. Bigger thefts, assaults, and finally rape and murder.

Joey told Phil that he remembered his mother telling him that he had been baptized as a baby in the Catholic Church. But he couldn't remember going to church more than once or twice before his mother died and never after that. After five or six visits, Phil asked Joey if he might be interested in talking about God a little. Joey hesitated but said he would. Over the next several sessions Phil talked about the life of Christ, emphasizing the understanding and forgiving nature of Jesus. Joey listened.

After about the tenth visit, Joey asked the priest what he'd have to do to "make it square" with God. Phil told him that it was easy. He told Joey to spend the next week thinking about his life and how his actions toward people offended God. Then the following week, Father Phil helped Joey make a private confession and receive absolution of his sins. He assured the criminal that, in God's eyes, he was completely forgiven and was dearly loved by the Creator. At mass that afternoon, Joey received Holy Communion for the first time.

That evening as Joey wept in his cell, Phil drove to the monastery absorbed in peaceful thought about Joey's conversion and the part he was allowed to play in it. Lost in these thoughts, he didn't hear the radio as it squawked about the debates between Clinton and Dole, the troubles in Bosnia, or the ongoing investigation into the TWA 800 crash. Instead, Father Phil was thinking, This *is what it's all about!*

In May, Danny Parton had another visit from Mike Benson. "How 'ya doin', Danny?"

"Oh, just great, lawyer man," whined the prisoner.

Benson did not respond to Danny's mood. He said, "Danny, I don't blame you for being mad. I. . . ."

"I'm not mad, Mike. They're gonna kill me in August for a crime I didn't commit. I just gotta get used to the idea, I guess. I'm just so damned tired of getting my hopes up and then hearing the legal system still won't open their eyes. I think they just wanna kill me so they can say they are tough on crime in Kentucky. They haven't had anyone die since the death penalty came back. They gotta 'send a message' and all that bullshit. Maybe I *am* mad, Mike. Not at you, but at the whole damn system."

"Are you scared, Danny?"

"Huh?" Danny looked surprised at the question.

"Are you scared?" Mike repeated.

"Naw . . . naw, I ain't scared. They're gonna do what they're gonna do. Nothin' I can do about it."

"I'd be scared, Danny."

"Yeah?"

"Yeah."

"Well, hell, yeah, I don't look forward to getting strapped into that chair and gettin' lit up like a light bulb, that's for sure." Danny was silent for some seconds. Then, "Jeez, Mike, I guess I'm scared as hell. I don't wanna die," he cried. "And it looks like I've run outta time, don't it?"

"Maybe. But that's why I came up to see you, Danny. We can try one more thing but I gotta tell you that I don't think it will do anything but buy some more time. We can appeal to the Supreme Court of the United States."

"Really?"

"Yes, but I don't think there is a chance that they will consider hearing the case. They just hardly ever look at these death cases, especially after the circuit court has upheld the original verdict and sentence. But we can probably get another stay while we wait for the big court to tell us they ain't gonna review our request."

"That'll just cost you and Cindy—if she still is in this deal—more time and money. Can you afford to waste any more time on me, Mike, when we both know all it will do is hold off the big day?"

"Yeah, Danny, we'll do it and we'll do it to win. Because even if the courts haven't believed us, we believe in you, pal. And there's always some chance, slim to be sure, that we could win. I just don't want to get your hopes up like we have before."

"Mike, I just gotta have some hope in my life. I can't just sit here every day thinking about what happens when they execute me. Let's go for it, even if it don't work. And thanks, Mike. I know I am a smartass and don't let you know I appreciate your help, but I do, okay?" Danny was contrite.

"I know you appreciate it, Danny. I only hope we can do right by you one of these days." Mike said goodbye to his friend and left.

The following week the circuit court in Cincinnati issued another stay pending the Supreme Court's decision to review or to decline to review the capital case of Danny Parton.

Chapter Twenty-nine

Two Years Later

It took almost two years for the U.S. Supreme Court to advise Mike Benson what he had expected: there was to be no review of the appellant decisions in the Danny Parton case. When Mike visited Danny in early June to tell him the news, Danny was surprisingly calm. "It's okay, Mike," he said. "I've been trying face the fact that I'm gonna die in this place. I'm glad it is finally over. Did they set the new date?"

"Not yet, Danny. But I expect they will. We'll still try the last minute request for a clemency hearing from the governor. There is a bunch of legal stuff the governor's office will want to review before the Gov decides. Politically, he's forced to consider it. But the word is that this governor wants to show a tough face on crime and is looking for chances to prove it. Especially since Kentucky's first execution since '76 happened only last year. So I think you're well advised to prepare yourself, Danny, even though we'll still fight 'til the very end. I'm sorry, my friend." Mike choked as the weight of his own words hit him emotionally.

"It's okay, Mike. I understand. Say hi to Cindy." Danny turned back to his cell and Mike stayed quietly for a few minutes in the death row conference room. For the first time, the lawyer felt he had finally lost the battle. Why had it been so hard to convince the jury and all the courts that his client was not the killer in the Bobby Collins case? What could he have done differently? He felt responsible for Danny's impending date with the executioner. Depressed and angry, Mike left the building.

The news of Father Phillip, the "prison confessor," was never published but was still sensational. His reputation spread throughout the institution. He played a role in bringing some nasty criminals to God. He encouraged men who had had some religion in their earlier lives to return there. He instructed men in the tenets of faith, even though they had never known a relationship with the Almighty. And he consoled many more. A simple word of encouragement. A question about something a prisoner might be interested in chatting about. Help with a letter to a girlfriend. The "padre" as he was known at Eddyville became the most popular man in the building.

There was one experience at Eddyville that he would not forget. It was the last weekend in June a year earlier, a sad one for Phil and the Eddyville community. Harold McQueen Jr., a man convicted of murdering a store clerk in 1980, was scheduled to die in the electric chair on July 1. McQueen's case had not received much attention since he'd been convicted. During the month of June, the usual last minute appeals of clemency had been underway; the outcries against capital punishment were becoming more vocal; even claims from the convict that a half-brother was involved in the crime were heard but ignored.

Phil had often greeted McQueen when the priest visited death row but he was not involved in counseling the inmate. The local chaplain had developed a solid relationship with McQueen. The prisoner was known to have become a "holy man ready to die" according to the chaplain. When reports that requests for a stay of execution indicated they were going nowhere, Phil had become more concerned that McQueen might actually be the first man in Kentucky to be executed in thirty-five years.

In the early morning of July 1, 1997, Phil had joined the crowd outside the prison in protest of what was about to happen. And when the signal was sent that McQueen had indeed died in the electric chair, Phil experienced a profound sense of sadness. He momentarily had suffered some serious doubts about the power of his own prayer that morning. How could God not have saved this man who seemingly had turned his life over to the Creator? He'd struggled the rest of that day with that question. He lingered late that evening to see if he could help console inmates, many of whom were visibly upset. Finally, as he drove back to the monastery that night, Phil found some small peace remembering that Christ Himself was also executed and somehow millions of Christians had found much meaning in that event over the centuries.

Phil gradually recovered from the sadness he'd felt over Harold McQueen's execution. But in August of 1998, he received some bad news. He was notified at the monastery one morning that his death row friend, Joey Anderson, had dropped dead, the victim of a stroke. Joey's case, like most others convicted of a capital crime in Kentucky, had been delayed for years in the courts. His latest appointment to die in the electric chair had been set for later that year. Phil took solace in his belief that Joey was headed to the right place in the next life. He was grateful to have played a part. And grateful, too, that Joey was spared the further anticipation and agony of a gruesome death.

Chapter Thirty

In March 1999, Jerry Sullivan, chief aide to the governor, contacted Mike Benson by phone. "I'm sorry it took me so long to reach you about the Parton matter, Mike. As you know, the governor has had all heads into the tobacco thing along with a whole bunch of other messes. I know your client has been sitting on death row a long time but we've been swamped here." Benson rolled his eyes. "Governor Matthews will, of course, grant the clemency hearing and is anxious to do so, but his schedule is so full that he can't see a clear open spot in his calendar for the foreseeable future. And naturally, he wants to give it the proper attention to assure your client serious consideration."

"So what's the bottom line, Jerry?" asked Mike.

"Well, Mike, he called the presiding judge and learned that the new date for the execution is not yet set. He asked him if he, the judge that is, could extend it a year. And, believe it or not, the judge okayed it. The execution will be in June of 2000. Or I should say, it will be *set* then. Naturally, Governor Matthews wants to give himself every chance to consider clemency for Parton which, if he grants it, will make the execution date moot. So, what I'm trying to say, Mike, is that the clemency hearing will be next May or early June. I don't know if this is welcome news or not, but that's everything I know."

"Jerry, my client oughta get off just for all the times he's prepared himself to die only to have some glimmer of what is probably false hope extend the horrible waiting time. I'll tell my client, but at this point I don't think he's gonna be happy about it."

After he hung up, Mike placed a call to Eddyville and left a message with the administration to have Danny call him. A half hour later, Danny was on the line. Mike said, "Danny, I just got off the line with Jerry Sullivan, the governor's top guy."

"Yeah?"

"He tells me that you'll get a clemency hearing but not for a year or so."

"Oh, shit!"

"No listen, Danny. That was my reaction at first, too, but I've been thinking about it. There's some possibilities here. First, if the Gov makes us wait a year there's gotta be a little pressure on him to be fair, I mean not just the appearances of fairness, but maybe his conscience will force him to really give us a chance."

"That SOB doesn't have a conscience, Mike."

"Danny, I'm just looking at the possibilities and some of 'em, well, are possibilities. Another 'possibility' is that we can bring witnesses who think you shouldn't die. Remember now, a clemency hearing doesn't consider the facts of your guilt or innocence. The courts have settled that, *wrongly*, but settled it. At the clemency hearing we simply try to convince the governor that you don't deserve to die. We talk about what a good prisoner you've been. We can bring the character witnesses. We *can* take some sideways shots at the case by saying how well you've accepted your fate in the wake of maintaining your innocence. Anyway, Danny, with a year to work it, and with a little help from the folks who are against capital punishment, we might just soften the ol' boy up and get a life sentence. What'd ya think?"

"Did they set a new date for the big day?"

"No, not exactly. Sullivan said the Gov asked the judge to set the date for June next year but they haven't given me the exact day yet. We'll have it soon. But what will happen is that the clemency hearing will be set for as close to that day as possible. Remember, this hearing will be the last chance to turn this mess around, Danny. I suppose you could tell me to tell the governor to pound dirt and the date would be set sooner, but I guess I'd like to ask you to wait."

Danny was quiet. It struck him that he and his lawyer were talking about his date with death as if it were little more than a scheduling matter. Since the McQueen execution, Danny was feeling more convinced that he was actually going to die. But he knew on a deeper level that Mike Benson was as good a friend as he ever had or deserved to have. He dreaded another year or more of waiting. It was so hard to wait. But with Mike's invitation to wait, there was also hope, slim to be sure, but hope. "Okay, Mike." With that, he hung up and returned to his cell to wait some more.

⌒

The abbot had given permission to Father Phil to listen to the radio when traveling to and from Eddyville. One warm early October afternoon as he was driving along the parkway, it had occurred to him that this permission was not such a wonderful freedom. Much of the news all year dealt with the president and his improprieties. He was sick of hearing about it and all the politically based reactions to the whole affair. He flicked off the radio and decided to forgo further indulgence in this passive activity. Instead, he would pray and enjoy the rolling sights of nature. Much better that a Trappist do that, he thought. It was the life he had chosen. What a relief.

That evening after supper, the abbot asked Phil to meet him in his office. When they sat down, the abbot said, "Phil, I have a special request from the warden at Eddyville. He knows about all the good things you have been doing at Eddyville, and he asked me if you could take on a special project for him."

"Oh, what's that, Father Abbot?"

"They have an inmate up there who is scheduled to die in the electric chair in about eight months. This fellow has been on death row for years and the warden thinks the man may not get a reprieve as others have in Kentucky. He has a clemency hearing coming up but the warden says he doesn't have much hope that it will change things for him. Apparently, the governor is thought to favor an execution if all the appearances of due process have been met, according to the warden. He, the warden, asked if you might take on just this one inmate and prepare him to meet his maker. You could continue your regular work at the prison and schedule whatever additional time you wish to meet with this fellow. That is, until his fate is sealed one way or the other. I'll approve the extra time if you'd like to do it."

Remembering his sadness when Harold McQueen died, Phil was not immediately elated with this invitation. "What crime did the poor fellow commit, Father?" asked Phil.

"Phil, in this case, I'd advise you not even to *inquire* about the man's crime or his guilt if you get involved with him. It hasn't even occurred to me to ask about that myself. Work on getting him ready to die. If he dies there, as the warden predicts, he'll need to be spiritually prepared, regardless of what he did or didn't do. If he gets clemency, your good work won't be wasted."

"What's his name?"

"Daniel Parton. He's an older man. I think he's in his early seventies."

"I've seen his name but haven't met him. There's some thirty-five men on death row at Eddyville now. Parton apparently never asked to see me."

"No, this request is coming from Adam Caufield. Parton doesn't know about the warden's desire to get him involved with you. Adam thinks you may be able to reach him in spite of the fact the other chaplains working at Eddyville haven't."

"Hmm, I don't know if I am qualified to specifically prepare someone to die in the electric chair. I've tried to fool myself that the fellows on death row are just gonna end up lifers. And my job there has been helping them to learn how to live, not die. That's what I tried to do with Joey Anderson. But after McQueen, I'm confused. What do you think I should do, Father?"

"I'm not going to decide that for you, Phil. This case may not be easy on you. But if you *do* decide you want to tackle it, I have no doubt you'll do a wonderful thing for this poor fellow. You *are* qualified, Phil."

"Okay, Father Abbot," Phil responded hesitatingly. "When would you like me to start?"

"You can start next week if you want. You know Adam; he'll fill you in."

That night, the priest had trouble falling to sleep. He had doubts he was up to this new assignment. Somehow this felt different than Joey Anderson. In the back of his mind, old memories haunted him. If fate had been different, he might be facing death in prison himself. Could he realistically help someone else awaiting execution? After some tossing and turning he was reminded by faith he'd left that guilt behind . . . that he'd been forgiven. He'd been transformed and was now employed doing the Lord's work. And in doing that work, he concluded he was making recompense for the terrible deed in his past. "Get over it, Phil," he told himself. He rolled over and slept.

Chapter Thirty-one

The next week, as Phil drove to Eddyville, he was apprehensive as he wheeled along the freeway. Some of the misgivings of the past week continued to bother him. He tried hard to focus on the help he might provide Danny Parton and rid his mind of any doubts. Would Danny be open to Phil's usual approach of slowly bringing the person to find a spiritual dimension, an eventual relationship with God? Or would the man be so hardened that the best Phil might do is provide some sensitivity and human comfort? Or would this fellow simply send the priest packing? At ten in the morning, he was at the gate of the old prison. Soon, he would begin to understand what he was up against.

Warden Caufield, a professor-like, thin man, was five and a half feet tall, balding, and wore glasses. In spite of his meek appearance, Adam Caufield had the reputation of being fair but tough. The two men had chatted briefly in the past and now the warden welcomed Father Phil in a business-like manner. But soon it became apparent that Caufield had genuine concern for Danny Parton. "Father, I don't know what you can expect from Danny," he said. "He has never shown any interest in anything religious or spiritual. I've never met a man who was on death row who was so adamant about his innocence. In his early years here, that's all he talked about. The past couple of years, though, I've noticed a subtle change in the man. He still proclaims his innocence, but he seems to have mellowed around the edges. He doesn't cuss and swear as much. He seems more resigned to the possibility that he may really die here in the spring. And by the way, I do think the governor may let this execution go through; it may be politically advantageous for him to do so. There was strong local support for the death penalty for Parton when he was convicted—that, of course, is off the record, Father."

Phil nodded and the warden continued, "I've spoken to Danny about you. I've told him of the fine reputation that you've developed at Eddyville. He was not enthusiastic about meeting you but finally agreed to do so. I think he may have just done so to accommodate me but then, in his situation, he had no real reason to do that. My hope is that deep inside, the man might have developed a certain curiosity about the hereafter that will allow an opening for you to help him prepare. Do you have any questions for me, Father?"

"No, I don't think so. I've been told not to discuss his case, which is fine with me. But what if he wants to talk about it at some point?"

"I don't think he'll want to discuss it other than to strongly assure you that he is not guilty of the crime he's sentenced to die for. However, if he wants to tell you his story at some point, I'm sure you'll listen. Isn't that part of your approach with prisoners?"

"Exactly," said Phil. "We try to respond to whatever or wherever the person wants to go. When a person gives us an opening that allows us to provide some help, we hope we recognize the opportunity and gently move in."

"Well, fine, Father." Then he changed the subject. "It's time I take you up to meet your new 'client.'" With that the warden stood and led Phil through the maze of locked doors and corridors to death row. Parton was sitting at a table in the common area reading a newspaper.

"Hi, Danny," said the warden as he and Phil walked into the room.

"'Lo, Warden," said Danny over his shoulder as he turned to look at the men entering the room. "And who's this guy? The priest or whoever you said you were gonna bring up here to console me?" Parton's voice was not without sarcasm as he studied the man dressed in a black suit and Roman collar.

"Right, Danny. This is Father Phillip from the Trappist monastery south of Bardstown. He's been working with some of the men here at Eddyville and seems to be helping quite a few, too."

"Yeah, I've seen you around. Weren't you a friend of Joey Anderson?"

"Yes, Danny, I knew Joey. I'm sorry he's gone."

"Hm, I wish I could go like Joey. A quick stroke and you're 'outta here.'"

"I can sure understand why you'd feel that way, Danny," said Phil. "I don't think he suffered much."

"Bardstown, eh? I have no happy feelings about that town. The people there hung me out to dry in Bardstown." Danny's face was turning red as the images of his trial ran through his mind. "I don't know if I trust anybody from Bardstown. Maybe some other day, Father, or whatever you call yourself."

The warden answered, "Danny, are you forgetting Mister Benson, your attorney? He's from Bardstown."

"Oh, yeah. I forgot." The prisoner calmed down a bit. "Okay, just what do you wanna do to me or for me, then?" said Danny, addressing the priest.

The conversation was moving so fast, it didn't occur to Phil to react to the Bardstown comment. For a fleeting second it crossed his mind that he might have seen Danny Parton sometime in the past but he didn't make any connection. Shaking off his curiosity, he responded, "Well Danny, I don't know if I can do anything for you. But I'll tell you what I'd like to do. I would like to spend some time just visiting with you and getting to know you. You can take the conversation any place you want to. If, after a couple of visits, you still don't feel comfortable around me or we've run out of things to talk about, it's easy to call it all off, right?"

"I guess so. What if I don't wanna talk about my damn case? It just pisses me off every time I think about it."

"Fine with me, Danny." Phil showed no reaction to Danny's language. Nor did he mind Danny's hands-off attitude about his case. Phil had topics of his own that'd never been discussed with anyone since Abbot Conrad died. "If I start talking about anything you don't want to discuss, just tell me and we'll talk about something else."

"All right. When do you wanna start?" Danny was feigning gruffness now.

"Well, I gotta little time right now. How 'bout it?"

Parton nodded and the warden quickly excused himself. After he was out of the room, the convict said, "Where do you wanna start?"

Phil responded, "You know, Danny, why don't we just start giving each other a short story of our backgrounds. We'll avoid any subjects that are private or that we just don't want to talk about. It's a way we can begin to get to know each other. You could go first or I could go first, whatever is most comfortable for you."

"You go first," Danny said quickly. "Then I can decide if I want to keep playing this little game."

"Okay. Let's see, where do I begin?" Phil started slowly. "Well, I'm a country boy from Mississippi, near Biloxi. I lived on a small vegetable farm. School was an on-again, off-again thing for me 'cause I had to work on the farm. I actually quit before I graduated from high school.

"Today, both parents are dead; both a sister and brother dead, too. But, I'm lucky in recent years to have gotten acquainted with my brother's wife and daughter and I've grown to love *them* very much.

"To tell you the truth, Danny, I didn't get along with my parents very well. I loved my older sister 'cause she stuck up for me at times. I didn't care all that much for my little brother since my parents kinda favored him over me. When I was about seventeen, I left home; went in the army during Vietnam. Got myself pretty screwed up over there on pot and booze. Even got mixed up with some loose women. Took some treatment for alcoholism but I never beat the scourge until years later when I started to live at the monastery."

Danny seemed to be listening intently.

"I met a real nice girl once in Chicago. Guess I fell in love with her." Phil's half-smile betrayed a hint of lingering melancholy. "When she told me she wouldn't marry me, I tried to find relief in the bottle. Drifted a lot; drank a lot for about ten years. Then one day, I was walking off a five-day drunk and fell asleep on the road near the Trappist monastery, about eight miles south of Bardstown. A nice old monk found me there and took me to the monastery. They got me shaped up and offered me a job. I took it, and one thing led to another and a couple a years later I joined the Trappists as a novice—that means a fellow who lives like a monk for a while but isn't one yet; kinda like a training camp. Anyway, I became a monk and eventually was ordained a priest." It didn't even occur to Phil to mention the crime he committed in 1981.

Parton said, "You probably know all about my case, then, if you lived near Bardstown."

"Actually, no. From about 1984 on, when I decided to join the Trappists, I was more or less cloistered."

Interested in the priest's story, Parton was warming a little to the conversation. "You were what?"

"Cloistered. It kinda means locked away from the world. Newspapers, TV, and radio were rarely available and usually very discouraged. When I was a novice before I made my vows, I didn't see a newspaper or hear a radio for two and a half years. And very rarely since then. Cloistered monks avoid the distractions of the world around them. It's rare we even speak to one another. It's only in the very recent past that monks like me even leave the monastery to minister to people outside our walls. So, Danny, I really don't know anything about you except what the warden told me. And that is only that you are facing possible execution and that maybe I can be of some service to you."

"Being a monk sounds wacky to me. You said something about 'making vows,' what's that all about?"

"Well, a vow is a solemn promise to God. I took three vows when I became a monk. One was a vow of poverty meaning I can't own anything in my own name anymore. Another is a vow of chastity; that means I can never marry. And the third vow is obedience. That means I do what I'm told by my boss. We call him the abbot."

A slow smile developed on the prisoner's face. He chuckled. Then he commented, "Sounds like I should be a monk. I don't own anything anymore. I ain't had no woman since my wife and I separated after the trial. And I gotta do whatever the warden or any guard around here tells me to do. Whatdaya think?"

Phil laughed. "You're right. We're kind of in the same boat." Phil didn't think it was a good idea to point out the differences. Instead he suggested, "Do you feel like telling me a little about yourself, Danny?"

"Oh, I dunno. We're not gonna talk about my case so what else do you wanna know about me?"

"Anything you want to tell me. Where were you raised? What things have you enjoyed doing in your life? Whatever you are comfortable talking about, Danny."

Parton sat quietly for a minute. Then he offered, "You know, I haven't thought about it for years, but I did *not* have a bad childhood." The convict smiled as he remembered. "I was pretty much raised by my gramma. First I lived with my mom and dad in the hills outside of Jonesborough. That's in Tennessee, by the way. When I was five, my mom and dad were killed when their jalopy ran off the road. They were comin' up the hill late on a Saturday night. Nobody knows what happened but the car hit a tree and killed 'em both dead. I still remember how hard I cried. I thought I'd never stop. When they put 'em in the ground, I wanted to jump in with 'em. Boy, I . . . uh. . . ." A tear shown in his eye as his words trailed off.

After a moment, he continued, "Well, Gramma took me in then. Had no other kin except an uncle and aunt on my mother's side. They weren't interested in takin' me but Gramma sure was. She wasn't too healthy but she looked after me real good. She fed me good and taught me how to live in the hills. She didn't care if I went to school or not, so I didn't go much." Danny half-smiled. He seemed as if he was talking more to himself than to Phil now. "She was even the one who taught me how to make 'shine.' And she taught me good. Real good."

Phil interrupted. "Are you talking about moonshine?"

"Yeah, of course. That was my business. I started making and running booze when I was eight. I worked for an old codger who lived up the hill from Gramma. Gramma showed me some great recipes, and I made up some batches using Gramma's recipes in the old guy's still. We used his ingredients, too. Never showed the old guy the recipes, though. But he was okay with that 'cause he made a lot of money off us for a while. I'd make up a batch. Then we'd bottle it up and the old man would tell me where to deliver two bottles at a time—COD. He let me keep thirty percent of the take which, of course, I collected every time I brought back the cash.

"After I got a little older, me and Gramma bought the old still from the man up the hill and went into business on our own. We ran the business the same way as he did until Gramma died when I was seventeen. By then I had enough money to junk the old still and buy a real good one from another neighbor. I moved about four miles to a neat little holler that was nestled between three hills. It was sitting there, perfect to hide our still and, even better, the way the winds worked through them hills, there weren't no way anyone could see any still smoke unless they was right in the holler." Danny was warmed up now, laughing while telling his story.

"I hired myself some 'helpers' and we grew the business. I was makin' big money by the time I was twenty-two. And when I was about thirty, we had three good stills hid away in the hills around Jonesborough. We even built a warehouse in the biggest holler and I had two trucks on the road delivering hooch. 'Course," he laughed, "them trucks didn't look like liquor store delivery wagons. One was marked like a milk truck. We used that one for home delivery. The other one was bigger and was painted like a commercial laundry truck. That's the one we used for the weekly trips to the bars. We brought in laundry baskets with cases of booze under a set of bar towels." He laughed. "Boy that same set of bar towels made lot's a trips in and outta bars.

"I'd be lying, though, if I told you we fooled everyone. We paid off a few cops, and a lot of folks just looked the other way as long as we only sold booze and kept our noses clean otherwise."

Danny suddenly realized he had fallen into talking more to himself than to the priest. Looking up, he said, "Well, that's enough about me. I'm kinda tired there, Father. Is that what I should call ya 'Father'?"

Phil answered, "Father's okay, or call me 'Phil' if you like, Danny. And it's time for me to head back to the monastery. Do we have a deal that I can stop and visit with you some then, Danny?"

"Yeah, I suppose. Gets quiet around here sometimes. But if I don't feel like talkin' sometimes, don't take it personally. Some days I just wanna be alone."

"Fair enough, my friend. I'll see you soon." Phil offered his hand and Danny shook it. Good grip, Phil thought as he moved back through the maze of doors and locks. He stopped for a minute to report to the warden that he and Danny agreed to some visiting. The warden was pleased and the priest headed for his car.

On the way back to the monastery, Phil let his mind lull over the visit with Danny. Not using his voice, he talked to himself. *I like this guy. He's about as screwed up as I was. Both of us have a big plate of sin in our past, although Danny hasn't gotta a grip on it yet. In fact, he kinda made his early days sound fun and a bit innocent. I bet the "devil's in the details" with my new friend. 'Course it took me a long time and I'm still not fully healed, am I? I wonder if I can help him. I guess I'm better off letting him take the lead in that department and if it's supposed to be, it's supposed to be.* His internal chatter continued in this vein until he reached the monastery.

Chapter Thirty-two

In November and December, Phil had six visits with Danny. During the first five visits, the two men did not speak of anything negative or threatening to the inmate. They talked about the Yankees since they were the favorite team for both. They shared more stories of their "country boy" childhoods—mostly funny stories, avoiding the sad. Phil talked about being a monk and life in the monastery. Danny listened, at first not believing one could live like a monk. As the visits went on, he seemed more interested, asking questions but not sharing his private thoughts about what he was hearing.

At their last visit of the year on Christmas Eve, Danny seemed nervous when Phil met him in the conference room. The two made small talk for a few minutes and Danny blurted out, "You realize I'm gonna die in this damn place next spring, don't ya, Phil?"

The priest realized in that split second that their relationship had just moved. He said, "I know that you have a date, Danny." His execution had been set for May 30, 2000. "Do you want to talk about it?"

"You're dammed right I do. That's why you're here ain't you?"

Phil smiled kindly. "Of course I'm here to help, Danny. But only on your terms. That's what we agreed to, right?"

"Okay, but now I wanna talk. I'll tell you, Phil, I'm scared. I don't want anyone else to know that, except maybe Mike and Cindy, my lawyers. But I been listening to you and think I might wanna know more about God and stuff. If there is anything to all this religion stuff, I wanna get in on it. Hedge my bet, kinda."

Phil spoke deliberately. "Well, good, Danny. Maybe you can tell me what you've been thinking about. We can take it from there."

Danny was excited and speaking quickly. "Jeez, Phil, I don't know. Let's see. Is God for real? Is there something after this life? If there is, and I ain't convinced yet that there is, do you think an old bastard like me can get in on it? And if so, how?"

Phil couldn't help laughing but showed no disrespect for the prisoner's comments. He gently suggested, "Danny those are great questions. And I can answer a big yes to all of them. But if it's okay with you, I would like to take each of your questions, and any more you have, take them one by one and spend as much time as necessary to answer each one as best I know how."

"We can't do that today?"

"No, we can't. But let's do this. Right after New Year's we'll start. I'll come as often as you want. By the time your date arrives—and by the way, I'm still praying you'll be granted clemency—we'll cover anything you want to the extent you want. Is that okay, Danny?"

"I guess so, but do we hafta wait 'til the first of the year?"

"Well, Danny, we do because of my commitments at the monastery at this time of year. But we can both be getting ready during the next week. You be thinking of all the questions you want us to discuss. Write 'em down if you can. And I'll try to think about some of the answers I need to be ready for. Okay?"

The two men agreed and both felt a great sense of relief and anticipation as priest and prisoner parted that Christmas Eve. They both felt eager to engage in a more serious relationship. On the way home Phil thought to himself, *I think Danny and I are moving forward!*

Phil made the trip to see Danny again on the first Monday of January. Phil had just come off a busy but exhilarating week. In their chapel, adorned with Christmas trees, wreaths, and poinsettias, the monks conducted all the beautiful liturgies of the season. Often the ceremonies were open to the public and Phil offered homilies at several of them. He'd also spent many hours hearing the confessions of people who came from miles away to receive the sacrament of reconciliation.

As he drove along toward Eddyville, he thought about how much satisfaction he had in his various ministries. He wondered about the year 2000 coming up and all the challenges and opportunities a new millennium might bring. Tired and happy, he drove on to Eddyville.

Danny, on the other hand, was edgy when the priest arrived. In the time since they had seen each other, Danny stewed. He had spent the entire time alone trying to come to grips with his situation. He forced himself to face the clear prospect of his execution. His mind wrestled with what would come after. Was it nothing or was it something horrible or could it be something nice? Over and over he would see himself die in the electric chair followed by the many scenarios. The more he thought, the more his brain hurt. When he saw Phil he yelled aggressively, "It's about time!"

"Whoa, Danny," said his friend. "What's goin' on?"

The prisoner took a couple of deep breaths and began to tell Phil about his mental merry-go-round. Phil listened carefully for a quarter hour as Danny dumped his load. When he ran out of words, Father Phil said gently, "I'm so sorry you had to go through this alone, Danny. I'm here now and committed to spend whatever time we need together. No matter what the outcome this spring, we will prepare you for what will come afterward."

And for the next three months, that's what happened. Phil made two and three trips a week to see the convict. The priest's manner soothed the inmate; his words provided information and solace. Phil started with telling Danny about Christ, His life, His miracles, His words. When Danny would have questions about the miracles, the followers of Christ, or His words, the priest plumbed his own understanding to share with Danny his deepest and clearest insights. Phil used examples that made sense to Danny, given his life and prospects.

For his part, Danny listened, eager to learn. He liked most of what he heard. Some was hard to understand. Over the weeks, one central theme came through to him—the idea that no matter what he'd done in the past, he could be forgiven. It was that idea that began to give Danny hope and courage to face his future.

One day in early May, Danny asked the priest, "Hey, Phil, what would it take for me to become a Catholic?"

"Is that what you want?"

"Dunno. If I can just get in on that confession deal and not join your church, that'd be fine with me, too."

Phil smiled and said, "It doesn't quite work that way, Danny. By the way, are you baptized?"

"No, we weren't church people. My gramma told me she believed in some kinda God but she didn't believe in religion or going to church. She said people had to take care of themselves and not bother God. She didn't think he cared that much about what we did anyway. She woulda told me if I was baptized, 'cause that's something you go to a church to do, right?"

"Usually, but sometimes not. But from your story, Danny, I'm convinced that you've probably never been baptized. And that means, just like in my case, you don't need to go to confession to be forgiven if we get you ready and baptize you."

"How come?" said Danny.

"Because when anyone is baptized into the church, all previous sins are forgiven in an instant. No confession needed. So, what we should do, if you're willing, is get you ready and baptize you in the next few weeks. Does that sound good to you?"

"Sounds good. I gotta shed this horrible feeling that I'm gonna fry in hell if I don't get things right with the Man Upstairs. In fact, Phil, I been thinkin'. Confession or not I think I *should* tell you my story, I mean about my case. I know I said I didn't want to talk about it but that was before you got me thinkin' about God and all. And I think it'll help you understand what I'm guilty of and what I'm not. And there's a whole lot more about me, too, Phil. You gotta know that I was a bad apple. Been stealin' and cheatin' since I was a little kid. I was always in trouble, runnin' booze, beatin' up folks, runnin' with the broads, you name it. And I used a whole lot of people, too. Especially my wife, Betty. She *really* got a raw deal from me. Yeah, Phil, it might make me feel better, to do the confession bit, that is."

The priest met the inmate's eye and spoke softly, "Danny, I'll be happy to hear about your case or anything else you'd like to tell me. Let's set aside some time after you're baptized and we can spend as long as you want to fill me in. But for the next couple weeks, we need to get you ready for baptism. Okay?"

"What'll it take?"

"Not a whole lot. We've already covered much of what you need to know. A few more visits and I think you'll be ready to receive the sacrament."

When the priest left that evening, Danny Parton found himself relaxing and even thinking, *Maybe, just maybe, this baptism thing is a no-lose deal.*

Chapter Thirty-three

As priest and convict worked on preparing Danny for baptism during the mild spring days of May, Mike Benson and Cindy Nolan were preparing a clemency plea to be heard by the governor on Saturday, May 27. They anticipated the prosecutor would call John Sedwick and George Cantrell, the coroner, to recall the horrible beating that Bobby Collins took the night he was murdered. Mrs. Maloney had passed away, but the prosecutor would have Steven Schumen and Clement Smith from the distillery speak about the wonderful person that Bobby was and how he didn't deserve to die. For their part, the defenders would ask Warden Caufield to testify to the model prisoner Parton had become. One ex-con, who served on death row with Danny and was proved innocent of his crime at the eleventh hour, would tell how Danny helped him face death in spite of not being guilty. The man was convincing in shedding doubt about Parton's guilt, claiming insights that only one like himself could have.

As a courtesy, the lawyers also asked and received permission from Father Abbot to subpoena Phil to speak in behalf of the *character* of the man he'd been counseling the past several months. Phil was happy to oblige. The abbot knew it would do no good to deny the lawyers who had the civil authority to force the issue if need be. The lawyers and the priests agreed that no confidential information that passed between Phil and Danny would be exposed. Phil's only job would be to show that society would not be served if the convict would die.

Mike and Cindy also planned to seed into the governor's mind the questionable facts in the case as he otherwise considered a pardon for Danny. While so-called facts were not to be considered as part of the hearing, the lawyers hoped those facts could provide some subtle help in drawing attention to Danny's actual plan to murder Collins. For example, the idea that a bomb was put in place and not disturbed until the police expert defused it many hours after the murder might give the governor some faint doubt of his own. Their hope was that any doubt left in the governor's mind might push him subconsciously toward clemency.

On Friday, May 26, at three in the afternoon, five men gathered in the small chapel at the penitentiary: Father Phil, Danny Parton, Mike Benson, Warden Caufield, and Father Winston, the prison chaplain. Phil started the ceremony by briefly explaining the theology behind baptism and how the sacrament provided entrance rights to eternal life.

With the lawyer and the warden acting as sponsors, Phil asked Danny if he believed in the Catholic faith and if he renounced Satan. After Danny responded positively, Phil poured water over the head of the prisoner and said as he did so, "I baptize you in the name of the Father and of the Son and of the Holy Spirit." Then he anointed Danny by taking specially blessed oils on his thumb and making a cross on the prisoner's chest and forehead. In a few brief comments toward the end, Phil explained that the *water* symbolized the giving of new life in the Spirit and the anointing with *oils* symbolized a priestly and royal nature bestowed on those baptized as ones anointed.

The entire ceremony was completed in fifteen minutes and each of those present offered their congratulations to the man they'd come to know as their friend. Warden Caufield even arranged for some coffee and cake served outside the chapel door to celebrate the occasion.

Later, when Phil and Danny were alone together in the conference room on death row, Danny said, "Phil, I wanna tell you something. I ain't been a very good man in my days but today I feel like one. I don't know what's gonna happen when you guys meet with the governor tomorrow to try and get me a pardon. But as far as I'm concerned, I'm ready. Ready to go and be with God. You and Mike and Cindy have done your best for me and I really appreciate all you've done. I have no regrets any more, Phil. And one more thing. I told the truth when I said I didn't commit the murder they're gonna execute me for."

"Don't say that, Danny. There's still a good chance you'll be pardoned."

"No, now listen, Phil. Here's what I'm gettin' at. I didn't commit *that* murder but I did murder a man in Tennessee years ago. And I beat the rap on that one. Got off by marrying the main witness. They had to throw the case out." Parton paused a few seconds and then said, "What I'm trying to say is that you have helped me find God. If I die on Tuesday, I'll just figure I'm taking my medicine for that old murder back home that I *did* commit. For the first time, I've felt some guilt for killin' that fellow back home, but I also feel peace and forgiveness. I'm thinkin' that maybe me and God are okay with each other now. You know, the baptism and all. So don't worry about me, okay Phil?"

"Danny, I uh . . ." The priest couldn't continue. He reached for his handkerchief.

"Phil, no matter what happens, you've done your job. We still haven't talked about my trial or the case and you never seemed to judge me. It doesn't seem as important now that I tell you all the gory details about my case. You've really given me all I need to face the future, whatever that is for me. And, you've given me the kinda hope that means something. But there is one more favor I gotta ask."

"Anything, Danny."

"If things go as expected and the governor don't let me off, I want you to be with me on Monday. I might just need a little more help to stay brave before they pull the switch. Can you make it, Phil?"

Phil spoke in a voice so soft, he could hardly be heard. "Of course, Danny. I don't like to think about it, I admit, but if it is your time, I'll be there." He looked at Danny and spoke slowly. "And we'll talk, if you want. About your case or *anything* else. Or we'll pray. Or we'll just be quiet together. I *will* be with you, my friend."

The two men visited for a few more minutes before Phil left for the monastery. Once in the car, the priest couldn't help himself. He broke down and wept until his body shook uncontrollably. After twenty minutes, he pulled himself together, started the car, and drove home.

The next morning the main parties were assembled at the long table in a modern state office building near the governor's office in Frankfort. Kevin Lawton, now the city attorney in Louisville, was there to defend the verdict in the Bardstown trial held fourteen years earlier. Mike Benson and Cindy Nolan were there to beg for leniency for their client. Governor Matthews and three members of his staff were there to hear the arguments pro and con. The witnesses supporting both points of view were waiting in a small room near the larger conference room where the hearing was to take place. The press lingered in the designated press room.

Phil was called first. Mike Benson greeted the priest officially and asked, "Father Phillip, you've only known Mr. Parton a few months and what can you tell us about him?"

"Well, I can say with great certainty that the man does not deserve to die. My assignment was to bring Mr. Parton solace and instruct him in the ways of religion, if he chose that. We never discussed the nature of his alleged crime. But in our time together, I learned a great deal about the man and was a witness to what he's become. Today, Daniel Parton is a God-fearing man without animosity toward any other human including any of you who might wish his death. He has indicated to me that he is prepared to die if that is your decision, Governor. But I would ask you to explain what kind of justice would be served by killing the man that Danny has become. As a priest I have learned a great deal about forgiveness. And assuming that Mr. Parton even needs forgiveness for the particular crime for which he was convicted, I can say that by virtue of his baptism yesterday, he has been fully forgiven by God for any wrongs he's committed in his entire life. And so my invitation to you simply is to consider the question, If God has forgiven him, why can't man? In my view society will *not* be served by killing Danny Parton."

The governor's face belied his thoughts. *This is the same stuff I get from all these religious people. They all think just because these criminals say they've found God when they are about to be executed, that we should just say "fine" and let 'em sit in prison for life.* He asked outloud, "Has Parton confessed to you that he committed the murder in 1981?"

"I think you know that if he came to confession to me, I could not tell any of what was said between us. But because he was baptized yesterday, he had no need of confession; all his sins were forgiven at the moment of baptism. And as far as our many discussions in his cell, I have already mentioned that we *avoided* any discussion of his actual case. And finally, I would add that, if he did tell me he did or did not commit the murder you speak of, I would not reveal any such information."

"Then you can't help us much," said one of the governor's staff.

"I hope you listened when I told you about the man you are about to execute. He is fully at peace with himself, and it appears to me that what evil might have *ever* existed in his heart is gone. Daniel Parton is a good—even holy—man and should not be put to death."

The governor listened but did not seem moved, his staff even less so. Benson felt that the priest did as well as could be expected, but he knew Phil's points fell on decided ears. The priest was excused and asked to wait in the witness room in case he was needed further.

The remainder of the hearing went as predicted. Mike and Cindy tried but could not maneuver the governor to delve into the weaker facts in the case. The other defense witnesses delivered their points of view, but it was obvious they did not impress the governor as much as the emotion shown by witnesses supporting the prosecutor. Three hours after the hearing started, the governor thanked the parties for their presence and said he would make his decision on clemency by seven A.M. on Monday morning. He said he wanted to carefully consider all that he'd heard and seek the private counsel of trusted advisors not present during the hearing. He asked an assistant to release the witnesses waiting in the room nearby.

Cindy and Mike felt the governor had made up his mind already but wanted to demonstrate the *appearances* of careful judgment. They felt defeated as they left the building. Phil caught up to them on the steps outside and asked, "How did we do?"

"Not good, Father. I think our friend Danny is gonna die on Tuesday," said Mike, dejected.

"I know how you feel. I know how *I* feel. You both did such a good job. Danny knows that."

"I know, Father." Mike fell quiet.

Then Cindy said, "Mike, I've felt all along that Danny never *did* kill that guy in the cathedral parking lot that night. It just breaks me up that he will probably die for something he didn't do. It makes me question if practicing law is what I wanna keep doing."

Phil stopped walking. His mind was suddenly processing. He thought, *This morning the governor had said the murder was in 1981. Cindy just tied it to the cathedral parking lot.* His throat tightened. His face turned red. His ears burned. His stomach rolled over. At first the two lawyers didn't notice until Phil ran to a nearby bush and vomited. The lawyers quickly joined him and asked how they might help.

"Leave me alone; I'll be fine," he gasped. "I'm okay. Really, I'll be fine," he lied. "My car is this way. I'll be fine," he yelled as he headed out running across the grass in the direction of a parking lot.

The two watched him run, wondering about his sudden illness and unusual behavior. Mike said, "Maybe the reality of losing Danny has finally hit the padre. He'll probably be all right when he gets into his car and gets the air conditioning going. Still, a rather weird reaction, isn't it?" Cindy and Mike visited a few more minutes and then parted, agreeing to be in touch when they heard the governor's decision.

Chapter Thirty-four

"Oh, God. Oh, God. It can't be. What have I done?" Phil didn't stop at his car. He kept on running. He had to. The flashbacks came one after another. *He was running away from Bardstown on that cold March night. Running, stopping to catch his breath, and running again. Then into the woods, sleep, then out again. Collapsing in the ditch. Cold, afraid, blackout.*

Finally, after he ran a mile and a half as fast as he could through the streets of Frankfort, he fell exhausted under a tree in a downtown park near the capital. He quickly stood again, gasping. He had to walk. His chest pounded and ached from anxiety and trying to catch his breath. "It can't be. Danny Parton is gonna die for the crime I committed? What do I do? What do I *do*?"

Phil was angry with himself, thinking, *Me and my fancy priesthood. Me, the helper to prisoners condemned to death. What a phony I am. I'm so damn professional that I don't even pick up a clue that this man is pegged to die for my crime. I hate myself.*

The priest continued walking and stewing. After about an hour the pounding in his chest subsided some. As he calmed himself, he thought about practical next steps. Should he go back to find the governor and confess? Should he call Mike Benson? Should he drive to Eddyville and tell Danny? Should he return to the monastery and think some more? It was this last thought that he pursued. He found his car and drove from Frankfort to Gethsemani with no memory of the trip.

As he walked into the monastery the bell rang for 5:30 vespers. He quickly changed into his white Trappist robes from his black clerical suit and took his place with the monks in the long white chapel. As they chanted the verses of the psalms, Phil could not think of anything but his predicament. Supper in silence followed and he continued engrossed in his thoughts. He thought through every scenario he could think of. Each one frightened him. He realized that he hadn't felt so much actual fear earlier, more sheer anxiety until he'd returned to the monastery. Now he was considering the real possibility he could lose his *own* life for his crime. He wondered if he could bear the disdain of those who knew him or even the spiritual relapse of those he'd helped, once his crime would be exposed.

His mind thrashed about for what to do next.

He continued this way through the night. He paced in his room, laid down, got up, and paced again. His mind didn't stop. He trembled, thinking that he and Danny had agreed to discuss the case in a day or two. What a scene that would have been! He questioned how he could have completely missed news of Danny's trial in Bardstown. Though very isolated from the world outside, he felt sure news that big would have found its way to the monastery. Then he realized from comments Danny had made that the trial must have taken place while Phil was a novice. During those two years, he and his fellow novices were *completely* out of touch with local or national news. And in the years that followed, he'd been isolated enough not to see or hear low-level news items about the Parton case.

When Sunday morning came, the monk was just as mixed up as the evening before. He wasn't scheduled to say a public Mass and he decided to skip saying a private one. He felt unworthy. He attended one of the public Masses and he showed up for the morning sessions of common prayer, but he was totally distracted. He wondered what he was doing even going through the motions. He saw himself as a complete fraud.

By mid-afternoon, he was exhausted; he decided to make a private visit to the chapel and see if some divine assistance might still be available to him. He prayed, *O Lord, I've almost given up on you today. But I couldn't have lived these past sixteen years in vain. I know You're out there. It's time I get You involved. Please show me the way.*

As he sat quietly in the chapel, something told him to carefully review each possible course of action. He prayed that he might do this carefully—that the Lord might help him recover what remained of his rational abilities. And so, calmer now, he began to think.

Danny Parton has committed a murder in Tennessee and he says he's ready to die for that crime. With God's help, I helped prepare him for this if he isn't pardoned tomorrow. Could it be God's plan that Danny should die and come home to Him, leaving me here on earth to do His work?

And it doesn't seem possible that God would have brought me through everything, cleaning up my life, becoming a monk and a priest, only to die disgracing Him and the Trappists and myself, does it? He must want me to continue His work.

And what of my family? Phil had only seen them once since his ordination when they stopped at the monastery for a short visit. Most of their contact was by mail now. *Why didn't I ask the abbot for permission to go to Sandy and George's wedding? Some brother-in-law. If they find out, Sandy and George could never acknowledge me—a disgraced priest who is a murderer? And Kerry will probably have her own family one day, too . . .*

how would they feel when they'd learn of me? I must think of their welfare in all of this, too.

These arguments were making sense to Phil. He felt some vague sense of relief now. Maybe God was speaking to him about a path he might take. He finally decided that he didn't need to make any decision until after the governor announced whether or not Danny would be pardoned. Then maybe he could consider his options in a different light.

As Phil pondered these thoughts, he realized just how tired he'd become. He found the abbot in his room and told him he was not feeling well and asked permission to skip the monks' schedule for the rest of the day and retire. The abbot agreed and Phil went to bed only to be awakened at three A.M. Monday for early prayer.

After having slept some, the anxiety of the past two days returned, but more slowly. Phil began to second-guess himself and rehash his situation. In the back of his mind, a thought floated that he might be compelled to turn himself in, even if Danny's life was to be spared. It was possible that if Phil admitted to the Collins murder, Danny would be freed from doing more prison time. His time at Eddyville would logically serve as recompense for his bootlegging crimes.

Phil tried to concentrate on the spiritual exercises but could not. He felt like he was floating aimlessly from thought, to fear, and back to thought. He couldn't get anchored. He struggled with himself to hold off making any decision until he would hear the governor's decision. He told himself he needed that information to continue his deliberations. Six hours would pass, however, before Phil would hear the governor's decision.

Chapter Thirty-five

By 8:45 A.M. on May 29, the crowded press room near Governor Matthews's office was buzzing with gossip and anticipation. All audio and video feeder lines were set and ready. National reporters were among those assembled. At nine on the dot, the governor walked in. His countenance serious; he stepped abruptly to the podium and spoke. "Ladies and gentlemen of the press, thank you for coming," he said quickly.

"This has not been a pleasant Memorial Day weekend for me. The duties one has in public life are sometimes crushing. I have spent the greatest part of the past three days listening to and considering the case of one Danny Parton, the man condemned in the courts to die in the electric chair tomorrow. Two central thoughts occupied my mind. On the one hand we have the crime. Parton was convicted of one of the most brutal murders recorded in our state. The verdicts were sustained through several appeals. The suffering of his victim, according to experts in these matters, must have been beyond contemplation. Such an action on the part of Mr. Parton cries out for adequate retribution.

"On the other hand, we have heard testimony from prison officials and others that Mr. Parton has become a docile and cooperative inmate. He has, I've been told, developed a deep and genuine sense of religion in the past year. I've also been made to understand that his conversion has been so complete that he claims to be at peace in accepting whatever fate awaits him.

"These two competing realities have tested me greatly as I wrestled with the decision. And I myself have sought divine assistance in considering clemency for Danny Parton. Therefore, considering his peaceful disposition in the context of his horrible crime, I've taken it as a sign that Mr. Parton should fulfill his sentence. Therefore, I will not grant clemency and the execution order stands. May God have mercy on his soul."

"Governor, Governor, what about. . . ." "Governor, will you attend. . . ." "Governor, will other inmates now get. . . ." In unison, ten reporters were yelling their separate questions at the governor. A few with stern faces were silent; still others were smiling and laughing. Most were talking or yelling, adding to almost unbearable noise. The governor started to add more rationale for his decision but could not be heard. He considered some political stumping for an end to violent crime and tougher sentences but thought the better of it. He mouthed the words "thank you" over the din and left the room. The reporters snapped open their cell phones or ran to their mobile units in the hallways to deliver their summaries of what was now already heard and known by those watching TV. The State of Kentucky would execute Daniel Parton at six A.M. the next day, less than twenty-four hours away.

⁓

Father Abbot had given permission to Phil to borrow a radio from the monks' room and bring it to his room. He kept the volume low and listened to Governor Matthew's press conference. When it was over, he quickly turned it off. He dropped on his bed, curled up, and wept; wept until he could weep no more.

After an hour, emptied in body and soul, he sat up on the edge of the bed and told himself it was time to form his own decisions. Having debated all the possibilities in his mind over the past two days, it was already becoming clear to him what he must do. He said a short prayer for guidance and started to make his plan.

As tough as it would be, he must first find the abbot and tell his story. He wished Father Conrad, the former abbot, were still alive. That man was the only one on earth who had known everything about him and would join in his planning. Father Robert, the current abbot, was a good and holy man but Phil did not have the close relationship with him that he'd had with Conrad. Phil feared the disappointment and shock that Robert would certainly feel. Yet, he knew he must tell the abbot and get his blessing and guidance.

Then the priest knew he must rush to Eddyville and tell Danny. He knew this would be bittersweet news for the inmate. Danny was prepared to die for the murder he *did* commit but still was resolute about his innocence in the Bardstown murder. The news that Danny would be saved from the electric chair would certainly be welcomed by the prisoner, but the knowledge that his spiritual mentor was the real murderer would cause him much confusion and pain. Danny might feel sorry for Phil or be very angry at him or both. He would likely question all that the priest taught him and wonder how valid was this new found religion he'd accepted. Phil shuddered, wondering how Danny would react. Yet he knew he must tell him all. He'd do his best to help his friend understand that he did not *know* that Danny had been taking the rap for him. He was confident that Danny would be released from prison, allowing time served to cover his bootlegging crimes. He hoped eventually the prisoner would put the pieces together, forgive the priest, and continue in his reformed outlook on life.

Last, he must turn himself in to the authorities in Bardstown. Phil figured that this would not be an easy task. The police would probably know that he was counseling Danny Parton. They might conclude that, as a Trappist monk, Phil just might be willing to die for Parton. He might be taken for nothing more than an over zealous religious fanatic trying to work his own brand of an eleventh-hour reprieve. With the time running short until Danny's execution, the authorities would not want to be criticized for patronizing the priest, so they might simply ignore him.

As Phil pondered these possibilities, he remembered the letter and notes hidden away in the envelope in his desk. Father Robert had given the envelope to Phil, unopened, after Father Conrad died. The bishop's letter proved that there was or had been a murderer in the monastery and there was an obligation to reveal the guilty party if another was accused. Father Conrad's note written before he died connected that murder to Phil. And Phil's note admitted his guilt. Phil reasoned the authorities could contact Bishop Hoffman, still in charge of the Louisville diocese, to verify that he wrote the letter to Conrad, without knowing who the killer was. And Phil would try to make the authorities understand how Danny's reluctance to discuss the case and his own living of the Trappist way of life, made it not only possible but likely, that he did not know until Saturday, that Danny Parton had been accused of his crime. Following this logic, Phil hoped the police would take the necessary action to at least stop the execution and allow an investigation into Phil's claim that he, not Danny Parton, murdered Bobby Collins.

Phil hurried to get himself cleaned up and dressed in his black clerical suit. He pocketed the envelope exposing his guilt and walked to the abbot's room. He saw a note on the door saying the abbot had been unexpectedly called to a meeting outside the monastery and would not return 'til later in the afternoon. He knocked on Father Bart's door.

"Bart, the abbot's gone and I have to head for Eddyville; Danny Parton is scheduled to be executed tomorrow, you know." Phil was fidgety.

"I'm sure it's all right for you to go. Don't you and the abbot have an understanding about that assignment?"

"Oh, yes, we do. I just needed to talk with him first. Tell you what. If he checks in, would you just tell him that I need his help with something and I'll call him later?" Phil figured he'd try to reach the abbot by phone from the prison after breaking the news to Danny. He'd spill his story to the abbot and then ask the abbot to meet him in Bardstown at the police station.

It didn't occur to him that he could end up being detained by the authorities at Eddyville. He quickly thanked Father Bart and headed for the garage.

Phil was anxious beyond distraction as he raced north on Highway 31E toward the Bluegrass Parkway. Lost in thought, he failed to turn west on the parkway toward Eddyville. He continued on 31E toward Bardstown.

Now that the decision was made to confess to his crime and save Danny Parton, his mind was preoccupied with the excruciatingly difficult things he had to do in the next several hours. He was rehearsing what he would say to Danny and to the abbot and to the police. He had to make them all see it and believe it and to understand how it all could have happened the way it did. He would not try to make any kind of plea for leniency; that might come later. For now he must only convince them all of the truth.

After he missed the entrance ramp to the parkway, the road took him past the Holiday Inn and down the hill through the wooded areas on both sides of the road, toward the narrow bridge that crossed the Beech Fork River. Suddenly, he had a flashback. *The bridge. Crossing that bridge on foot that dark night in 1981, he was throwing his wallet over the railing. Once over, he was running back to the middle of the bridge to ditch his ring, the ring that tore the flesh from his victim's face.* He saw it now as if it was happening before him.

Caught up in this dreadful replay, Phil didn't notice the semi-truck and trailer carrying a load of full whisky barrels heading down the hill on the opposite side of the bridge. Both vehicles entered the bridge simultaneously. Given proper caution and speed, they could have passed successfully. But both were driving too fast. The truck held its lane but it was too late for Phil to maneuver clear through in his own lane.

Truck and car hit full force. The truck's two-foot high reinforced steel bumper served as battering ram and sheering instrument against the car. The crash sounded like a bomb, heard more than a mile away on Stephen Foster Avenue in Bardstown. In a split second, three feet of the whole left side of the car was sheared away, rolled and compressed, and then hurled a hundred-eighty feet back along the bridge deck and onto the roadbed behind. What came to rest was a crunched-up, tangled mess of twisted steel, busted upholstery, and body parts. Father Phillip Norton was dead, two-thirds of his body sliced and shredded throughout the severed wreckage.

The other driver somehow managed to keep his truck from going over the side of the bridge after the violent impact. His seatbelt and quick reactions saved his life. He swerved several times as he exited the bridge and finally brought the truck to a stop fifty yards beyond the point where Phil's crumpled half-auto and shredded body lay ensnarled. Overcome, the driver fainted.

A motorist who happened on the scene two minutes after the crash called 911 on his cell phone and in another three minutes the police, fire trucks, and paramedics from Bardstown were on the scene. The road was temporarily shut down on both sides of the bridge, the traffic turned around and rerouted.

There was little damage to the truck. Amazingly, the cargo was also undamaged. The driver had come around by the time help arrived and was immediately aware of extreme pain in his left leg. The paramedics assumed his leg suffered multiple breaks. They made a quick check of his vital signs, stabilized the leg, and carefully lifted him from the truck to a gurney and into an ambulance. In two minutes, the ambulance made the short trip to the Bardstown hospital and the patient was delivered to the emergency room.

At the same time, the police and firemen were examining the two parts of Phil's car, one left on the bridge, the other on the road bed. After impact, the section of the car remaining on the bridge had bounced off the side wall, careening and spinning to the left before it stopped, blocking both lanes of the bridge. The exposed side where the car had been severed was ugly at the cut, but relatively untouched within. The human remains left there were also ugly at the cut. The priest's head was gone. His right shoulder, arm, hip and leg were left intact and still clothed in what was left of his black suit. Blood poured from the tangled mess of broken bones, severed tissue, and blood vessels where the rest his of body had been torn away.

A paramedic from a second ambulance joined the others peering into the section of the car that had been ripped away and rolled down the highway. Each was repulsed by what they saw. One fireman's visceral reaction sent him into the woods next to the road. The paramedic went to his van and radioed for a hearse. Then he changed his mind and asked that the undertaker bring some sort of plastic big enough to be tied over both pieces of the wreckage. He hung up and radioed a local wrecking company and ordered a flatbed truck to pick up the entire remains of the car and its driver. Forty-five minutes later, the professionals on the scene working together under the direction of the undertaker were able to secure the entangled remains of man and car on the flatbed and cover it with a tarp turned shroud. A police escort then led the truck to the mortuary. It was four in the afternoon before both sections of Phil's car were removed and the road reopened.

The police had traced Phil's license plate to the Trappist monastery. The police sergeant asked to speak to someone in charge and was put through directly to the abbot, who had just returned. The sergeant explained that there had been an accident involving a car registered to the Trappists and it involved a fatality. He asked if someone could come and identify the car. The abbot asked about the victim. The policeman indicated that direct identification was impossible but it would be appreciated if the abbot might view the remains of the car and the man to help sort out clues leading to the identity of the driver.

The abbot agreed and hung up. He sat down. He knew it must be Phil. He'd received Phil's message earlier and wondered what he might have wanted. How could the accident have happened? Fighting back tears, the abbot walked to the garage, and drove to Bardstown.

When the abbot arrived at the mortuary, the funeral director asked if the priest might accompany him to the large garage in the rear of the mortuary building. The abbot shuddered seeing the flatbed truck holding the wreckage containing Phil's body. The funeral director spoke. "First, Father, let me offer my condolences. This is a terrible tragedy. I must say, I have never seen such a horrible accident scene. What I recommend is that you *don't* climb up and view it. We have removed additional remains from a separate part of the wreckage to our laboratory. They are more intact, yet most gruesome. I also recommend that you avoid viewing those remains."

"I'm sorry, sir, this is something I must do. I'm certain this is Father Phillip, one of our Trappist monks. I must see and then pray." Some temporary steel steps had been rolled in place and the abbot started up the steps followed by the director. The abbot waited until the man stepped in front of him and removed the tarp.

Father Robert was horrified. What he saw of flesh and bone entangled in twisted steel could hardly be identified as a human. The tears he'd fought back earlier now flowed freely. He held his handkerchief over his mouth and nose for fear of vomiting. After a few moments, he slowly encircled the wreck and its mutilated contents, holding back sobs as he went. He blanched, noticing what looked like a whole eyeball lying alone on a part of the frame of the car.

Completing the circle, he nodded to the director, took a prayer book from his pocket, and began to say the Prayers for the Dead in Latin. After five minutes, he went down the steps as the director put the shroud back in place. The two men left the garage, and the abbot asked that he be taken to view the human remains that were in the laboratory.

The mortuary technicians had draped the severed side of Phil's body, so what could be seen was only what was left of the naked right side of his body. The abbot gasped. He paused, then cried, "Oh my God, Phil. What has happened to you?" He wept for a number of minutes looking at the body and then turned to the funeral director.

"Father, we assume you'll want us to discard what clothing was left on this part of your monk's body," said the director. The abbot nodded. "But we *did* discover an envelope in the breast pocket of the coat. I'm surprised that it was somehow not destroyed in such a violent accident. I have it in my office. Should we move over to the office now?" Still in a daze, the abbot nodded and followed the man to his office.

The funeral director was a slim, pale-faced man with thinning hair. He wore metal-rimmed glasses and spoke in a soft, serious voice. "Father, again, I am so sorry for your pain. No one should have to see a beloved colleague have his life ended this way." He paused, then offered, " If you'll permit, I would like to offer something in the way of a suggestion?"

"Yes?"

"Perhaps you'll allow our staff to remove the human remains from the wreckage on the flatbed. This would involve a very careful procedure trying to separate the remains from the steel and other material. For example, I noticed what might be personal effects like some shredded pieces of a wallet and some small bits of clothing and so forth. We will burn all of this type of material that we're able to separate because it's obvious there is nothing there worth salvaging. However, it's also likely that some small amount of non-human material may unavoidably be gathered, mixed in with the human remains. This can't be helped in order not to leave any human remains behind. We would then place all of your monk's remains, including the large portion of his body that you just viewed, in a heavy plastic bag, seal it carefully, and lay it in the casket. The casket would then of course, be sealed shut. We would deliver the casket to your monastery where you would be free to conduct the funeral and bury your monk there in your cemetery, as is your custom. Does that make sense to you, Father?"

Father Robert was distracted, thinking about Phil. He was recalling with some melancholy, when he was Master of Novices, how he'd helped this sometimes over-enthusiastic convert through the process of becoming a brother monk. And what a successful Trappist he'd become. The abbot was suddenly aware that the director had finished speaking and said apologetically, "I'm sorry, could you go over that again?"

The funeral director kindly obliged and the abbot agreed to his suggestions. The director mentioned the envelope again and handed it to the abbot, who had no curiosity about it at the moment and put it in his breast pocket. They discussed a few more details and Father Robert returned to his car. On the twenty-minute trip back to the monastery, the abbot, mustering considerable resolve, forced himself to begin thinking about the necessary steps he must take in planning Father Phil's funeral. The monk's family must be notified and invited to come and stay in the retreat quarters at the monastery. A list must be compiled of those known to have sought

Phil's help and counsel. They must be invited, too. And the warden and perhaps some of the guards from the prison should also be included. The abbot had a fleeting regret that he'd ever asked Father Phil to take on the special ministry at the prison.

The abbot forced his attention back to the planning. He considered whom of his Trappist monks should be directly involved in the funeral mass, who should welcome and provide for guests, and who should organize the quiet reception after the funeral. The abbot would make sure that Phil's funeral would maintain the humility and dignity characteristic of a Trappist monk and yet be a fitting tribute to a priest who'd helped so many.

As the abbot drove into the drive way of the monastery, he felt he must set aside the planning for a time and go to the chapel. There in the silence, he would allow himself to pray and grieve for his brother monk. But then he remembered: before he could go to the chapel, he must first call the prison chaplain and let him know the terrible news. He wondered how poor Danny Parton would take it when he heard.

Chapter Thirty-six

It was seven o'clock and still very hot on this Memorial Day evening. At the prison in Eddyville, Danny Parton was pacing the floor in the larger and more comfortable holding cell that he'd occupied since early that morning. The cell was painted in soft tones. It offered a large TV and a six-foot table that could accommodate several people. The bed was larger than normal prison issue and had a thicker mattress. Danny yelled to no one in particular, "Where the hell is Phil? He said he'd be here no later than six."

The guard on duty, a burly fellow everyone called "Andy," walked to the cell and said gently, "I don't know, Danny. I'm sure he'll be here soon. Probably got caught in the holiday traffic. We'll get him up here as soon as he steps in the door. Can I get you anything?"

"Naw, just find me my priest. Doesn't he know it's NOW that I need him!" Then he asked Andy, "What's goin' on outside?"

"The crowd is already forming just outside the fence. A couple of kids in pony tails and cut-offs have guitars and are starting to sing some kinda hymns. Lot's of folks with signs, some starting to march in a circle. The weather is nice so I bet were gonna have a big crowd all night."

"Why don't they just go home and leave me alone?" Danny bellowed. "This ain't no circus, is it?"

Andy answered, "Well, Danny you never know. Even though the governor said 'no clemency,' he can change his mind right up to the last minute. It's happened. Maybe he'll listen to these folks outside."

"Yeah, sure," said Parton sarcastically.

"Well, I don't know. Anyway, some people get their jollies demonstrating like this. And if you ask me, the press loves it, too. They're out there now takin' pictures of the protesters and all."

"Damn it, where is Phil?" yelled Danny, not really listening to Andy.

Just then, Warden Caufield and Father Winston walked into the death row unit. Both looked solemn. The warden joined the prisoner at the table in the holding cell. "Danny, I have real bad news."

"Yeah, I know I'm gonna get the chair in the morning. I'll be ready. But where is my priest?" Danny was agitated.

"I'm afraid that's the bad news, Danny. This afternoon on his way to see you, Father Phil was killed in an auto accident. It happened on a bridge south of Bardstown; hit by a truck . . . a real mess, I understand. I'm sorry, Danny."

"What?" The prisoner's face broke into compete disbelief. He was stunned. Tears began to flow. After a long pause, he looked at the floor and mumbled, almost inaudibly, "Where does that leave me?"

Father Winston answered quietly, "Danny, I don't pretend to be any kind of stand-in for Father Phil, but I want to help you in any way I can. We can pray or just talk or just be quiet together."

The condemned man didn't answer. He stood up and began pacing again. After about five minutes, he suddenly stopped and stood still with a curious look on his face. A slight smile started to turn in the corners of his mouth. Then a broader smile. Then a giggle that turned to a hearty laugh. He sat at the table, slammed his fist on it, and said, "He told me he'd be with me but I didn't get it. That-son of-a-gun. Last week I told him I wished he could come to heaven with me because I was gonna miss him when I died. That it might be years before we could visit again. He told me not to worry because it would seem like a heartbeat to me before we met in heaven. Wow! He'll be waiting for *me* when I arrive tomorrow morning."

Danny got up and moved over to sit on the bed. He chuckled and shook his head back and forth as he continued to contemplate the profound. The warden and the chaplain were dumbfounded. Neither wanted to interfere with Danny's meditation. Eventually, they stood quietly and left the cell. The prisoner didn't seem to notice. On the way out of the unit, the chaplain whispered to Andy, "We'll be downstairs in the warden's office. Call us when he stirs and starts talking again."

Chapter Thirty-seven

When the abbot returned from the chapel he took off his clerical suit coat, starting to change into the simple Trappist white robe worn by all the monks in the monastery. Laying the coat on the bed, he noticed the white envelope still inserted in the breast pocket of his coat. He sat on the bed, opened the envelope, and began to read.

He first read Phil's note acknowledging his guilt in the death of Bobby Swanson. The abbot was startled and confused. He quickly read the other pieces and the truth dawned. Father Phillip, his fellow priest and friend, had murdered someone. The abbot quickly stood. He shook with panic. His throat felt like it would close. His mind raced. He immediately was tempted to destroy the documents to protect Phil and the Trappists. He resisted. Back and forth he paced in his small room. He flopped backward on his bed, pumped his arms heavenward, and yelled a muffled, "Phillip, what have you done?" And the abbot wept.

Slowly, he began to regain control of himself. His panic and fear slowed and turned into a profound sadness. He tried to put the pieces together. He speculated how Phil must have taken refuge in the monastery and later somehow found religion. He must have confessed his guilt and sought direction concerning what obligation he would have to turn himself over to the police. The abbot's predecessor, Father Conrad, must have asked the advice of the bishop, and together they decided that Phil had reformed his life so his crime could therefore remain hidden unless some other person was indicted in the matter. Then it hit him. BOBBY SWANSON!

The abbot, the only monk to routinely review the newspaper as part his singular role of being generally informed of the ongoings of the outside world, had been aware that Danny Parton was going to die for the murder of one Bobby Swanson. He was holding the note from Phil admitting the murder of Bobby Swanson. Panic returned. Phil must have just recently learned that Danny's victim was really his own. Could this be? The abbot thought he remembered Phil mentioning once that Danny didn't want to discuss his case. Phil must have been on his way to turn himself in when he was killed. "Oh my God. I have to stop the execution. Oh my God. Help me."

The abbot tried to gather himself. "Let see. Call the prison. No, call the bishop. No, call the governor. Yes, the governor is the only one who can stop the execution of Parton." Not sure how to reach the governor, he dialed 911 and told the person who answered who he was and that he had an emergency message for the governor. She put him through to the general number for the governor's office, and the phone was answered by the security person on duty there. "The governor's office. Security here."

"This is Abbot Robert. I am in charge of the Abbey of Gethsemani, the Trappist Monastery south of Bardstown?"

"Yes, Father. I've heard of the Trappists. How can I help you?"

"I need to talk to the governor immediately. Can you reach him for me?"

"Gee, Father. I don't think so. It's a holiday weekend. He is probably at his retreat on Lake Barkley. The rule is he's not to be bothered there unless it is an extreme emergency."

"Listen, son, what's your name?"

"Billy Kline."

"Billy, I *do* have an extreme emergency. Are you aware there is a man by the name of Parton who is going to die tomorrow morning in the electric chair?"

"Yes, of course."

"Well, Billy, I have conclusive proof that Parton did not commit that crime and that if the governor doesn't stop it, an innocent man will be sent to his death."

"Gee, Father, we were told that we would probably get this kind of a call from someone tonight. In fact, you are the third caller. I'm sorry I really can't put you through to the governor."

"Listen Billy. One of our Trappist priests was killed today on his way to bring this new evidence to the authorities. I am in possession of this evidence now. I *must* speak to the governor. You must believe that this is not a crank call. In fact, why don't you quickly use your resources to get the phone number here at the abbey and call me back. Ask whoever answers to put you through to the abbot."

"Well, I. . . ."

"Do it now, Billy. You'll never forgive yourself if you don't give me a chance to at least try to reach the governor." The abbot hung up hoping the security guard caught his sense of urgency.

Ten minutes later the phone rang in the abbot's room, and the priest answered on the first ring. A hesitant voice on the other end said, "Is this the person I talked to a few minutes ago? This is security at the governor's office."

"Yes, Billy. Can you help me reach the governor now?"

"Well I don't know, Father. What I can do is call the security shack at the governor's retreat and tell him I am convinced you're not a quack. If you call in five minutes, it will be up to you to get ol' Charlie to interrupt the governor." The guard gave him the number and hung up. The abbot waited a long five minutes and made the call.

"Charlie O'Brian here. Security."

"Abbot Robert here. Did you just get a call from Billy at the governor's office?"

"Yeah I did, Father, but I don't know if I can help you. The gov told me not to disturb him unless the president called or we went to war."

"Charlie, I promise you that by tomorrow night you'll regret it terribly if you don't help me reach the governor."

"I'll try, Father. Billy gave me your number. I'll call you back."

It was twenty minutes before the abbot's phone rang again. It was the governor himself. "Listen Father what-ever-your-name-is, I really resent you and that other monk trying to influence me because your religion is probably against capital punishment. I thought you people stood for honesty and here you are trying to pull a fast one on me. Danny Parton is guilty and unfortunately, tomorrow he'll pay his debt to society. Now then, is there anything else you have to say to me? If not I would like to get back to my friends and my dinner."

The abbot took a deep breath and said, "Governor, I can understand why you feel the way you do. People must lie to you all the time to get what they want. If you just give me a few minutes, I think you'll agree that what I learned just an hour ago makes an enormous difference in the Parton case."

"Okay. Let's get on with it, then." The governor still was annoyed.

The abbot verified that the governor remembered Father Phil and explained the monk had died that afternoon, presumably on his way to convince the authorities that *he*, not Parton, had committed the murder in 1981. The abbot summarized the contents of the three documents that were found on Phil's body. He explained the theology that allowed Phil to remain at large as long as he did not know Parton or anyone else was accused of the crime the monk himself had actually committed. He also tried to explain to the governor how for a cloistered Trappist monk, it was indeed possible that what seemed preposterous, especially Phil's late knowledge of the truth, indeed could and did happen. He finished, begging the governor to stop the execution.

The governor's response was not polite. "This is the most abject example of religious interference that I've ever encountered in my life. You ought to be ashamed of yourself, Father, creating a story like that at the eleventh hour to push your cause against the death penalty. I am disappointed in you *and* the Trappists." He hung up.

Chapter Thirty-eight

Nighttime was setting in and the crowd outside the prison was growing. A portable amplifier was set up and the leaders took turns calling for an end to capital punishment. Candles were lit throughout the crowd. Between the speeches, people armed with their signs marched up and down in front of the area covered by the press. From time to time the musicians would step to the microphone and lead the group in songs and hymns that would catch the mood of the crowd. The TV cameras were running.

At eleven, Andy asked Danny if he wanted to eat his final meal. He seemed ambivalent and told the guard he might just like a Coke or two. He was thirsty but not hungry. Andy called for the sodas and also alerted the warden and chaplain that the inmate seemed to be more communicative. The guard reported that he thought that Danny was still quite peaceful but more aware of his situation.

A few minutes later, Father Winston appeared bringing the Cokes. He entered the holding cell and said, "Here're your sodas, Danny. How are you doing?"

He answered in an even voice, "I'm okay, Father. I don't need to go to confession or anything. Phil and I pretty much took care of everything. But maybe you could stay with me and pray a little?"

And so it went. The chaplain and the condemned man sat in his cell as the hours passed. Sometimes silent, sometimes talking, sometimes praying together. It was not strained. A mutual presence.

The governor was still awake. It was four-thirty in the morning. He rehashed his phone call with the abbot over and over again. He'd been angry when he first went to bed. He carried on with several imaginary conversations with the abbot as he tossed and turned in bed. He saw himself telling off the abbot six different ways. "How could a so-called man of the cloth try a deceitful trick like that? It must be a crime in itself to do something like that!" he reasoned. "I'll have the attorney general look into that, I will."

But neither peace nor sleep would come to the governor. He got out of bed, got a drink of water, and sat in the stuffed chair in his bedroom. He gathered himself and thought, *Why am I so upset? If the abbot is a crank, I should forget him and get some sleep. Or am I upset because if what the abbot said is true, I'll have to let Parton go free and that could make me look weak?* "Oh man," he groaned, "this is one thing that politics should not touch." He paused as he wrestled with that thought. "By gosh, I think I *am* affected by the politics of this thing. I'm concerned about my image here. What if I call off the execution and nothing comes of this Trappist's claim? I'll look foolish. But if it's proved the abbot *isn't* lying, and I let Parton die, my political career is dead. And, if I grant a *temporary* stay and reschedule the execution and later it looks like I've been had, people will see me as adding punishment to Parton by making him go all through this again. No, I've *got* to find an answer now." Another pause as he pondered. "I think I'll start with the bishop."

"Bishop Hoffman, this is Courtney Matthews. I'm sorry to wake you."

"No Governor, you didn't wake me. I just got off the phone with Abbot Robert a few minutes ago and actually I was just about to call you. The abbot had been trying to get me all evening and finally tracked me here at my niece's home in Baltimore. I just called my residence in Louisville and had the porter put my personal number on call forwarding. I am so glad you called, Governor. I take it you wish to discuss the pending execution?"

"I do, Bishop. What can you tell me about this story the abbot told me about Parton's priest being the real killer?

"Well, I can't speak with *absolute* assurances, but my instincts tell me that what you were told by the abbot is true. I'll never forget that case, even though it was many years ago and I never knew the identity of the murderer or who was murdered. The late Abbot Conrad brought me his question regarding the right of a man to remain silent about a crime when no one else was accused. I sought concurrence from a fellow bishop and gave my opinion, with several caveats, of course, that the abbot could advise his 'client' of his obligations and stay close to the situation.

"What convinces me that the priest who was killed yesterday afternoon is the guilty party are the documents that Abbot Robert read to me. My own letter *is* the one I did send to the last abbot. And Father Conrad's own letter and the confession-like note from the Trappist priest, Phillip Norton, convinces me that Norton is your man."

"So, you are convinced, Bishop. Even if this embarrasses your church?"

"Well, Governor, I'm inclined to believe that the church will survive. I remember this fellow. I actually ordained him, not knowing, of course, that he was the murderer. Knowing Abbot Conrad and the Trappists, I'm sure Norton was fully repentant. And, the way he's spent his life since his crime, doing good work and counseling countless people including the prisoners, has become well known in the Catholic community here in Kentucky."

"But hiding his crime when another was going to die for it. That isn't so heroic, is it, Bishop?"

"Not if he knew, Governor. Think about it. If he knew, how could he have ministered so effectively to the poor fellow who was going to die for his crime? Abbot Robert has been very close to Norton's work at the prison and he is positive that the priest did not know who he was helping."

"How could he *not* know, Bishop?"

The bishop explained what the abbot had tried to explain to the governor earlier that evening. "Governor, these Trappists are among the most secluded monks of modern times. Their rule keeps them sheltered to the concerns of the outside world. They force themselves away from curiosity about our world. They do this in order to gain a higher level of spirituality. I couldn't live like they do. But they are for real, Governor."

"Yes, but this Norton was working a special mission at the prison. He was working specifically with Parton. I just can't believe he couldn't figure it out!"

"Two things convince me it *is* possible, Governor. A Trappist would not pry; he would listen but would not pry. If Parton didn't want the priest to know anything about the specifics of his crime, the priest would not ask. The other thing that makes me believe it's possible is the note that Norton wrote years before, admitting to the crime and asking that if anyone else was accused that it be made known that he, Norton, was the murderer. To me that says he was serious about his obligation to come forward if and when he knew. And, the fact that he was carrying these documents when he was killed also shows he wasn't hiding anything at that point."

There was little to say after that and both men were polite as they signed off with no resolution. The bishop had hoped for more but all he could do now was pray.

Chapter Thirty-nine

At five A.M. the warden appeared and said it was time for the preparations. A special unit of the guard staff called the "death team" arrived to shave and dress Danny. With the chaplain praying aloud and walking behind, two members of the team escorted the prisoner through the death row unit to a door on the far end of the room. As they passed the cells of the men also awaiting their own fate under a death sentence, Danny stopped several times and exchanged a somber and quiet goodbye with each man inside. All were tearful except Danny who, while serious, seemed at peace.

The door led to a hallway. The second door on the right was called the "isolation room." It was next door to the death chamber where the execution would take place. The isolation room was small. It had a single chair. It had large inside windows on three sides. The chaplain gave Danny his blessing and the inmate entered the room and waited there alone. Other members of the death team were busy checking the equipment that would end Danny's life.

Governor Hoffman sat in his chair. He felt very alone. He couldn't delegate this decision. Nor would the advice of his staff help now. He searched his mind to find what he believed at this moment. Slowly, gradually, he reviewed what the abbot and the bishop had told him. He could feel himself resist as the bishop's logic started to make sense to him. He had felt so much commitment to this particular execution. Political, yes, but also it had seemed so right that this Parton fellow was guilty and should suffer the supreme punishment. But what was the right thing to do? And to do *now*? As he dug deeper into the core of his mind, he acknowledged that there was now a greater probability that Norton, not Parton, was the killer. And that was what he must act on.

The governor stood and jumped to the phone. He called the security shack. "Charlie, get me the prison and hurry."

"But Governor, I understood you released your open line to the prison yesterday afternoon before you came over to the lake."

"Oh, damn. You're right. I was sure I wouldn't need it. Now, of course, all their registered phone lines are closed off to avoid complainers and masqueraders from driving them nuts. What time is it, Charlie?"

"Almost five-thirty, Governor."

Lake Barkley, in the southwest part of Kentucky, is one of the world's largest man-made lakes. This fifty-eight thousand acre lake is popular for all forms of outdoor recreation and water sports. Besides the untouched wilderness surrounding the lake, its shores hold numerous resorts, camping sites and private homes. The governor's retreat was eleven miles across the lake from the Eddyville prison. Due to bridge repairs the only open road around the lake to the prison was a forty-two mile trip. "Do you think we can get to the prison faster in the Blazer or the boat, Charlie?"

"Probably the boat, Governor. But the wind is coming from that direction; could slow us down some."

"Let's see, the execution is scheduled for six-fifteen. If we leave now we can just make it. Meet me at the boathouse in three minutes, Charlie."

As the earliest tinges of orange shone in the eastern sky, the two men were in the state-owned CrisKraft inboard cruising at twenty-one miles an hour toward the somber gray structure near Eddyville.

Fifteen minutes before the appointed hour the witnesses were escorted into the viewing room. The group included retired Detective John Sedwick; Kevin Lawton, former D.A. from Nelson county; Tommy Kendrick, the foreman on the original jury; Mike Benson and Cindy Nolan, Danny's attorneys; Warden Caufield and two of his assistant wardens. Father Winston would not be there.

All were in place when Danny was moved from the isolation room a few steps into the side door of the death chamber. Two team members strapped him into the chair and connected the electrodes to the various parts of his body. Then the two guards joined a third team member in the control area. There, each would hold a lever, one of which when all were pulled at the same moment, would deliver the fatal charge to Danny's body.

The curtain was pulled back and each witness looked directly at Danny Parton and he at them.

He was asked by the warden if he wished to say anything. He nodded. "I was not a good man before I found God. I hurt a lot of people and if any of them read what I'm saying now, I hope they might forgive me. I *am* guilty of one murder in my life and I accept *this* punishment for *that* crime. But I did *not* kill Bobby Collins. I forgive anyone who has done me harm. May

God have mercy on me."

A voice was heard in the corridor outside the viewing room. "Hold it. Hold it. I'm the governor. Stop the execution. Please, please let me in there."

The warden was about to signal the team to pull their levers when he heard the rumble. He thought it might be someone who had sneaked by security and gotten into the corridor. Someone with false credentials who was against the execution and wrongly thought he could save Parton's life.

The door opened and the governor walked into the viewing room. Mike Benson was the first to react. He jumped to his feet and welcomed Governor Hoffman. "Thank you for coming, Your Honor. I'm sure you wouldn't be here if you weren't here to stop the injustice that was just about to take place?"

The others in the room sat dumbfounded, not knowing what to think. The governor satisfied himself that Parton was still alive and turned to the small group assembled there.

"I apologize for scaring you all half out of your wits." He turned to Danny, sitting in the electric chair, mouth wide open, face white as a ghost, looking like he was going to vomit. "I especially apologize to you, Mr. Parton. But I am sure you will accept my apology when you hear that I am here to void your death sentence. I will also do my best to see any federal charges for bootlegging be set aside for time served here." Danny gasped and passed out. He was carried from the chamber back to large room where he had spent most of the last night.

The governor then told the Phil Norton story as he knew it. Doing so, he did not paint an evil picture of the priest. He explained why he had come to believe what he'd been told by the abbot and the bishop. He ended by saying, "I think I may have also learned something about myself these last few days, at least I hope so."

Epilogue
One Year Later

Unannounced, Danny Parton showed up in Mike Benson's Bardstown office one afternoon. The two greeted each other with a bear hug and smiles and laughs all around.

"So, how *are* you, really, Danny?"

"I'm fine now, Mike. But I sure had a couple of rough months after the gov pulled me out of the chair. I was sick to my stomach and jumpy for six weeks or so. Kept thinkin' it was a fluke and the cops were gonna show up and take me back to death row. After they sprung me, I went back to Jonesborough, found myself a little apartment and just sat around for the first couple of months. When I left prison the warden told me about Phil and how he died and all that. To tell the truth, I was really pissed—oops sorry—I was really angry at Phil. I fought with myself not to believe he was a complete hoax who was gonna let me die for killin' Bobby when he did it himself. That's all I could think about sittin' there in that apartment. And tossing that around in my head all the time made me even sicker. And believe it or not, Mike, the whole time I didn't even have a drink."

"So how did you pull yourself out of it, Danny?" asked Mike.

"Well, I couldn't stand it, just sitting there, sick and mad. So, I decided I would head back to Kentucky and pay a visit to that Trappist place that Phil lived at. Thought maybe those people could help me understand what was going on with Phil. Well, those fellows, the monks I mean, couldn't have treated me better. They insisted I stay with them a while and I ended up staying a whole week. They showed me how they live and I even attended some of their prayer services. They explained how they believe Phil really went through a change of heart. That he wasn't just a killer that they were hidin' in the monastery. The abbot also convinced me that Phil didn't really know until the very end I was gonna die for *his* murder.

"I guess the more I thought about it, the more I came to believe that Phil was the real thing, too, Mike—even if he did kill Collins. Me and Phil never got to talk about my actual case. He never pushed me. He must not have known I was gonna die for the *Collins* murder. I guess those Trappists don't stay up on things 'cause they're kinda sequestered there in the monastery. And, when he did figure it out, looks like he was on his way to get me off the hook but never made it. Besides, the guy couldn't have been a phony and teach me religion the way he did. The religion's stuck with me, too. I figure that couldn't happen if something real wasn't happening between me and Phil."

"So, where did you go after meeting the monks, Danny?"

"Lot's of places. I was a real tourist. Phil talked a lot about his sister-in-law and her daughter. So one place I went to was Mississippi and met his people. Stayed three weeks. They treated me like family. They wanted to learn all they could from me about Phil that last year before he died. And, I've stayed in touch with the family, too. The daughter, Kerry, is married now and is gonna have a baby. If it's a boy they're gonna name the kid 'Phillip.' How 'bout that, Mike?"

"Gee, Danny, seems like some good has come out of all the sad things that happened to you and Phil."

"You bet, Mike. And there's more. This morning, I had a long visit with the detective who set me up for Collins' murder."

"John Sedwick?"

"Yep. I got a letter from him a month ago in Jonesborough. He invited me to come to Bardstown to visit him. Said he had some information for me. Turns out he went back into the old records and examined what they said about how Bobby Collins died. Seems he studied the coroner's report a little harder and noticed some things about how Bobby's face was wrecked. He said he finally figured out that the blows to Collins' head almost *had* to come from a right-hander. Then he checked my records at Eddyville and learned I'm a lefty. And he said he called the Trappists and found out Phil was right-handed. Why you all missed that twenty years ago, I can't tell ya. But that's finally convinced Sedwick that he'd tracked down the wrong man."

"Danny, I. . . ."

"Forget it, Mike. I ain't blaming you. You and Cindy did a great job for me and I'll always thank you for it. But before I left, this Sedwick fellow actually cried and asked me to forgive him. If it weren't for all the things Phil taught me about forgiveness, I would have probably punched him in the kisser. But, Mike, I told the guy he was forgiven. I couldn't believe it myself. And I felt good about it. Can you believe it?" Danny laughed, standing as if to leave.

Mike joined in the laughter. "So, what's next, Danny?"

"Well, Mike, I've been thinkin' about that. The Feds have released me from all the old charges. Gave me credit for all the time I served here in Kentucky. And Tennessee can't try me for the murder I *did* commit—double jeopardy, you know," he chuckled. His expression turned more serious.

"Anyhow, seems people over there think I've reformed and have done enough time in prison to get another chance.

"I don't have a lot of years left, Mike. I want to do some good. The folks in Washington County, Tennessee, are building a home in Johnson City for teenagers in trouble with the law. They contacted me and offered me a job. Seem they think I might help some of the kids reevaluate their game plans a little. Can't you just see it. Ol' *Danny Parton* teachin' kids how to be good."

Both men laughed again at that. A quick handshake and Danny was gone.

8828

NORMANDALE COMMUNITY COLLEGE
LIBRARY
9700 FRANCE AVENUE SOUTH
BLOOMINGTON, MN 55431-4399